MW01126910

This is a work of fiction. While, as in all fiction, the literary perceptions and insights are based on experience, all names, characters, places and incidents are either products of the author's imagination or are used fictitiously. No reference to any real person is intended or should be inferred.

ISBN 978-0-557-58799-5

The Emperor's New Music

By Alex Langford

Chapter One

Blood Red

Music saved my life once. Can it save me again, because I'm in the battle of my life.

I'm fighting well for a man who's never even been in a fight. This guy is three inches and thirty pounds bigger, but he's slow, and he's drunk. I can dodge his punches easily; just have to find an opening to knock him in his fat head. He throws a left fist at my face. I sidestep, but my foot slips on something wet.

It's blood. I look over and see my best friend, Jason, lying in a pool of it. The bright red stuff is streaming from his right temple. He's three feet away from me, but a crimson channel is flowing my way; it tripped me off my feet. His skull hitting the marble must have been the sound I heard a minute ago: a loud, unnatural cracking behind me. Like the sound you make snapping a chicken bone, times ten. Jason probably went down on the first hit he took.

I can smell the warm, coppery stench of his blood. Life seems to be draining fast out of his body, but I can't help him. I'm fighting for my own life.

I lose my balance and fall hard on my back, onto the marble floor. The guy jumps on top of me, his stomach pushing the air out of my diaphragm. Damn, I was doing so well.

At least Demetrius is still on his feet. I catch a glimpse of him landing a solid combination on one of the two guys he's holding off. But now there's a trickle of blood coming down the right corner of his mouth. Two against three: three hip-hop thugs who want to make a name for themselves by attacking my friends and me. And now Jason's out cold.

I work my arms under the guy's midsection, and push him up an inch off my body so I can catch a few shallow breathes. But I'm getting weak holding up the weight of this smelly, stoned brute, trying to keep him from pinning me down again. I hear a faint sound from Jason; a death knell, and I know I'm his only hope.

My opponent pulls his left arm up, and grips my neck with a sweaty, cold hand. Sausage fingers come together until there's no space between them, blocking my air, making me lightheaded.

Is this how it ends – my young life, on my back rumbling with gangbanging rappers? Fifteen years in L.A., and I'm dying in a senseless fight after I just produced a nationally-televised rap awards show. How ironic: to be killed doing a show where I thought rappers would be killing each other.

Images flood my mind. I see the bouquet of carnations that seemed so peaceful between the nearby elevators, the bloodshot eyes of the guy trying to kill me, the sad, bloody wetness around Jason's head. Man. Blood like I've never seen before. Not since, what was it, way back when?

I'm battling the urge to pass out, to find a peaceful sleep. Fight on, Anthony. But a voice says, *Just let go.*

My brain is disconnecting, held together by the thinnest thread. Were those flowers red, or were they pink? Anthony, you could be home in Chicago now, safely raising a family and teaching music.

Music. What was the name of my band?

Ice Age.

I remember how everything changed when the Ice Age came to an end.

Everything was so much simpler back then, in 1977.

Wait, there was nothing simple or nostalgic about it at all. Chicago was a nightmare. My first band was a disaster, and all we did was fight. The bass player thought the drummer played too loudly. The keyboard player argued with the guitarist about chords. The guitarist thought that I, the lead singer, didn't sing with enough of a rock edge in my voice.

I was annoyed with the guitar player: his tardiness for practice, his girlfriend who came to rehearsals, even the red leather pants he loved to wear. We spent as much time arguing as we did rehearsing. I knew the band needed changes, but they weren't so severe that we couldn't work out the problems. Or so I thought.

Our last night together, we discovered the bass player was dating the drummer's ex-girlfriend. She knocked on the door to pick him up after rehearsal. One of the guys made a smart remark, and they started fighting and rolling around on the floor. After one broken nose and a cracked keyboard, Ice Age was finished.

In most bands, the singer is usually the leader and peacemaker, a role natural for me. So the next morning, I tried to get the guys together for a band meeting, but after three calls, it was clear everyone wanted to go separate ways.

When I walked outside after the last call, I was surprised to feel not sorrow, but a peaceful calm that signaled the end of two years of struggling to keep the band together. It was a clear April morning in 1977, the kind of Chicago day when the air was filled with high clouds dotting the blue sky like penguins in the ocean.

I walked back into the house, past my mother who was cleaning the kitchen. In my room, I ran my finger across the embossed diploma that arrived the day before. "Anthony Richard Adams, Bachelor of Arts, Journalism." No more papers to write and no more homework to be done. But now there was no band to help fill my time and earn a few dollars. I had been looking for a newspaper job for weeks, but the nation was in a recession, and I was having no success. My father was pressuring me to start making money. I wondered if he would actually put me out like he threatened.

Under the diploma was a postcard from Jason Brown in California. I had met Jason in a music theory class. He graduated a year before me and moved to California before the ink was dry on his diploma. He wanted me to come west and join him, saying how hard it was to meet people in the real world compared to college. I put the postcard on top of the diploma. The green palm trees of Hollywood matched the green school color of the diploma's padded case.

That night, my father helped me decide what to do. Every evening at 6:30, he would arrive and plop into his chair in front of the TV, still wearing his mail carrier's uniform. If it was a good day, he would call for a beer. If it had been a bad day, he would demand something stronger and faster-acting. He called for whiskey, which my mother mixed with a tiny amount of soda; she quickly brought it and slid the wet glass into his hand.

I sat at the dining room table in the dark and watched him drink.

Children of alcoholics look for small signs of warning or expectation. It's like living in an unpredictable shell of anxiety. I watched my mother scurry into the kitchen and emerge this time with a second round, two glasses: one for him and one for herself. The only competitive bone in her body was in the sport of drinking.

"Get over here, boy," my father said. "How's that job search going?"

"I didn't go out today," I said, walking toward him. "The band broke up. I spent the morning trying to call a meeting, but the guys are fed up with each other. I just wrote a new song, though."

"I didn't ask you about your damn band, I asked if you found a damn job. You better get some work before you get put out."

"Dad, you're getting an early start. And it's not even dark yet."

"Are you trying to be smart with me, boy?" He glared up at me with his thick eyebrows coming together in a typical Virgo's frown.

"Not at all, Dad. Things are not good for me right now. I don't even have gas money for my car. Nobody's hiring."

"Yeah, right," he said. "What about all that affirmative action? With a black daddy and a white mama, you should be just what they're looking for. Black, but not too black. Ha."

I backed away from him and stepped into the kitchen.

The only time my father talked about race was when he was drunk or nearly drunk. I didn't like it when he joked about me being biracial. We were the only mixed family in the neighborhood, in a city known for being segregated and polarized, and it was not a safe feeling being surrounded by angry, ignorant neighbors.

"Try not to upset your father," Mom said quietly when the swinging kitchen doors closed behind her. "I'll fix your plate after I fix his. I'm sorry about your band, baby. You know, this might be a good time for you to think about making a big change. You're my *big* baby now." She stepped behind me and gave me a gentle hug. "Sometimes, it's like *you're* the grownup around here."

"You might be right about me doing something, Mama. Just hurry and get him some food. He's drinking on an empty stomach."

After dinner, Dad calmed down and went into the basement to play his saxophone. Crazy me, to think my father would sympathize with the pain of losing your band. Thirty years ago, he toured the east coast and the south in half a dozen jazz bands, and each band lasted no more than two years. His groups broke up either because someone got strung out on heroin, or a band member got locked up for a petty crime. Surely my dad knew what it was like to have a promising band fall apart. But I remembered he was not a sympathetic man.

His fire and stormy personality were what attracted my mother. They met when she was a hostess at Chicago's Playboy mansion. My dad's band played there. Mom was one of Hefner's cadre of blonde beauties, and they fell in love. Three months later they married, and in a year, I was born. When his music failed, he didn't turn to crime or drugs - he turned to liquor. But now I was faced with the prospect of being a failed musician just like him: delivering mail and watching TV on a Friday night, instead of playing a gig somewhere.

I collected a few quarters in my room and went to the pinball arcade five blocks away. My father's saxophone music was still in the air when I got halfway down the block, but the neighbors never complained about the noise, either out of appreciation or fear.

I came home around midnight. A lamp was broken in the living room, and a trail of tiny blood drops led from the kitchen to the bathroom. *Here we go again*. I followed them, like a hound, down the dark hall. They ended inside the bathtub, a bright red bloodstain, the size of a small puddle, with a faint bloody handprint sliding up the side of the tub.

I realized why I always hated the color red. I turned on the hot water and washed away the stain. The image would be harder to erase in my head.

After cleaning away the red, I picked up the trail, expecting the worst. But when I reached their room, Mom and Dad were safely asleep in bed, with moonlight falling on their heads. It had just been another one of their emotional rows, fueled by Johnnie Walker Red. I heard them snoring, peaceful to the pain of their crazy worlds.

Back in my room, I decided it was time for a different kind of search. This time, it was for Jason's number in California.

Chapter Two

The World Was Different

1977

I'm on my way.

Those words were stuck in my head from Chicago all the way to California.

I needed to write a song about all this.

Days on the open highway gave me a chance to think. My father had given me two hundred dollars and a gas credit card. My '65 Dodge would surely make it to Los Angeles in spite of a loud, bad muffler. I was roaring across the country's midsection, where one flat state looked and felt just like another.

Before leaving home, my dad had given me what he thought were wise words of advice. "Never give up on your dreams, son. Your mother and I are proud of you - the first college graduate in either family. I just hope you stay with your music. I don't understand the whole rock thing, but give it another chance. Just don't let drugs and women cloud your mind. Leaving this rusty town might be the best thing for you.

And, for God sakes, when you get out there, cut off some of that hair if you want a job."

He was an unpredictable man. A typical musician.

Still, in spite of his encouragement, I had serious doubts about life as a singer in a rock group. Being in a band is like having four wives. Every musical choice and decision, from the songs you play to the clothes you wear on stage, is up for debate. As much as I loved singing, I knew my personality, as an only child, would make it hard to constantly compromise.

But life as a music journalist? That seemed ideal. The independence, the thoughtfulness, the chance to make a difference were all appealing. Two reporters had brought down Richard Nixon, which was the main reason I majored in journalism.

I was finally in Los Angeles County, thundering down a mountain pass, radiator cooling after a long, steep climb. It was mid-afternoon, and Jason had promised to leave a key to his flat under his welcome mat while he was at work. He mysteriously said he had something to tell me when I called him that morning before I left a Nevada motel.

I pulled into the driveway of a pink duplex bungalow house on Hardy Street in the heart of West Los Angeles. The key was there. Inside, I lay across his sofa and took a deep breath of California air.

Egyptian posters and artifacts were throughout the living room. Two lovebirds in a cage were making chittering sounds in a corner. A faint smell of incense was in the air, and I heard a soft hum coming from a back room. I got up, walked toward the sound, and peeked through an open door. It was coming from a window air conditioner. The cool air was strong enough to make gentle waves on the cotton Indian print fabric covering the waterbed nearby. I retraced my steps to the sofa, and lay back down. The hum was soothing. It lulled me to sleep, with those words "I'm on my way" still in my head.

"Anthony." I woke up with a start. Jason came through the front door, followed by another man. I could see the sun was setting behind him. He darted toward me, and I quickly stood up, seeing he wanted to hug. He was just over six feet tall and built like a tight end, but he often acted like a big kid.

"Anthony finally made it west," he said.

"Yes, indeed. I took your advice and made the big plunge." The guy was still standing in the doorway. He was a tall, thin man with short curly hair. He reminded me of Jason's boyfriend in college. "Is that your friend?"

"Oops. I'm so bad. Come in, Samir. Anthony, this is my friend, Samir. He's from Cairo."

"Good to meet you, Samir."

Samir nodded his head once.

"He doesn't speak much English yet," Jason said, "but I'm working on him. We met when he came to town, with the King Tut exhibit. Isn't he beautiful?"

"I guess, Jason. I see you're still chasing guys, man," I whispered in his ear.

"Chasing?" he said. "This one is caught. Which brings us to our little problem. Samir is staying with me now."

I stared at him for a few seconds. "So *that* was the telephone surprise. Do you think you could have told me this before I left Chicago?"

"Don't get uptight, man. With a little creativity, a little patience, we can work this out. I didn't want to tell you because I was afraid you wouldn't come. You'll find a job in no time, then you can get your own place, maybe even move in upstairs if I can get rid of that witch living up there. What do you say, you still want the spare room, and your very own sofa bed?"

He opened his arms, tilting his head like a bad puppy, and I stepped into his hug. I was wary of living in another unpredictable household. But he was genuinely happy to see me. I figured the three of us could manage until I got my own place. The situation would be an incentive to find a job quickly. "Show me where to put my things, roommate. I need to mellow out."

The transition from Chicagoan to Californian took exactly two days. That was the day I drove to the beach to see the ocean for the first time. Lake Michigan had waterfronts, but Los Angeles had beaches with pretty women. I'd go to the beach to girl-watch after a long day of handing out resumes, and it took my mind off the sounds of Jason and Samir doing…whatever it was they did.

Three weeks later I had my first job interview. None of the big newspapers were hiring, but I got a call from the head of a new music magazine called Hype. Their offices were on Hollywood Boulevard near Highland. Wendy Robinson was the young publisher and editor.

I was led through a large office where a staff of 15 energetic young people were darting around. It sounded just like my college newspaper production room, which we used to call "the hive."

Wendy sat at her desk, dressed in all black, with long raven-colored hair. She reminded me of another Jewish girl I dated in college. Her office walls were covered with four previous magazine covers, and posters of the Rolling Stones, Neil Young and other rock and rollers. I sat across from her, and she described her vision for the magazine.

"We've only been in business for six months, but I want Hype to become a household name for people under thirty," she said. She went on and on. I was happy to let her do most of the talking. "I want this magazine to cover music the way Sports Illustrated does sports."

"Music is my life," I said when she took a breath. "I've either been playing it, writing about it, or hearing it at home since I was five. Rock and roll changed the world, and I've always wanted to write about it."

"Well, after looking at your writing samples, you're clearly the best writer to apply so far. And the best-looking, if I do say so."

My future boss is flirting with me, I thought. I can handle this. Wendy was not a bad-looking woman. She told me she had inherited a million dollars the year before from a trust fund when she turned twenty-five. It was her brother's idea to start a rock and roll magazine. He was not involved in Hype, though, and I wondered why, but didn't ask.

"Two articles a month, $150 a week," she said after an hour-long interview, then she leaned back in her chair. I accepted the offer eagerly. "Welcome to Hype Magazine, Anthony."

The world was different when I stepped back onto Hollywood Boulevard. Different in the way I looked at the fine cars and beautiful people driving them. With a great job, I could be as successful as they were. When I thought about it, it was me who was different. It was the same feeling I had the first time I did a live newscast at my college radio station. Now I had a voice. I could add it to the sounds of the city.

When I got home, Jason and Samir were on the sofa, shirtless, smoking weed. The air was filled with sex and smoke; Jason looked at me and started laughing while his friend reached for corn chips that were scattered among the mess on the coffee table.

What happened to you out here, my friend, I wondered. Jason was equally skilled at violin and piano. He had dreamed of becoming a concert violinist as a young man. But by the time he got to college, he had been teased and beaten so many times for carrying a violin case, that he changed his major to accounting, and made music his minor. Now he worked as an insurance adjuster, and there were no signs of violin or music anywhere in his home.

"What are you laughing about, fool?" I said to him.

"I'm laughing at that tie and those shoes you have on," Jason said. "They so don't go together."

"Well, I may not be the fashion guy like you, but at least I have a job."

"A job!" he screamed, jumping up to give me a hug. He was only wearing boxer shorts, and his cologne and body odor added to the thick smell of the room. "I knew it, I knew you could do this. Tell me."

"I'll be writing articles for a new magazine called Hype. Mostly I'll be interviewing musicians and profiling people in the record business. They publish twice a month, and I'm doing one story for each edition. I start tomorrow. It's a dream job, man."

"All I can say is, you've arrived, brother."

I went to the back of the house, to my small room in the den past the bathroom. I wanted to celebrate, but Jason was the only one I knew in the city, and he wanted to spend every spare moment with his new friend. Where can I meet some females in this big town, I wondered?

I celebrated by shopping. I found a small stereo system with a turntable at a nearby Sears, and went to a record store, where I looked through the latest hit songs. For the first time, I noticed how many songs were about California, about searching for your dream on the road.

I bought "Hotel California," "Hollywood Nights," and "Running with the Devil." They were all songs that spoke with a weird mix of hopefulness and alienation. Each song was layered with the sharp and heavy guitar sound that my old band Ice Age was developing before we broke up.

It was dark when I got back to Jason's. A piece of paper was taped to the door of my room. I eagerly opened the stereo system and connected the turntable to the amplifier and the speakers. Then I opened the note, which I assumed was a phone message. It simply said, "Anthony: We're moving to Cairo. You'll need to find a place in a few days. Sorry for short notice. See you in the morning."

Chapter Three

Crossover

Jason's bedroom door was still closed when I left for work in the morning. His car was parked out front, so I assumed he was still asleep or going in late. I'd have to wait until evening to discover why he left such a note.

I snaked my way through the L.A. streets toward the freeway. Everything was new compared to Chicago. The streets looked clean, and almost seemed to shine. Most strikingly of all, there were no people walking the streets. Cars were rushing everywhere, but no one was walking. I jammed on the accelerator and joined the herd.

Wendy had promised to have an assignment for me soon, and I was so eager to work that I agreed to start right away.

At the office, someone had written my name on a piece of paper, and placed it on a desk right in the middle of twenty other desks in the Hype editorial room. Wendy was at a meeting, as the rest of the staff trickled in.

The editors, photographers, graphic artists, secretaries, and workers seemed friendly as they came to my desk and introduced themselves, usually in pairs. They were a similar-looking bunch: white, young, attractive, mostly blonde.

When Wendy arrived, the energy in the room changed immediately. People snatched up phones and started making calls or began typing. The big boss was dressed in all black just like the day before, except for a lacy white shawl draped over her shoulders.

Her eyes scanned the big room. "Good morning, all," she said, and the people replied reluctantly, like children addressing their grade school teacher. She walked through the office, straight toward my desk.

"And good morning, Anthony. How do you like your new job thus far?"

"So far, so good. I've done absolutely nothing. Just getting used to the space here."

"Good, good. I have something set up for you. Follow me."

In her office, she told me about Jim Mancini, a record company executive she had met at a recent party. He told her there were big changes happening in the music business, and he had a good story. Wendy gave me his number. "I'll try to have an article in a few days," I said.

I called Mancini, the vice president of promotion for Atlantic Records. He was leaving town the next day, and suggested I come now if I wanted to catch him. His Hollywood office was a few blocks away. I left.

Atlantic Records was having the best success in its history. The Rolling Stones, Bette Midler, Aretha Franklin and Yes were the names on the gold records in Mancini's office. Jim was a dark-haired Italian man, taller than me, and full of energy.

"You're writing for Hype Magazine, huh?" he said when I finally sat across from his desk. "What do you know about that boss of yours, is she, like, available?" He winked.

"I don't know much about her. I just started today. You're my first interview. She said you had a great story for us."

"Let's get down to business," he said. He loaded some papers into his briefcase. "The record business is changing, son, and I can sum it up for you in one word: disco. It is here to stay, and it's going to change everything."

"Disco?" I said, taking notes. I noticed the "Hollywood" sign in the window behind him. "I hear it on the radio sometimes, but I didn't know it was so big."

"I'm telling you, disco is the story. Clubs are popping up across the country. It's on TV commercials, they're making movies about it. Write this headline: 'How Disco Will Rule the World.' I've got this great new act called Hot Sugar, and they'll be around for the next ten years. People are always gonna dance, people are always going to want a good time. There's your article, kid. Now what questions you got?"

"Tell me about some of the disco acts on your label. How can you be sure it's not just a fad, a dance craze, like the twist?"

"Listen, Anthony, I've been in this business a long time. Rock and roll, the way I knew it, is dying. Peace and love, the Beatles, that wimpy stuff, is long gone. Nobody ever danced to that crap. Now, disco has all the bases covered. Kids and adults love it, it's fun, you can roller-skate to it, it makes you feel good. But mainly, you can dance to it. These gold records on the wall are all dinosaurs, man. In five years, this wall will be covered with ABBA, Chic, the Trampps. The record business is changing, and guys'll either perish, or adapt."

He walked to a shelf, lifted a heavy cardboard box, and dropped it on the desk in front of me. "Listen to these," he said.

"I can get you an interview with any of them. They're the future. They're all hot, hot, hot."

"The problem is," I said, "Hype Magazine is geared toward a rock-and-roll audience. I could be wrong, but I don't see the disco thing fitting in with their demographic."

"Am I wasting my time with you here, or what?" He slammed his briefcase shut, and locked it with a loud click. "I gotta catch a flight. There's your story, do what you want to do. I don't know what else to tell you."

"Tell me," I said, "about other trends you see happening in the music industry. Outside of disco, what's happening in music today, tomorrow?"

He thought for a few seconds. "There's something bubbling under the surface that'll be big, too. I'll give it to you in one word: crossover. It's what happens when an act appeals not just to blacks or whites, but to blacks *and* whites. Crossover. Hall and Oates used to sell to just whites until they did 'She's Gone.' Now they're selling millions. Same with that black guy who won all those Grammys. Softened up his sound, now he's selling millions. Crossover is the future. It's going to be, you know, hot, hot, hot."

I lifted an album from the record box; it was a new record by a black performer I'd heard of, but there was a white model on the cover. This disco is some kind of weird joke, I thought.

"Last question, Mr. Mancini." I practiced the question several times in my head before I spoke. "If you take the soul out of soul music and the rock out of rock and roll, don't you just end up with a boring, colorless mess with no heart or soul?"

He looked at me like he had just swallowed a bitter pill. "Son, how much do you know about the record business? What are you, like, twenty-one?"

"I was music director at the college radio station, and yes, I'm twenty-one."

"I'm going to tell you one thing, one last thing, then I'm out of here. A song called "Rock and Roll Is Here To Stay" was a big hit years ago. Take it from a man who's been in records for a while. It ain't true. Rock is dying. Half the top records this year have been disco. Radio stations are going disco. The freaking Village People were at the White House with that moron Jimmy Carter. You just listen to these albums and let me know which group you want to spotlight."

He grabbed his bags and stuffed his business card in my shirt pocket as he left. I lifted the heavy box of records, and realized I'd have to walk back to my office with the awkward load, unless I could find a cab. There were no cabs.

I must have looked odd: duck-walking down Sunset and over to Hollywood with a cardboard box filled with twenty-five albums. A thin layer of sweat was on my face when I caught the elevator up three flights to the Hype offices. Half the people had left the editorial room: gone out to make sales calls, interviews and meetings.

I found a turntable and a music system in the central conference room, where I sat and listened to some of the records. Like many musicians and rock people, I was disdainful toward disco. It was all drum machines and faceless singers. I had grown up listening to the rock and roll guitars of Jimi Hendrix and Eric Clapton. Disco was repetitive and robotic. From what I had heard, rock's rebelliousness and intensity was contrasted by disco's hypnotic hedonism.

I listened to the music. The songs were fun and full of energy, and many of them were funky and even soulful. I loved the complex arrangements of horns and strings. The singers were mostly women with big voices who sang with passion and conviction. Some of the lyrics were clever, with something rock and soul music rarely had: a sense of humor. Reading the album notes, I was surprised to see how many of the records were produced in Italy and Germany. Each album was good for only two or three songs, but those few songs almost made me into a disco convert.

"Nice beat," Wendy said, standing in the conference room doorway.

"I like it," I said. "You know, I never really listened to it before, but it's actually okay in places. I interviewed the record guy. He wants me to profile one of his disco acts."

"Disco?" Wendy said. "*That* was his story? You're kidding me."

"I was skeptical, too, but after listening to some of this stuff, maybe he's right. Dancing is a powerful thing."

Wendy walked to the turntable and lifted the needle from the album, making a scratching sound on the record. "Listen, Anthony. Let me tell you who reads Hype Magazine. White guys between 15 and 27 are our biggest audience. Guys who listen to Van Halen and the Eagles. These are guys who just want to clear up their skin and get laid. They don't want to dance. The fags want to dance. You aren't doing a story on disco."

"Whoa, no problem, chief." Wendy surprised me with her attitude, even though I had shared her opinion about disco ten minutes earlier. "The guy *did* give me another story about changes in the music business. It's called crossover. It's when black music and white music kind of meet in the middle somewhere."

"Here's what you do," she said. "Screw all the crossover and disco stuff. Write five hundred words introducing yourself to the readership. If you're going to be a featured writer in every edition, you've got to let people know a little about yourself. Tell them what you like, where you're from, what you'll be writing about - which will be rock music, by the way. I'll get Phoebe to design you a logo with palm trees and stars or something. What do you think?"

"I think that's a great idea. I'll have it for you by Tuesday."

"*Now* we're on the same page. Meanwhile, contact some agents to set up a few interviews, talk to people, look around for stories. Don't let me down."

She left the room, and I piled the records back into the box to take home. Seconds later, she poked her head back into the office. "And, Anthony, never, ever call me 'chief.'"

My new job had started with a bang. Then I remembered Jason's note, the one that said he was moving. The one that said I had to get out.

Chapter Four

Studio West

Jason's car was parked exactly as it was when I left in the morning. I had forgotten about his note in the excitement of the first day at work.

He was sitting alone in his spot on the sofa, wearing a tennis outfit, and watching the evening news.

"How was work?" he asked when I walked into the living room.

"It was great. I think I'll like it there. I got your note. What's up, man?"

He got up, walked to the television, turned it off, and went back to his seat. He looked at me.

"Samir's visa is up. He's got to go back to Cairo, and I figured, why not take a chance and live in the Middle East for a while. I quit my job yesterday. We're leaving as soon as I can get some money together."

"That's all great, Jason, but where does that leave me? First you convince me to move out here, almost under false pretenses, now you're moving away, leaving me without a place to stay? I mean, what is this? I thought we were cool."

"Anthony, buddy. You'll be fine. I did some thinking. You can sublet this place. Samir and I are in love, and if I can't be with him, I think I'll die, man. I *have* to go to Egypt to be with him. You've got to understand." He stood up and wiped his forehead. It seemed like he was close to tears.

"What a scene," I said. "Is he here now?"

"He's at work. He drives a cab at night. Probably at the airport right now. Anthony, you're my only friend, and I don't want you to hate me."

"Don't get all melodramatic on me, man. I'm just going with the flow. If staying here is an option, then I'll be cool. It's just weird that you're moving away right when I get here."

"Who knows what'll happen," he said. "I may not even get my money together, even though it's really cheap to live in Cairo." He wiped his eyes with a small white tennis towel, grabbed his wallet from the coffee table and took out a gold business card, showing it to me.

"What's this?" I asked, reading it. "Studio West?"

"Yes. A new club downtown where everybody goes. Let me make it up to you. Let's all party this weekend. Maybe you can meet some—what is it you straights call it—oh yeah, chicks."

Later, the sun had set, and the three of us were out on the town. Jason treated me to dinner in Hollywood. He and Samir took me to Studio West, an enormous discotheque in L.A.'s dark warehouse district.

We stood in a long line behind a red rope for a short while. The doorman walked down the line, stopped at me with a quick once-over, and signaled for me to go in. "My two friends are with me," I told him. He looked at Jason and Samir from head to toe, then he smirked and made a step toward the end of the line. Jason quickly slipped a ten-dollar bill into my hand, which I gave to the doorman. He undid the red rope, and we were in.

We walked through a foyer, the dance floor opening up before us like nothing we had seen before. Gold and red balloons covered the ceiling, and peacock feathers lined the walls.

"Something special's happening tonight," Jason said. It was their grand opening party, even though the club had been open for three weeks. "Isn't disco supposed to be an underground thing?" he yelled over the music. "Once the straights get a hold of it, it's over."

There were beautiful girls everywhere. In fact, everyone at the place was beautiful: the girls, the guys, and a lot of people whose gender was indeterminate. Hollywood stars were sprinkled throughout the crowd. Truman Capote, Telly Savalas, Sonny Bono and George Burns were the ones I recognized. They were not what I'd call beautiful. They looked strangely old and out of place.

Jason and Samir were already on the dance floor. I pushed my way to the bar to get some water. A deep voice spoke to me before I could get the bartender's attention.

"Are you having a good time?" I looked up at the tall man who was talking.

"I just got here," I said. "My friends are out there somewhere. I'm winging it."

"Good," he said. "Let me get you a drink. Bartender."

"Thanks, buddy, but I don't drink."

The man looked slightly disappointed, then he ordered more white wine for himself. I told him my name and profession. He told me his name was Stan, and he played professional basketball.

"I think writers are sexy," he whispered in my ear.

"Some people think that's true. I don't know why."

"It's the opposite of what I do, and I like that," he said.

"Well, I'm not gay, dude. I'm looking to meet females, myself."

"Yeah, I do that too," he said, "but when I get a little bit drunk, like now..." He finished his drink. "I like 'em like you: light-skinned, curly hair, nice lips, all skinny. I'm sorry. But if you ever decide to cross over to the other side sometime, look me up. Just between me and you."

"I'm sure you're a cool guy, but I don't think so, partner." After several moments of silence, I turned and watched the action on the dance floor and off to the sides. A news crew was interviewing Andy Warhol in the glare of a spotlight under a balcony. The light made his white hair glow like a distorted halo. A woman spoke to me from my other side.

"It looks like they let out the Hollywood old folks home for the night," she said. She was about my age, and she looked like she was watching animals in a zoo. "Have you ever seen so many washed-up celebrities in one place before?"

"You know," I said, "I knew something was a little off about this crowd. You'd think mostly people our age would be here, but this is like a dinosaur convention."

"I hear you, brother," she laughed.

Her name was Linda Fleming, and she was a production assistant at one of the TV stations filming the party. I was glad to have someone else to talk to. The basketball player had disappeared into a VIP area. "I *had* to come here for my job, what's your excuse?"

"I'm here with my friends. They're moving to Cairo. I'm new in town, and I got a new job as a magazine writer, so we're celebrating."

"Some celebration. Leaving you at the bar alone."

"You know what? You're right. What the hell am I doing here? I don't drink, and a guy just hit on me. But I have to say, the music is not bad. At first I thought it was crap, but I'm liking it more and more. Plus, somebody pitched me an idea for an article on dance music. Disco's not for our audience, but this is good research just in case."

Sammy Davis and Wolfman Jack walked past us and went upstairs to a roped-off area in a balcony.

"This is like some kind of dream," Linda said. "Or maybe it's a nightmare."

"Look at the bright side," I said. "We've got young and old, black and white, gay and straight all together here. I'm a musician and music is the only thing that can bring people together this way. It's like a fantasy world where people can live out their dreams for a night."

"True," she said, "but what do they do in the morning? They have to look in the mirror to their wrinkled old skin and faded youth. All the drugs and plastic surgery in the world won't let you dance away from the grim reaper. It's pathetic and sad, in a funny sort of way."

We stood at the bar, watching the old white stars and the young black wannabes twirling the night away under the lights of spinning mirrored balls, trying to find another reality in the beat of the music and the chemicals in their blood.

"I better find my crew," Linda said. She handed me her card. "Keep in touch, new kid in town. You seem like a loner, like me."

"But I'm not a..." She was gone, three-deep in the crowd before I could correct her.

Nice job she has, getting paid to party, I thought, unaware that *my* job was about to blow up in my face.

Chapter Five

Incomplete Pass

Monday morning I began writing my first piece. It took a while to focus after everything that happened over the weekend. My parents were arguing when I called yesterday and Mom said she might want to come live with me if things continued to get worse. The only people I met at the disco were a gay basketball player and a girl who seemed like she just wanted to be friends. On top of everything else, Jason was having trouble with Samir, who said his religion was making him think twice about their relationship.

I eventually hammered out an essay introducing myself to Hype's readers:

"Last winter, Chicago had the biggest snowstorm in its history. The Blizzard of '77 dropped ten feet of snow, from the Windy City all the way to Buffalo. From what I hear, out here in the streets of Hollywood, storm clouds are gathering over the music industry. I'll be here at Hype not just to interview great music makers, but also to report on the constant changes happening in the world of rock and roll."

I snatched the last page out of my typewriter and took it to Wendy. She was standing in the editorial room drinking black coffee.

"This is good," she said. She handed the papers back. "We'll go with it. What else are you working on?"

"Elton John and Steve Miller are in town now and Pete Townsend is doing a farewell tour with the Who. I'm going to try to get all those guys."

"Super," she said. "How are you settling into California life?"

I told her the basics of my relocation saga, but as I was talking, I remembered what she said to me back at our first interview. *Did she say I was cute?* As she stood there, I rambled on about the disco and my roommates and other odds and ends, wondering if I should invite her out. I tried to catch a look at her breasts, but her eyes were locked on mine. What the heck, I thought, isn't she close to my age, like 25? It would be risky, but no more perilous than moving out here alone in the first place.

"Wendy, I was wondering if we could, I don't know, have dinner together sometime. I want to get to know more of the big city."

She froze mid-sip and seemed to let the coffee drain from her mouth back into the cup.

"Dinner? Together? Anthony, you're an employee. We work together. What kind of a boss do you think will be respected if she's doing the employees?"

She must not have known how loud she was speaking. "Wendy, that's not what I meant."

"Anthony, I don't know how it works in Chicago, but the casting couch thing doesn't work at this company. It won't get you more money or a better job here. Please just do your little articles and interviews and remember this is a place of business." She turned and walked away.

Incredible. More mixed signals from a nutty L.A. chick.

I looked around and noticed that everyone within earshot in the editorial room had stopped what they were doing to tune their ears to what had just happened. Now they were looking at my face for a reaction. Phoebe, the graphic designer, had been standing nearby. She walked up when Wendy disappeared.

"Incomplete forward pass," she said. "F.Y.I., she only dates Jewish guys. And she's a big tease, so don't freak out."

"I didn't ask her for a damn date. Can't a guy invite his boss out to dinner without the world stopping?"

"Anthony, lunch means 'let's be friends,' dinner means 'let's screw.' Hey, you're a kid, you didn't know. Anyway, here's the logo artwork for your piece."

"Palm trees and shooting stars. That's just great. I hope my job didn't just go up in flames, too."

Jason was seated on the stairs of the house when I pulled up after work.

"He's gone," he said before I was even out of the car.

"What are you talking about?"

"He's gone. Samir is gone. He packed up his cab and took everything. The TV, my clothes, my jewelry, everything. Everything is gone."

"When you say 'everything,' Jason, he didn't steal your furniture, did he?"

"No, whatever he could fit into the car, he took. I'm the biggest fool in the world."

"Did he leave a note? Did you call the police?"

He stood up, and I followed him into the house. "There's no note. Even if there were, it'd be in that gibberish language of his. That brown bastard. And what would I tell the cops? *My illegal alien gay boyfriend who lived with me moved out and took my stuff?* Baby, the cops would arrest *me*. And I wouldn't blame them." We looked around the living room.

"Jason, I never trusted that guy anyway. Now, I don't know much about people, but I know a best friend can't come between new lovers. But I didn't know what to say. I didn't even try to tell you my suspicions."

"Okay, okay, I'm an idiot, I get it now. And guess what? I was at the embassy today, applying for my visa to go to Egypt like a damn fool. I can't believe I quit my job. Oh my god."

The only thing I noticed missing from the living room was Jason's small color television. He went to his room; moments later I heard him softly crying and ripping up papers, probably photographs or travel plans for Egypt.

Look at me, I thought. Jason is a year older than me and I came to California thinking he could help me get settled, but his life is more chaotic than mine.

I walked into my room. Samir had also stolen my new stereo system.

Chapter Six

The Next Big Thing

A YEAR LATER, APRIL 1978

After interviewing half a dozen great rock superstars, I learned they all had one thing in common: they loved talking about themselves. Talent was their only commodity and they apparently spent every waking hour focused on nothing but their artistry and how to mine it. As a result, they didn't know much about politics, science or current affairs. All they knew about was themselves.

By now, I had interviewed and written articles on Joni Mitchell, Eric Clapton, and other musicians with various levels of greatness. I was spending half my time out of the office, which was good since Wendy and I developed an icy relationship. She loved my articles, but things were never the same after I asked her out to dinner. L.A. women were odd: beautiful, tightly wrapped packages of neuroses just waiting to unload on the next unsuspecting guy. I had occasional flings, but hadn't yet found a girlfriend who didn't seem like a psycho.

Jason resurrected his life after Samir moved away. He found a job as a rehearsal pianist for the Conservatory of Music and was thrilled to be playing music again.

From time to time, Wendy, or one of the editors, would leave information on my desk. Ideas, leads, or press releases would be in my box. One morning, they left a clipping about the Sex Pistols and how the punk movement could be the next big thing. The group was having hits in Europe and they were on their way to conquer the states.

I got an interesting note from Wendy about a famous singer who was trying to make a comeback. He had been a huge star, part of the hippie generation ten years ago, but now he was washed up and nearly bankrupt. I called and arranged an interview.

The first clue that Bobby Gold was on hard times was the fact that he lived close to the airport. I took the freeway, exited, and drove past three seedy adult bookstores and a strip club. My once-famous star answered the door in a Hawaiian shirt, shorts and flip flops. In his wrinkled red face, I could barely see remnants of the guitar player who made so many beach songs I heard as a kid, songs that helped form my impressions of California.

"It's me. Hard to believe, I know." I must have had a surprised expression on my face. "Time has not been kind." He laughed, then started coughing like a phlegmy cigarette smoker.

The room was barely furnished. An old beige leather sofa was pushed against a wall. The sofa was as dry and wrinkled as his face. I walked in and sat down, taking out my notebook. He told me about a new album he was working on; he was full of quiet excitement as he spoke about it, but I wanted to talk about his recent past.

"This music business," he said slowly, "is not for the weak of heart. Vipers at every turn and they only live to suck the life out of you. I had two number one songs and I sold eight million records around the world. Now I can't even get promoters to return my calls."

"What happened?" I asked.

"We tried to change the world, but the world didn't want to change. When '69 began, it was all about peace and love. You could taste the excitement in the air. You have no idea what it was like to be at Golden Gate Park or Greenwich Village or anyplace back then. A spirit was in the air. Music could change people, solve problems, stop the war.

"But honestly," he thought for a moment, "I don't know what happened. Nixon happened. J. Edgar Hoover and Richard Daley happened. The Allman Brothers had a great line about how cool it would be when all the war freaks died off and left us alone. But it looks like only the good die young. Evil and greed are eternal. Now they want to flush all the old hippies down the drain and make way for, I don't know, K.C. and the Sunshine Band?"

"And yet you're still making music," I said. "How has the music business changed since you were at the top?"

"Man, it's all crap now. Rod Stewart and the Stones are doing disco. Those guys used to be about something. Go back and listen to "Street Fighting Man" one day. The record company wanted me to do a disco song to get a deal. Nothing but garbage. The Captain and Tennille. What the hell is a Captain and Tennille and why is it in my life?

"But to answer your question, the record companies are getting too big for their britches, too corporate and impersonal. There was a time bands could send their tape to Capitol or Columbia and get a deal based on their merit and their music.

Now all the labels are merging. One day there'll just be three or four labels running everything and calling all the shots."

He was out of his seat, pacing back and forth, forehead covered with sweat. "They're just throwing these oddball acts against the wall, seeing which one'll stick. They don't want to develop talent like they used to. They're just following trends and squeezing them dry until the next big thing comes along. They're lawyers instead of music men." He paused. "On top of all that, it's hard keeping a band together, simple enough."

He talked more about the music business, then he gave me a depressing account of his finances, his divorce, and his bad health. The one thing that made him smile was his teenage daughter, and how she was singing in a new group. "A voice like an angel," he said. "She loves to sing and people seem to like her. She's my last hope for this crazy world."

He lit a cigarette as we walked to the door. I wanted to ask for his autograph, but I resisted the urge. I was becoming less star-struck as I interviewed more and more famous people. I wished him good luck and promised to call if I had further questions.

Driving back to Hollywood, I thought about Bobby Gold's daughter and her group and wished I was still in a band. I thought about Ice Age. Some of my best times came when I was rehearsing and performing with the band. Nothing can compare with the sheer joy of being in front of an audience, at the height of your powers, knowing that people are there to love you and your music. But, like the man said, it could be torture trying to keep everyone together. Egos clash, people refuse to compromise, guys are afraid of failure and afraid of success. And for some reason, the more talented a musician, the crazier he is.

Making music together is like sharing your soul. It can be torture being in a band that dislikes each other. But nothing, not even sex, compared to the thrill of putting on a good show. I was aching to perform.

When I got back to the office, I noticed some new faces sitting at desks; apparently they were new employees. I wrote a "where are they now" piece based on the interview and thought about the possibility of getting back into a band.

I called Linda Fleming for one of our weekly conversations. We hadn't seen much of each other since meeting at Studio West the year before, but we were what she called "phone friends."

"What's new?" she asked.

"I just interviewed a guy who used to be on top of the world. Now it looks like he's two steps from being homeless. It'll make for a good article. Take me about an hour and a half to write."

"Wow, you're fast," she said. "I bet you'd make a good TV news writer. We need a few more real people around here. You know, ones that aren't made of plastic like most of these L.A. people."

"That's something to consider. Linda, I've been thinking. I used to sing and play in a rock and roll band back at school and I'm debating if I should give music another try. I don't know."

"Look," she said, "if it's something you really want to do, just go for it. You really like performing? They couldn't pay me enough to get up on a stage."

"I love it. I love being up there, singing and telling stories, feeling energy that you can only get from an audience. Promise not to laugh, but I once had a psychic say my voice had the power to heal. I know that sounds dumb, but it's a gift to be able to make music. Man, I miss it."

"Then, start a band. What have you got to lose? It sounds like you have a real passion for it. Believe me, if I had an ounce of talent, I'd be out there whoring myself every day. Why don't you put an ad in the Times and see what happens. Better to do it now before you're old and thirty. Speaking of old people, have you been back to that disco where we met?"

"I'm not a night person," I said, shaking my head. "The cigarette smoke and the noise are a real drag, man. I mean, I want to meet people, but that whole scene is a little desperate."

"I have to get back to work. Remember, you promised to come visit the station soon."

I hung up. I knew I had no interest in visiting her station. To me, television represented the worst kind of journalism: pretty faces with titillating stories of random violence with a smile. But I thought for a moment about something else she had said. Do it now while you're still young.

When I got home, I found my old guitar and sat in the middle of the floor. I hadn't written a song since coming to California. I closed my eyes and started playing. *Now, what was that lyric, that melody?* I thought about what I had done in my life so far and what I wanted to do. *So, you jumped into a car alone, and drove 2,000 miles to a strange place with no job and ten twenty-dollar bills in your pocket. So, you want to be a rock musician – or maybe a music journalist.* The words started to come, slow at first, then they poured out as I sang.

Well, it sure does feel like I'm climbing uphill
When nobody's by my side
So I change my name and I dream about fame
I try to pick up my pride
Yes, I'm on the road, and I won't be back no more
I'm on my way.

After I finished the song, I got the phone book from the kitchen, and looked for a number to the L.A. Times. *I'm in Hollywood,* I thought as I dialed, angry at myself. *How the hell am I not in a band?*

Chapter Seven

Something in the Air

Another chance to make music.

Another band.

I did some serious thinking after placing a call to the paper. But it was official. I was jumping back into music.

My ad said: "Rock singer/guitar player seeks new band for local performances. I have the songs, the look, the voice, and the fire."

I felt the fire, but I also had doubts about returning to music. Ninety-five per cent of me was happy and satisfied working as a reporter. The other five per cent was a lingering hunger to sing and perform. You know, like that small spot in the middle of your back: you can't reach it and you can't scratch it.

I decided to remove any doubt and commit myself all the way. I would invest in a top-of-the-line guitar.

I had saved up just enough money over the past year. So, shortly after placing the ad, I picked up Jason and drove to a large professional music store in West Hollywood. It was late in the evening but there were a lot of shoppers. In the middle of the store was a large room where three of the walls were covered with guitars. Black, white, red and orange guitars, and every shade of brown imaginable. A baby grand piano sat lonely in one corner of the room.

"This is like a candy store," I told Jason. "I remember the first guitar my dad ever bought me. We got it at Woolworth's, if you can believe that." I picked up a cheap one near the door, and strummed the strings. They were out of tune. "I'm sure I was the only black kid in my high school who played in a rock band. Talk about being out of tune with your peers."

I looked up at the array of glistening new guitars. My eyes stopped at one that was honey-colored and beautiful, high on the wall amid dozens of others that now seemed invisible. Something was special about the way it looked. I used a small stepladder to bring it down. When I played it, the sound was beautiful and almost magical.

"I wonder how my new song will sound on this. I wrote a new one, man. It's called 'I'm On My Way.'"

"A little corny, but okay. I need to start writing again my damn self."

I played eight bars of my song, then I went into the beginning of James Taylor's "Fire and Rain," which also dealt with the breakup of a promising rock band. When I finished, there were a handful of people standing and listening.

"There's something about this guitar," I said quietly to Jason. But he was distracted by something else.

He was looking at the people's faces, some of whom had their mouths open in disbelief. I saw a glint in Jason's eyes – a brief spark of light he sometimes got when he was hatching something.

He strolled to the baby grand piano, sat, and began to play a complicated piece by Bach. I began to improvise something along with his playing, but he started playing louder, drowning out my poor six strings with his eighty-eight powerful strings and hammers. I held my own until he played so loudly I had to stop out of futility.

When he finished, the room was silent, and a dozen people were standing and watching. They must have been amazed to see two black men playing at such a high level. They didn't applaud, like people would have done in a movie; they just stood in awed silence for a few seconds, then drifted out of the room, back to whatever they were doing - fingering flutes and checking out cheap keyboards. I bought the guitar and a case and we headed for home. I strapped it around my back and felt special walking down Sunset Boulevard.

Jason and I were able to spend more time hanging out after his boyfriend disappeared. But with Samir gone, he began a phase of having casual sex with numerous men. He said he was bitterly against relationships now and even chose to have anonymous sex in parks and public restrooms. When I came home one Saturday night and saw a gang member and a Nation of Islam guy both putting on their clothes, I knew it was time to start looking for my own apartment.

"But we're good roommates," he begged when I told him I wanted to move.

"After your friend left," I said, "it was cool for me to stay and help you with the rent. But, man, this scene is wild around here. I need to have my own space. And I want to be up in Hollywood, closer to work. Aren't you making enough so you don't need a roommate?"

"I don't really *need* one, per se. I just don't like living alone. I actually prefer having someone else around. But I'll be okay. We all need to do our own thing."

The Los Angeles Times classified section was filled with thousands of job listings and hundreds of personal ads. There were only about a dozen ads for musicians who either wanted to sell an instrument or find a new band member. I checked mine; it was nestled between a group that needed a bass player and a guy selling drums.

Three days after placing my ad, I got a call from Sam Stone, a piano player who was putting together a rock group with jazz and R&B flavor. It sounded like just what I was looking for.

I took my guitar to Sam's place in Venice Beach. He had a cozy garage that was perfect for band rehearsals. The first thing I saw when I walked in was Sam's head peering over a speaker cabinet that he was plugging in. He stepped from behind the cabinet to shake hands and I was surprised to see how short he was. He was dark, with a slight resemblance to Idi Amin. His brother, Don, was taller; he was standing in a corner leaning and looking cool like bass players always do, tuning his guitar by ear.

They wanted to hear original songs, so I played "She's The One" and "Down to the Water." It was exhilarating to be able to sing in front of people after such a long time, even though it's more nerve-wracking to perform for two people than for two thousand, especially when they're critical musicians. They listened attentively and bobbed their heads to the rhythm.

I wanted to hear them play as well, so the three of us did "Hey Joe," by Jimi Hendrix. Not a challenging song for me to sing or play, and I had a chance to hear Sam's natural talent at the keyboard and Don's mastery at keeping the beat, even without drums.

"Nice, brother, very nice," Sam said. "I think we can do this. We would still need a girl singer and a drummer to round things off. But I like your voice and I think we can move ahead, that is, if you're interested."

Don said nothing; he was obviously the youngest, letting his big brother make the decisions. Sam gave me a tape cassette with several of his songs for me to learn. He said he wanted to take it slow while he searched for a female singer. We agreed to write new songs together while looking for the right girl.

A few days later, I finally got together with Linda. We were on our way to becoming good friends and the fact that we had no romantic chemistry made things easier.

Television City, where she worked, loomed over its Hollywood neighborhood like a white whale in the sky. It sat on four city blocks functioning like a self-contained village. I wound my way through a maze of security checkpoints and parking lots to reach Linda's building. A receptionist telephoned her. She came to meet me in the lobby.

"Welcome to the zoo," she said, "or as the squares call it, Television City."

"Seems like an interesting place to work," I said. "Do we have time for a tour before lunch?"

"Sure, follow me, but I have to eat soon." She led me through halls lined with pictures of television stars. Jack Benny, Judy Garland, Mary Tyler Moore, and the sheriff guy from "Gunsmoke" were prominently displayed. "And here," she said at the end of the hall, "is the queen, Miss Lucille Ball, the broad who helped make this place possible. Say you're a fan of Lucy. Say it."

"I love Lucy," I said, and we laughed together. "How many production studios do you have here?"

"Keep in mind the network and the local station are separate, even though we're in the same building. The station has two studios, one for news and one for local programming.

The network has ten studios spread over the lot, including Big Bertha where they shoot specials and musical numbers. The squares call it Studio B."

"There's a lot a buzz happening down the hall. What's happening?"

Four men in suits and a tiny woman in a red dress were entering a room down the hall from us. Each person was talking at once, except the tallest man, who was listening to them. When they entered, we walked a few steps, and Linda peered through the small glass window above the words 'Studio One.'

"It looks like Ronald Reagan," she said. "That puppet head is running for president again. They're taping an interview with him for one of the news shows. Now *there's* a man who should be president: a bad actor. Won't happen in a million years."

We walked around the lot, which was bustling with shows in various stages of production. Carol Burnett was rehearsing in one of the bigger studios and a local children's show was taping in a smaller one. It must have been like working on a big playground.

"Can I start you off with drinks?" the waitress asked. We were seated at a small cafe table on the sidewalk of the crowded Fairfax Grill, across the street from the studio.

"I never drink during business hours," Linda said, staring at the menu. We both ordered Cokes. "So what do you think about applying for a job at the station? I'll introduce you to the news director if you want."

"I think I should stick with the music journalist thing for a while at least. I like the lone cowboy aspect of being out in the field doing my interviews. Actually, I *could* do all my writing at home. So, technically I never need to go into the office except to hand in a story and get mail."

"I'm telling you," she said, "it's a great place to work. TV reaches millions of people every day. How many people do you reach with your magazine? And how can you tolerate covering the crap they play on the radio today?"

"Good point. It could happen, if I could find a way to do what I do now, but just do it for TV. I love music, whether it's writing about it or making it. It's dynamic like nothing else."

"You're right about that part," she said. "Television is the same as it was thirty years ago. Dumb jokes, laugh tracks, and commercials. Carol Burnett is just Lucy in a different format."

"Exactly. But, music is always going to change. There'll always be a trend or the next big thing. Sinatra, Elvis, the Beatles, now it's disco - in a few years it'll be something else. You gotta love it."

"It sounds like you just began your next column," Linda said. "I guess the music scene is not all bad. You've got your Osmonds, your Jacksons, Carpenters, you've got Barry Manilow, disco fever…" Her voice trailed off; she closed her eyes and shook her head. "On second thought, I'm going to have a little drink. Music sucks."

"There's something in the air," I said. "I'm interviewing all these people, right? The more I hear, the more it seems like we're in some sort of transition period for music. The old sixties and seventies people are being pushed aside, and everybody seems to think disco won't last. I'm wondering which way pop music is headed."

I told her about the band I was joining and how hopeful I was about making music again. I had to yell because of the noise from street traffic. A car was stopped at a nearby red light. The driver was playing some loud, rhythmic music I had never heard before. No one was singing on the song; a guy was shouting - sounding angry and boastful at the same time. I listened closer, but the car sped off as the light turned green. I noticed the car's New York license plate. It wouldn't be long before I learned what that music was.

Chapter Eight

Street Corner Symphony

ONE YEAR LATER

"Five million dollars!" Linda said.

"Five million in cash," I repeated into the phone. "At this point it's just a rumor. Wendy won't talk about it, but word is, a big company is offering her that much to buy this little magazine."

I was standing at my desk looking around at all the new faces in the office.

"If I were her," she said, "I'd cash in quick enough to make your head spin."

"Wendy's a weird chick," I said, lowering my voice so no one would overhear me. "I've been at *Hype* two years now, and she's practically a stranger to me. As far as the buyout goes, she likes being the head of her own company with nobody to answer to. I don't think she'll sell at any price. The record business is red hot right now, and so are we."

It was March of 1979 and *Hype* had tripled its readership since I arrived. Fleetwood Mac, Michael Jackson, and other big acts were helping the music industry sell more records than ever before. That also meant predatory corporations were looking for attractive companies to gobble up. Already bought out were Alliance Records, Soultown, Rolling Rock Magazine, and Groove Records. Could *Hype* be next?

Business-wise, we benefited from the bulging readership; the magazine became a primary place for advertisers to sell their snack foods and motorcycles to record-buying young people. As a result, Wendy doubled the number of pages in each issue; now there were 80 pages instead of 40. The increased number of ads also meant longer articles and more employees.

One of the new employees, the one I was looking at as I spoke to Linda on the phone, was Charlene Sweet.

She looked up from far across the office and saw me staring at her. To my surprise, she stood up and walked toward me.

"Let me get back to you later, Linda." I hung up the phone.

Charlene's high heels clicked with a rhythm on the tile floor as she walked in my direction. She had been on the job two weeks, as production assistant, but we had never had a real conversation, since I did most of my interviews in the field. She had a white envelope, swinging in her left hand as she walked. The clicking stopped, and she was standing over me.

"You. You must be the famous Anthony Adams. I've been trying to catch up with you." She put out her right hand, and we shook. Soft hands, nails the same crimson shade of her thick lipstick.

"I don't get to hang out in the office much," I said. "Most of my games are on the road."

She was uncomfortably close – so much so that if I stood up we'd be face to face.

"Wendy wanted me to give this to you. I was hoping we could..."

My phone rang. I needed to take the call. I put up a finger for Charlene to wait a minute. She stood for about ten seconds, then she handed me the note with a Hollywood smile, spun around and walked away.

As I talked on the phone with Steve Miller's manager, I opened the note; all the while watching Charlene disappear around a far corner. What was it she wanted? I remembered how Phoebe called her a "teacher's pet" because of her close friendship with Wendy. But I had no idea why she wanted to talk to me.

I ripped open the note. It was a memo from Wendy.

Anthony,

This disco thing keeps hanging around, so let's consider doing some articles on it; Saturday Night Fever just may become the biggest record ever.

Here's an idea. There's a black gay guy out of San Francisco with a couple of hits who calls himself "the Queen of Disco." He dresses in women's clothes. Maybe you could write a fun piece on him."

The note went on, but I was thinking of the way Wendy liked to use the word "fag;" maybe she wanted me to make fun of this guy. At least it was something new for a change. *Hype* had avoided the word "disco" like Ronald Reagan would soon avoid the word "AIDS."

I read the last line of the note. "P.S. Charlene wants to talk to you."

The weekend finally came. I packed my guitar on Saturday morning and drove to meet Sam Stone at his Venice garage. This was only going to be our fifth rehearsal in a year. We had co-written three great songs and now he said he finally located the right girl singer.

His house was nine short blocks from the ocean. It was a cool, funky neighborhood. On weekends, shop owners and artists turned the district into a colorful street fair and flea market. Many of them were setting up their booths as I walked down Rainbow Lane.

I parked several blocks away and walked down the beachfront street, hoping and wondering if this was going to be a good experience. I was greeted with several smiles along the way, especially when their eyes went from me, to my guitar, and back up to me.

As I walked up his street, I could hear Sam playing electric piano. He was playing a sweet, soulful song that had complex chords and changes. I began humming to go with what he was playing. My ears caught a little three-note melody line and the words *one good love* popped into my head.

The garage door was open to the street. Sam was alone in the garage. There were two microphone stands in the middle of the room. He was riffing with his eyes closed. I stepped up to a mike, and began to improvise with him.

"One good love is all I need
With one good love, you're guaranteed
no more lonely nights.
But one good love is hard to find
And one good love will change your mind
about everything."

"That's awesome, bro," Sam said.

"I just made it up walking here, man. That was some sweet, funky stuff you were playing."

"You need to write those lyrics down, boy. I can definitely do something with those. 'One Good Love.' That's a winner, son."

Someone knocked on the open door. The sun cast a large, round shadow on the garage floor.

"Yoo hoo, it's me, LaWanda."

"Hey, girl," Sam said, "come in, we're just warming up."

"You must be Anthony. I'm LaWanda. I heard you're a good singer, and a great songwriter."

"Well, I do okay," I said. "I'm just looking forward to getting out in front of the people again."

LaWanda was cheerful and pleasant, but she was also extremely overweight, and quite short. I wondered what kind of visual impact we would make on stage at a time when Donna Summer and Diana Ross were the standard body types for girl singers. With my height of six feet, and her less than five, maybe we could call ourselves Number Ten, since that's what we would look like on stage. This is "just the right girl singer" we've been looking for?

Sam's brother Don walked in, and Chuck, the drummer, was last to arrive. They set up their equipment, and we were ready to play. Sam was the clear leader of the band. He barked out instructions and knew exactly how he wanted us to sing, play and sound.

We ran through the four songs that were on the rehearsal tape, doing each number three times. I was impressed by LaWanda's beautiful soprano voice. Don was good, too, thumping and plucking the bass strings and keeping perfect time. Chuck was a weak point; his drumming sounded mechanical. Don tried to get him to loosen up and play with more feeling. Sam was the best musician of us all. His natural talent and confidence poured into his piano playing.

After an hour, Don said his wife wanted him home by three, so we had to cut rehearsal short just when we were feeling juiced. Before we left, Sam announced the name of the group: Night Club. We thought it was a short and sweet representation of the smooth, jazzy music we were developing. Overall, it was a good first meeting and I left feeling confident, energized and exhausted at the same time.

Singing is a strange mixture of the spiritual and the technical. You have to be technical to hit the right notes and stay in the right key. You also have to access your spirit in order to touch people's souls. I was never the most soulful singer, but I hit the right notes and brought just enough soul to make it sound interesting.

It felt so good to step into the warm, still, ocean air. I needed a few seconds to remember where my old Dodge was parked. As I walked, I noticed there was one street musician on each block of the avenue. *They must have to stake out their territory like squirrels in a park.*

One man was playing a folk guitar, singing songs by Bob Dylan. His guitar case was open and empty, waiting for dollars or coins to drop. On the next block was a black man playing saxophone. His wailing notes sounded lonely and tortured. Hungry tourists were rushing past him to get into a nearby restaurant. His hat had a dollar and three quarters in it.

I crossed the street and walked toward two men playing congas. They looked like brothers and they both had cigarettes dangling from the same sides of their mouths. The men played in perfect sync with each other. As I listened, there were times when the guitar, sax, and congas fell into time together, like an abstract street corner symphony. Most of the time the sound was dissonant, but every few seconds there would be a small wave of beautiful music, sounding raw and free, like a mixture of souls.

I stepped back and listened. The passing people mostly disregarded the street musicians. If these same players were on "The Tonight Show," I thought, these folks would stop and applaud. But without a corporate seal of approval, the musicians were ignored, with only the odd person dropping a coin or a crumpled bill their way.

I wanted, against all odds, to be a working musician again, hoping Sam Stone's band would be my ticket. It was a good thing we weren't a disco act, because that term, that music, was about to die a quick death. And I would be there to see it die.

Chapter Nine

Divas

JULY 1979, FOUR MONTHS LATER

Sex was Jason's middle name for half of 1979. For every girl I connected with, he hooked up with three guys. "The neighbors must think we're selling coke or doing something illegal in here," I said to him once.

But in July, I noticed only one guy coming around. Omari, the gang member who dressed in bright flashes of red, never showed up before midnight, and always smelled of weed.

One night, the three of us went out for food, and on the way home, I sat in the back seat of Jason's car as the two of them sat in the front. While Jason was rambling on about something, I felt a hand rubbing my left leg. In the darkness, I saw Omari's arm creeping up my calf, his red sleeve like blood in moonlight. I slid to the other side of the seat, and told myself to start looking for an apartment the next day.

At the magazine, more office rumors were spreading about Charlene Sweet. The word was that she was in training to become a writer or editor, that she was Wendy's drug dealer, that the two of them were lesbian lovers. Wendy's casual management style only allowed the rumors to spread more. But as long as the magazine was successful and good, she was unconcerned about morale or rumors.

Months ago, Charlene had asked me for tips on becoming a music journalist. She wanted to eventually tag along on some interviews and basically have me train her. My field work and schedule allowed me to avoid her for months. I wasn't naïve enough to train my own potential replacement. But I knew I'd eventually have to confront her.

I was sitting at my desk for the first time in weeks. Without fail, Charlene came click-clacking toward me. "Whatcha working on?" she said. I looked at her, and got an image she had probably been a cheerleader in high school: an Orange County beauty queen type, using her looks to get her way.

"I'm on a deadline, doing a piece on Marvin Gaye's comeback. I really can't talk now."

She playfully fingered a stack of papers on my desk. "Well, what do you think about me coming out on your next interview?"

"Charlene, I don't have time to think about that right now."

She leaned in closer.

"Wendy says it's cool if I get out in the field with you sometime, so you might want to *find* time to think about it." She straightened up, turned, and walked away. After a few steps, she whipped back around, "And soon."

Going from one diva to the next, I spent that night with Sylvester, the disco singer Wendy wanted to profile.

It had taken a few weeks to schedule a meeting with him, but his manager was excited about getting some exposure in a mainstream magazine. When he said "mainstream," I realized how important and widespread *Hype* was becoming. It was no longer Wendy's little rich girl toy. We were players and I loved it.

Sylvester was in town visiting his parents for the Fourth of July, so his manager and I arranged for a meeting at a bar in West Hollywood. The singer had scored big last year with a couple of disco songs that crossed over onto the pop charts. He was also known for dressing in flamboyant outfits, and for being openly gay, to the extent of calling himself "the Queen of Disco." I remembered Linda saying she once saw him perform at a club, and that he was becoming an icon in San Francisco's burgeoning gay ghetto.

I stepped into a bar on West Santa Monica Street. Sylvester was the only black person in the Black Knight bar. Four thin blond men were flouncing around the table where he was sitting. Each man was holding a drink. It looked like a black queen surrounded by white pawns. A small amount of daylight was still in the sky, but the club was dark and Sylvester was wearing black sunglasses like so many rising and falling stars did. His hair was pulled back into a tight short ponytail. I squeezed between two of his minions to reach his table.

"I'm Anthony Adams from *Hype* Magazine. I spoke to your manager Harvey."

"Of course you did, doll," he said. "Have a seat."

He flicked his wrist twice for the young men to move away, and they danced to the beat toward the bar and the dance floor. They were like drunken little angels, trying to drink their way back to heaven.

"How are you enjoying your success?" I asked.

"It's wonderful," he said. "I've always been a singer, at home and in the church. It's such a blessing to be paid and appreciated for doing what you love, like music."

"Well, tell me what else you like to do. When you're not working or performing, what does Sylvester get into?"

"I like to dance, I like to shop - my music is my life, and that's what I do, all day and all night." He laughed and lit a cigarette.

I asked him about his childhood, his life as a young gay man, his big break in music. He had a mildly interesting story, but nothing unlike the hundreds of singers and actors in Hollywood who get a break and disappear. I didn't think *Hype's* readers would know or care about Sylvester, and I didn't know how to make it interesting. I *didn't* want to make him look comical or foolish, which Wendy may have wanted. After an hour of questions I still needed something to hang my story on. Something was missing.

As a reporter, I've found that some profile interviews are a joy. The person has a story to tell. They give details of a life of struggle, failure and achievement. Whether they're famous or not, they open themselves and reveal a complicated story that I have to summarize in a few well-chosen words.

Alternately, you'll find people who present a challenge to just get something to write about. Either their stories lack complexity or depth, or they're unresponsive and disinterested in talking. Sylvester was the latter.

Toward the end of our hour, we grew quiet and I found myself quietly bobbing my head to the beat of the music. I was more fascinated by the growing crowd of free-spirited young men in the bar. I couldn't tell where Sylvester's eyes were focused behind his sunglasses, but he seemed as distracted now as I was.

Sometimes a change in venue can affect the energy of a profile. The Queen of Disco was scheduled to sing the national anthem at Dodgers Stadium in a few hours, so I told him I would get myself a press pass and meet him on the field.

That gave me time to call the office for a photographer. Nick made it just in time; he had two long cameras hanging around his neck as he burst into the Dodger's press office. He got his pass, and the two of us headed down to the field. The sellout crowd was seated and ready for baseball, fireworks, and beer. Sylvester was standing with his manager in the walkway behind home plate. He was wearing a gold lame cape, sequined sunglasses, white platform shoes and a hat with tall ostrich feathers.

Harvey, Sylvester's manager, was talking with the press manager about some kind of problem.

"Hi, Sylvester, it's me again," I said. "What's going on?"

"They want me to go out across that muddy field in my new pumps, and oh no, they had better do something about that."

He wasn't angry, just annoyed and concerned about ruining his shoes, which were glossy white. I looked at the baseball field, which had been slightly watered down before the game, as teams often do. Even so, the heels on Sylvester's shoes would have certainly gotten dirty if he walked behind the tall fence where we were standing.

Harvey was trying earnestly to see what could be done. The man from the Dodgers was calm—obviously he had to deal with star attitudes on a regular basis—but game time was coming, and it was time to sing the national anthem.

The press man called for someone to bring him a golf cart. The cart came right where Sylvester was standing. "Get this," I said to my photographer, who started snapping pictures. The press man and Harvey lifted Sylvester onto the cart, which sped onto the field near a waiting microphone. The mike stand was lifted onto the cart, and Sylvester stood in the cart.

"Welcome to Dodger's Stadium," the announcer's voice said. He made a few more announcements then said, "Now singing our national anthem, disco star, Sylvester!"

The crowd became quiet. Sylvester clutched a chain around his neck and began to sing a capella.

"Oh say, can you see..."

I heard a quiet rumbling among the crowd, restless anger.

"...by the dawn's early light..."

His falsetto voice was crystal clear as it echoed beautifully around the stadium. But with each line he sang, the crowd became more agitated and loud. His eyes were closed as he concentrated. The photographer swung around to get a shot of the crowd, which was now a storm of boos and whistles.

"...and the home of the brave."

Only when Sylvester opened his eyes did he realize there were 40,000 people jeering and booing his performance. He took off his sunglasses and looked around the stadium in disbelief. His eyes and mouth were wide open, then he squinted his eyes like a villainous Bette Davis. In defiance, he unbuttoned his cape and lifted it over his head like a giant peacock, and took a bow. The crowd unleashed itself with the sound of fury.

"Disco is dead," I heard Harvey say.

The cart came back to where we stood behind the fence. Sylvester was anxious to leave, so I volunteered to take him back to his hotel, where Harvey would meet us. The photographer said he had more than enough. He'd send me proofs in a few days.

Sylvester was silent on the drive down Wilshire. His manager was already in the hotel room when we arrived. Harvey and I talked while Sylvester began making phone calls.

Harvey had been in the music business since the days of do-wop music. After do-wop, he said, he became part of a soul music band, then he found success at Motown Records, then funk took over. Now he was doing disco, though he seemed apologetic and a little embarrassed about the music he was making now. He was a strong but gentle older man who would have made a great profile interview himself, but for a different magazine.

Sylvester called his mother, a boyfriend in San Francisco, and some other friends while Harvey and I talked. Harvey's voice was extremely deep, like the color of mahogany wood, and he spoke with weary confidence like a man who had spent many years on the road with many musicians. He said he was working with a girl group he recently discovered. I told him I was also a songwriter and a musician.

"Really now," he said. "Everybody's a songwriter, I guess."

"I have a lot of songs I wrote for my band. Maybe I could send you some."

"Put together your best three songs," he said, "and give me a call." He handed me his business card. It was bright gold with black lettering. "The group is called Two Tons of Fun and we're looking for traditional ballads and upbeat tunes."

"I know just what to send you," I said.

"But no disco," Harvey whispered. "It's too black and too, too gay."

I joined them for dinner in the hotel. Harvey left and I took Sylvester back to the bar where I first met him. He danced most of the night as I sat sipping soda, trying not to look out of place. The music was hypnotically diverting, and before I knew it, it was nearly two in the morning. Sylvester said he found someone to take him back to his hotel; he had latched onto a tall, wide-shouldered blond man who could have been a Viking a thousand years ago.

The L.A. streets were bare. I had to figure how I could get 800 words out of someone whose sole interests were shopping, dancing, and men who looked like Norse gods. I decided to use the day's events to write an article on the inevitable. The title:

"Disco is Dead."

Chapter Ten

The Conference Room

Gay, gay, gay.

I felt like I was surrounded by gayness, from the closeted movie stars I interviewed, to Sylvester, to perhaps Wendy and Charlene at work, to my roommate at home. I loved my job, but I wanted to find a new place to live.

The day after the ballpark incident, I found an ad in the Sunday paper for an apartment in a good West Hollywood neighborhood. It was close to the magazine office and central to city life and activity.

The El Dorado.

A sprawling apartment building with twenty-one modern units splattered across a fourth of a city block on Cole Avenue in the heart of town. I called and made an appointment and at one in the afternoon I drove up and parked under the tallest palm tree I had ever seen.

Mina, the apartment manager, buzzed me in. She lived up front in apartment 101, where she could see everyone who came and went, and whom they were with. I knocked on her door. "Be right there," she yelled through the closed door. I heard keys jingling. She opened the door and quickly examined me from head to toe, squinting through a thousand tiny wrinkles around her eyes.

We walked up the stairs, and headed to the vacant unit. "You black or white?" she asked. A vile mix of cigarette smoke and liquor were on her breath. "I'm probably not supposed to ask that question anymore, but my eyes ain't so good now."

"I'm just a regular man, just like anybody else," I said. "A man who can afford $200 a month with no problem."

"Touché, honey," she said, then she laughed with a phlegm-filled cackle. We stopped at apartment 205, where she fumbled again with her set of keys, pushing her long, yellowing hair from her face, and opened the door.

"So, you're a music writer at, what did you say on the phone, Cake Magazine? I used to be a chorus girl at MGM, would you believe that? Long time ago, that was. Then, I went to school and became a teacher. It's funny: when I told people I was a chorus girl, they'd get excited and curious. Then when I told people I was a teacher, it was like they felt sorry for me. Ain't life grand?"

She continued to talk while we walked through the unit. The living room faced west, with a lot a natural sun coming in the windows. It was a clean and spacious apartment, and seemed like a quiet area. Perfect in every way, I thought, so I signed a lease to move in over the weekend.

As I walked outside, it struck me how massive the building was, and according to Mina, full of people on the edges of show business. In 103 lived a young lady who worked as a nurse for Paramount Pictures. Apartment 107 was home to a violinist who played for the Los Angeles Symphony. My neighbor in 204 was Dave Nelson, a retired man who used to be an arranger for Frank Sinatra and Nat King Cole.

The building was half a block from Melrose, which meant it would be a short, straight drive to work. Seven tall palm trees lined the front of the long structure, and a quiet courtyard was in the center of the rectangular building. It had a bubbling fountain at one end of the yard, making soothing water sounds. This will be a great place to write, I thought.

Around the corner and down Melrose was a club called Small World. I'd probably passed it dozens of times, but I only noticed it the first time I left my new apartment building. It was hard to tell what kind of club it was, though most Hollywood clubs were either new wave, metal or straight rock and roll. I knew it wasn't a disco; those all seemed to vanish in the same week, around the time "My Sharona" displaced "Good Times" at number one on the charts. The place looked like a renovated movie theater that had been converted to a club. Maybe my band could do some shows there, I thought. I'd have to call my running buddy, Linda, so we could check it out soon. I owed her a call.

I entered the office on Friday morning, and the first sign of trouble was a meeting in the conference room. Wendy never had meetings; she let her editor-in-chief handle those. Wendy, Charlene, and a man I'd never seen were huddled at one end of the long table. After I settled at my desk, Phoebe walked over.

"Something's going on, everyone's talking," she said in a whispered tone.

"What's happening around this place," I said, "everybody is so damn paranoid."

"Well, mister innocent, that happens to be Wendy's brother she's sitting with. Charlene told me. This is the first time anybody's ever seen him. You *know* something's happening." She waited for me to respond, but I had nothing to say.

Phoebe moved on to someone who offered her more energy, and I began working. A half hour later, Wendy rolled her chair to the conference room door, opened it slightly and peeked her head out.

"Anthony Adams, could you join us in the meeting, please?"

The big editorial room instantly became silent. I could feel the warmth of co-worker's eyes following me as I walked toward the meeting. Some of the eyes were searching my face. And everyone seemed to know what was about to happen except me. In my naïveté, in my first job out of college, I didn't suspect trouble. I was still focused on my half-written article, and thinking of my new apartment.

"Have a seat, Anthony," Wendy said. "This is my brother, Tom Robinson. He's going to be doing some work at the magazine. He's a photographer." She paused for a few seconds and looked out the window. "Let's get right to it. Charlene and Tom are getting married, she's a writer, they're going to be a team. I have to let you go."

Tom whispered something to Charlene, and the two of them left the room. I looked into Wendy's eyes, not believing what she said.

"Wendy, this is unreal. Are you *firing* me?"

"You're not being fired, Anthony. Consider it kind of a layoff." She paused. "I want to give Charlene a chance to prove herself. She did a great interview last week with Peter Frampton, and she can write. It may or may not work out. But I'm giving her a chance. You can easily find something else in this town. I'll give you a great reference."

"Has there been a problem with my writing or my work here?" I asked, still unbelieving what I had heard.

"Well, funny you should ask. I told you long ago, ninety per cent of our readers are white. So, what's with all the black stuff lately - Marvin Gaye, Sylvester..."

"Wendy, you *told* me to interview Sylvester."

"Look, let's make this easier. I'll pay you for three months. But this is a done deal. Issues are in play here that you don't know about, family issues. So let's not make this into a thing, and maybe I'll see you again sometime down the road."

We sat in awkward silence together for three seconds, until I realized there was nothing left for either of us to say.

As I walked away from the conference room, people were no longer staring; they diverted their eyes and looked down at their papers and coffee. Phoebe came up to me while I cleared out my desk. She simply gave me a hug, then scurried back to her work area.

It was hard to believe I had worked at *Hype* for two whole years; the time went by so fast. I looked around, thinking of saying goodbye to people, but I realized I hadn't made a friend in the place.

I went to the parking lot and got in my car. Jason was right about making friends in L.A. Two years, and my dream job had come to a crashing end.

How could I have been so clueless not to see trouble coming with Wendy and Charlene? I wanted to talk to someone. I thought about calling Jason, or Linda, or even my mother in Chicago, but pride and embarrassment took over. Instead, I drove to Venice and walked up and down the beachfront, surrounded by colors and life, listening to music, thinking about what had just happened, and what to do next.

Chapter Eleven

I'll Get Back To You

Being unemployed in Hollywood is like being a broke, hungry kid in a candy store. Money and the good life are all around, but you can't have any of the sweets because your pockets are empty. Nose pressed against the window, wanting for what you can't have.

As always, Jason had something to say. "Now, Anthony, you just need to quit getting fired all the time." We were loading boxes into a small trailer hitched to my car. "In the meantime, you should just stay your ass with me until you find another job."

"I thought about it, but there's the little problem of the lease I signed. Man. Who would have thought I'd lose my job the day after I finally get my new place. But it's good to know you got me covered if I go belly up after my severance runs out."

Plus, I thought, I'm ready to live alone for the first time in my life, away from parents and roommates.

We got in the car, and drove the short distance northeast to the El Dorado. I was hoping for a quiet ride, but Jason kept on chatting.

"You know what? I think it's fate you got fired. Bad things happen for a good reason sometimes. You can focus on your band now, 'cause you *know* music is what you're meant to do. Your group might be the next big thing."

Jason was starting to talk like L.A. people. Fate, karma, inner purpose and other phrases just sounded like nonsense to me. Spacey, New Age babble. I was here on earth, a midwestern boy trying to keep my feet on the ground, still reeling from the sting of rejection, thinking of how I'd be able to pay my bills in three months. He was my bro, but I didn't want to hear his platitudes.

We turned onto Cole Avenue, and Linda was waiting in her car to help us unload the trailer.

I was worried how my two best friends were going to get along.

She hopped out of her car as I was parking, and slowly walked toward us. I introduced them. They shook hands, and in exact unison said "I've heard a lot about you." We all laughed, but the ice never broke between them. On Jason's part, he never had any female friends since being teased in the seventh grade; he was nervous around women. And Linda was a loner who would rather read a book than be around people. But with their combined help, my move took less than two hours, and I made it to band rehearsal on time.

Night Club had been together just over a year, and we had done several small shows in bars over the past few weeks. We acted like professionals, unlike my previous band, which was immature and chaotic in comparison. Sam Stone was a charismatic leader who got musicians to work hard and do their best.

"My vision," he told me once, "is to create a soulful version of Manhattan Transfer: lots of vocal harmonies over a tight rhythm section, presented in a stylish, sophisticated show."

LaWanda and I shared lead vocals, with Sam singing background. Don and Sam worked with the drummer to get more feeling out of his playing. Overall, the band was sounding better every week.

On this day, I was first to arrive for rehearsal, as usual. Sam was behind his electric piano, and he stood up quickly when he saw me knocking on the old-style garage doors that swung open wide as I stepped in.

"Anthony, Anthony," he said. "Get in here, man, how's it going?"

"What's up, Sam?"

"Big stuff, some big stuff. I wish everybody would hurry up and get here. I got us a new booking, a *big* booking."

"Really? Where? Tell me."

"We're..." He looked around the empty room. "I should wait until they all get here. Just to be fair. Where are they, goddamn it?"

"It's still two minutes to one, cool out, man. This must be big, whatever you got."

"All right, all right, I'll tell you quick, but you have to act surprised when I tell the whole band. We are to open for—are you ready—Chic, the disco band. One of their people saw our show last month in Burbank, and they want us to do their Labor Day weekend show in two weeks. This could be the big break, man."

I felt a shot of adrenaline hit my heart at the idea of opening for such a great band, in front of hundreds of people. Sam and I high-fived each other, just as LaWanda entered the room, followed shortly by Don and Chuck. Sam asked for everyone's attention as people were settling into position.

"Ladies and gentlemen, I have good news, and better news. The better news is that I'm proud and happy to be a part of this great union called Night Club. Everyone is doing a tremendous job, and you are all great performers and musicians. The good news is that we, Night Club, will be opening at the El Rey Theater on Wilshire in thirteen days for one of the funkiest groups around, none other than Chic."

Everyone was ecstatic; Don said "yes" and pumped his fist, Chuck said "all right," and LaWanda gave me a hug while I said, "Sam, you're kidding, wow."

Time stretched out like a slow-running clock for the next two weeks as I anticipated the big show. Without a job, I spent most of the days in my apartment, enjoying the space and the solitude, and getting caught up with my friends and family.

I called my parents. They were having a rare period of peace since my father cut back on his drinking due to a bad liver. He was impressed when I told him all the musicians I had interviewed over the past two years. He had a great idea, suggesting I compile all of the interviews and put them together in an anthology, called something like "Talking to the Stars" or "Music in Their Own Words." I thought it would work. So did Linda.

"That book would sell like hot cakes," she said when I phoned her. "People are insane about celebrities these days. There's a new magazine called "People" that makes movie stars seem like gods. Hey, maybe you could get a job at "People Magazine."

"I'm sure they're based way out in New York," I said. "But I think the book idea just might fly. I could do it, if I got a decent advance from a publisher. With some cash up front, I wouldn't need to get a nine-to-five job."

Then it hit me: *Hype* Magazine owned all the rights to my interviews. I knew Wendy wouldn't give me the rights, and I couldn't afford to pay her for them. If I wanted to do the book, I'd have to start from scratch and do a whole new set of interviews. I needed to get at least a dozen topflight names if I wanted to get a book deal.

I said goodbye to dad and hung up. My *Hype* files, story ideas and contacts, were in two boxes in the kitchen. I looked through them, and found the names of some people who were labeled "possibles." There was a musician named Narada Michael Walden that Wendy had met in San Francisco. I called his office to arrange an interview. A man answered.

"Tarpan Studios, can I help you?"

"My name is Anthony Adams, and I'm a journalist. I'm doing a book of interviews with great musicians, and a friend of Narada's suggested I contact him."

"Interesting," the man said. "First of all, is there any compensation for Narada in this venture?"

His question caught me off guard. "No, it's just an interview. It'll take two hours. I'm doing this as a freelancer."

"Freelance?" he said. "You don't have a publisher?"

"Not as yet, no."

"Have you published anything in the past?"

"I was a writer for *Hype* magazine. I did lots of interviews there."

"You *used* to write for them? Okay, good, good. Well, let me get your name and number, and I'll see what Narada's schedule is like. I'll get back to you."

I never heard from them, and I actually never expected to. It didn't take long for me to figure out how the game is played in L.A. It would be nearly impossible to get interviews as a freelancer. Without a publisher or Hollywood contacts to throw around, I might as well be a homeless guy with my face on the glass outside a Beverly Hills restaurant. I shelved the book idea.

A week before my band's big show, I asked LaWanda to record some songs for Harvey, Sylvester's manager. I picked her up, and she practiced the songs on the way. It was a small studio on La Brea that only charged eight dollars an hour, including use of a piano and drum machine.

I remembered Harvey said he wanted ballads and up-tempo songs; the three songs I chose were midtempo ballads: "Harmony," "Heartbreak Fever," and "Moving On." I programmed a basic drum track for the songs and laid down the guitar and piano. LaWanda sang the lyrics.

The next day, I called Harvey, who seemed happy to hear from me. He told me to meet him at his studio, just off Sunset Boulevard, in a few hours.

When I got there, he was in a control room, speaking to a drummer and bass player.

"Excuse me for a second, fellows," he said to the musicians. "This is Anthony. He's a young songwriter, and he's got some dynamite songs that'll explode if I don't hear them soon, so take five."

"This must be where it all happens," I said. "Nice studio. Thanks for letting me come down."

"Hey, talent's not hard to come by in this town, but drive and initiative are what make the difference. That's what I saw in you. Now, what do you have?"

I handed him a cassette tape, and he slid it into a tape player nestled among a dozen components above his mixing board. I looked at the drummer and bass player, who were in the recording room drinking coffee. They turned away when we made eye contact.

Harvey listened to the songs.

Many people, when hearing new material, will chat, or do work, or make phone calls, but Harvey was actually engaged in the music. This was a good sign. His head wasn't nodding to the beat, but he did tap his toe every few seconds. Does he like them, I wondered. I had dreamed of hearing my songs on the radio since sixth grade, and this could be my big break. When the last song ended, he stopped the machine and handed me the tape.

"Well, son," he said, "you write some nice songs. The lyrics tell a story, and the guitar's got a nice, sweet sound. Right now I'm dealing with all these record company people and they're out of their minds. They're giving me a hard time, because my new act is a couple of women who are really big. I don't mean big-famous. I mean big-fat. The business is changing in ways I don't understand. Disco might have killed black music from the way it was. I'm saying all this because it might be a while before things come together. But when they do, I'll definitely get back to you."

Three days went by, then four, then five. I wondered if Harvey had lost my number. I thought about calling him back. Finally, on the morning of our show, I took his card, his gold-colored business card, and flushed it down the toilet. If I was going to make my name in music, it would have to be from up on the stage, where people *have* to notice you. I was ready to play and sing like my livelihood depended on it. It did.

Everything was on the line.

Chapter Twelve

All Together Now

LABOR DAY WEEKEND, 1979

Don's right leg was rocking up and down, like he was playing a silent beat.

We were seated together, huddled in a small dressing room backstage at the El Rey Theater. One hour before show time.

I looked again at Don, next to me, and I wondered if bass players always had a rhythm in their heads.

"You nervous?" he asked me in a quiet voice.

"I don't get nervous, believe it or not." I thought for a moment. "Ever since the third grade when we sang songs from 'The Sound of Music.' My class got a standing ovation. I always thought they were standing for me, you dig."

"I can dig it," he said. "But, wait, what are black folks doing singing the damn 'Sound of Music?'"

"Well, the music world was different in those days. On one radio station you could hear the Supremes, the Beatles,

James Brown, and Tom Jones. And, remember, I'm only half black."

He looked at me with one eyebrow raised. Maybe I'd never mentioned being biracial to him. He was very dark-skinned, and darker people sometimes had issues with my light complexion. He looked away, and we were quiet for a while.

Sam and LaWanda were sitting opposite us, talking. Chuck was in a chair, rat-a-tat clicking his drumsticks on the vanity counter. And Don's leg just kept jackhammer bouncing. Maybe he would calm down if I kept him talking.

"Not much to do before a show, except warm up. And maybe find a way to settle the nerves. In my old band, they used alcohol and pot. Some people meditate, some screw…"

"Let's go for a quick walk," he said. "It'll help calm you down."

"I told you I'm not nervous, man, but if you need to calm *your* nerves…'cause your leg hasn't stopped moving."

He stopped and looked at it. "My leg? What are you talking about? Come on, let's just take a quick peek out front."

We got up and headed for the door, as his brother gave us a "what the hell are you two doing" look.

"Taking a walk before a show," I said, stepping out into the hall behind Don. "This is something new."

The theater was starting to fill. We passed a plaque on a column that said the place was built in 1932. I looked up at the fixtures of naked women holding globular light bulbs on the walls. Soft-glowing chandeliers and red velvet walls that looked like candy coating I imagined all the great music that must have been played there over the years: big band, jazz, bebop and swing. And now, disco and rock. *What would Count Basie think?*

We observed the lobby crowd for a few seconds.

"Look at her," I said, "check out the big platform shoes."

"That butt is pretty smokin', too. Boy, if I wasn't married now. And look at that turkey she with. In a three-piece suit."

"When we're famous," I said, "we won't be able to do this."

"Yeah, right. But we better go back before bighead starts tripping."

We doubled back the way we came. Don was moving faster now. I put my hand on his shoulder and stopped him.

"This is beautiful, man," I said, nodding my head back toward the crowd. "Look at the people - folks from everywhere. Music is the only thing that can bring people together this way. Back East you'd never see a crowd like this. It's why I love California."

"It's true," Don said. "And this is why I became a musician." He rubbed his hands together, and we walked toward the dressing room. "Let's get ready for the show, bro."

The curtain went up.

The first thing I felt was the lights on my face. I loved how the spotlight set me apart from the crowd, and I used its energy. The music started, and still more electricity came at me from the audience. It sounds corny, but there is a power I can feel up on stage. My guitar was sounding good, and so was I. And the people were loving us. We were blowing them away.

Then I found it. The Face.

I don't know if people realize how well performers can see audience members from the stage. Depending on the lights, a singer can see you just as well as you see them.

And every audience has that one person, with their arms folded, who's just not digging the music. Not rocking at all. I liked to find The Face in the crowd and sing directly at them, try to make them move. She was a brown-haired girl in the third row.

I put some extra juice into my voice. I wasn't thinking about being fired and unemployed, or drunken parents, or Hollywood phonies who didn't return phone calls. Midway through "One Good Love," her head started to nod, then her shoulders moved. A little at first, then she let herself go. I had her.

"You young cats did great," Bernard Edwards said. I was sitting across from one of the great bass players of all time, the man who gave Chic its heavy bottom sound. While at *Hype*, I had read how influential "Everybody Dance" was to other musicians. And working there had also given me the nerve to knock on his dressing room door after their performance.

"Thanks, man. We're just getting our feet wet. I hope we can do even half of what Chic's done."

"I think the key," he said after sipping water, "is to just stay together. My band, we started out as friends, and friendship is the thing that should keep you together during the rough times. You might have money problems, problems with women, contracts, offers to join other bands. But if you're in a tight unit, just stay together, 'cause you might not find a band as good as the one you're in. So just go with the flow, man." He grabbed the towel from around his neck, and wiped his forehead.

I asked him about a song, "Rapper's Delight," that had been a big hit a few months earlier. It featured three guys rapping over a tape of his bass line from an earlier Chic hit.

"Crazy story behind that record," he said. "I was in a disco in New York last year, and that song came on. I thought the DJ was just playing "Good Times" and talking over it - live, right there in the club. I went to the booth to give him props, but little did I realize it was a record - a 12-inch record on the turntable."

"You didn't know about it in advance?"

"They did not have permission from us in any way. They basically took our song and called it theirs. Of course, we threatened to sue. The next thing I know, Nile and I are in the back of the club, with guns to our heads. These gangsters, straight up gangsters, are threatening us, telling us *not* to sue."

"So what happened?"

"Their song went gold, and they ended up giving us half a million dollars - in cash! We didn't even have to go to court. Is that weird or what?"

"What did you think of the song itself?" I asked.

He blew on his fingers, which were probably sore from the way he attacked the bass. "Piece of garbage, man. I thought it was cute the first time I heard it. But the rapping part gets kind of annoying after a minute. As an artist, why would you want to take somebody else's work, talk over it, and put *your* name on it? That blows my mind."

"It sounds like they're making it up as they go along, kind of throwaway. I'm sure this rap thing is just a fad that'll blow over in while."

I stood up and walked over to shake his hand. "I think you're the best."

I couldn't see his eyes behind his dark glasses. He just said, "Keep it funky."

There's a letdown that happens to a performer after a show. I spent weeks preparing, musically and mentally, to get up in front of a sea of energy that washes over the stage in waves.

Suddenly it's over. The applause stops, and I'm just another guy at the gas station or the checkout line.

I returned to my quiet new apartment, and started sending out resumes to newspapers and TV stations, hoping for another job soon.

Unemployment lasted long enough to make me appreciate what it used to feel like to get a steady check. Wendy sent me a final check from *Hype* Magazine, which clearly meant I needed a job soon.

Linda talked to her boss about me, and he called to set up an interview. I met with him, and he explained his plan to produce some new public affairs shows that would air on Saturday evenings. He said he would get back to me soon.

I'll get back to you. Here we go again.

Linda worked on her boss. He called and offered me a month-to-month contract as a freelance producer. The job offer came on Thursday, and he wanted me to start the next week.

Linda and I celebrated. I picked her up Saturday evening, and I was curious to see what her apartment looked like. She lived on the first floor of a modern security building on Fairfax.

"Nice place," I said, "I've known you for two years, and this is the first time I get to see your apartment. That's crazy. That's just insane."

"Has it been that long already? Some people in L.A. I've known for *five* years, and we've never been to each other's places. It's that kind of town. I think L.A. stands for 'lonesome angels.'" She walked into the bathroom to finish getting ready.

"I like your record collection. Looks like you have good taste in friends *and* music."

"Play something. Visitor's choice. Keep in mind I'm really going to judge you by this one song you play. I'll be ready in a few shakes."

Her albums were in alphabetical order, from Aerosmith to the Zombies. The records were strictly rock—she had no soul, classical or country records. I chose "All Together Now" from a Beatles album.

"Awwww," she said, coming into the living room, "that's so sweet." She was wearing her brown hair long and straight, like one of the girls in the "Charlie's Angels" TV show. She had on black jeans, and she was wearing no makeup.

"You look good, you know, for just a friend," I said, even though she looked like a plain farm girl. "I've never had a female for a buddy before. This'll be interesting. So are you trying to catch a man tonight, or what?"

"I'm not dressing to catch a *guy*," she said, "I'm dressing to keep guys away from me."

"What does that mean? Are you telling me you're a lesbian?"

"I'm not trying to be anything except just me, whoever that is." She looked around the room, then picked up her keys from the top of the TV. "What's the latest on your new job?"

"I noticed how you changed the subject. Anyway, Galen wants a magazine format, with three segments per show. And he wants it to focus on cultural events and arts. I'm going to talk to him about doing pop music stuff once in a while, too. You know, things that people actually want to see. I hope he goes for it."

We left the apartment.

"Does he have a name for the show yet?" she asked.

"He wants me to brainstorm some ideas with him first thing Monday."

The Beatle's song was still playing in my mind as I thought about her question. I put the key in my car door. I froze. Maybe a twinkle was in my eye because Linda didn't speak; she stood there watching my idea germinate. "I got it. What about 'All Together Now?'"

"All Together Now." She just smiled.

Neither of us had been back to Studio West since it opened. Disco music had been a billion-dollar industry, but there were clear signs it was fading from the mainstream. In fact, my "Disco is Dead" article was still on the newsstand, in *Hype's* latest edition.

I turned the car at Third and Figueroa, and there it was. But the glittering "Studio West" sign was now replaced with the words "Velvet Spike." *Velvet* was written in thin rounded cursive, and *Spike* was made from bolts of lightning. It looked like a ninth-grade art student might have made the sign for twenty bucks. We walked inside. Gone were the feathers and balloons. The walls were black and the crowd was all white. They were playing new wave music, punctuated by an occasional punk metal song. Everyone was under thirty, and they seemed angry. We stood at the bar, in the same spot where we had met so long ago. But now instead of being disgusted, Linda was enchanted.

"These are my people, Anthony," she said. "I think I have found myself a home."

She faded into the dance floor crowd, where dancing took the form of neck swiveling and pogo stick bouncing, with a spastic flourish here and there. At least *she's* happy with the change, I thought. I had the feeling there were even bigger changes ahead.

Chapter Thirteen

New Wave

OCTOBER 1979

Things came to a grinding halt for my band. Instead of being the big break we were hoping for, the Chic concert seemed like it was going to be our high point. We didn't get a record deal or a big tour; we spent the fall of '79 doing weddings and county fairs in the valley. Sam tried to keep things fresh by adding an occasional new song to our repertoire. But nothing was working. I wanted to feel again the power I felt at the El Rey, like a junkie needs to score a hit. It's hard to play a bar mitzvah after performing on stage for a thousand people.

How was the band? Sam and LaWanda were at each other's throats over her refusal—or inability—to lose weight. He thought her image was holding us back; the way he spoke to her in front of the group bordered on ridicule. Chuck was a typical drummer: going with the flow, and usually clueless. Don was being pressured by his wife to spend less time with his bass and more time at home. She was a religious woman who thought music should only be played in service to the Lord. He was starting to show up late for rehearsals.

He was last to arrive on Saturday morning. Sam smirked at him and shook his head. Then he spoke into his mike. "If I could have every one's attention. I think it's time for a change. Time for us to keep up with, well, the times." He took a deep breath. "I think we need to go new wave."

"New wave?" LaWanda and Chuck said together.

"It's simple," Sam said. "New wave is just what it says - the new wave in music. Disco is, like, so over. Rock is not happening. R&B is lame crossover music now. Just take a listen to what they're playing on the radio. I'm telling you, if you guys want to make it big, we need to start doing new wave right now."

"Look at us, Sam, sweetheart," LaWanda said into the microphone. "Two black guys, two white guys, Anthony - whatever he is, no offense, sweetheart..."

"None taken. Happens all the time," I said.

"...and a fat chick. Who in the world is going to come see the country's only interracial new wave band? What do we *know* about new wave? You want to ditch everything we've done so far and start over? Sam, man, you're losing it."

"LaWanda, it's all in the beat and the attitude," Sam said with a smile. He walked to the drums. Chuck got up and stood behind him, folding his arms; Sam sat at the drums and played a quick-paced, frenetic rhythm - faster than any of our song arrangements. "Now, Don, play this. Boomp, boomp ba boomp boomp." He voiced a sharply syncopated beat, which his brother played on bass. Chuck dashed behind Sam's piano, and joined in. After a few minutes with the new groove, the guys seemed to enjoy the freshness and energy of the sound. They smiled and nodded their heads with the beat, signaling approval. Sam spent the next forty minutes rearranging two of our old songs into a new wave sound.

At 4:30 we were all dripping with sweat. Sam spoke.

"In less than three months it'll be a new decade, people. It's the eighties. The eighties! And if we make a commitment to the new sound, you can all be there on the stage when the awards are being handed out. Or you can be sitting at home watching the Grammy's, and playing with yourself 'cause you're still doing old-time music. Who's with me on this?"

In quietness, we all looked at the ceiling or the floor, unwilling or unable to challenge Sam. At that moment, we were a new wave band. Don and Chuck seemed to have fun with the high energy level of the new songs, but none of us were entirely confident enough to make a drastic change. Sam used the power of his personality to convince us it was worth a try. We were going nowhere with our old sound. And anyone who challenged Sam might have been kicked out of the band.

We revamped every one of our song arrangements and lyrics to make them sound more like The Talking Heads, the Pretenders and other bands that were having success with new wave. Sam wanted us to dress in colorful clothes, and to develop quirky dance moves during rehearsals. He also planned to look for an additional keyboard player who would add a thicker synthesizer sound to our songs. Maybe jumping on the new wave bandwagon would get us a record deal. Maybe it was worth a try.

At the end of rehearsal, before anyone left, Sam came beside me, put his arm around my shoulder, and walked me out of the garage. "So, what's up, Anthony?"

"What's happening?" I said.

"I heard you and LaWanda had a side gig or something. Made some demos for a hot producer or something? What's that all about?"

"A guy asked to hear some of my songs, so I had LaWanda do a few vocals on the side. What's the problem?"

"The problem, Anthony, is that we're a family here. And if people are going off doing secret little projects, on the side, as you say, then that compromises the group and creates problems. And we don't need problems or outside projects right now. I'm just giving you a heads up."

"Sam, I'm a grown-ass man, not a baby. You can't imply I'm causing a problem by using her—for one stinking hour—to do a demo. We're not under contract and we're not children here. Come on, man, you're kidding." I moved his arm from around my shoulder. "Are you, like, threatening me?"

"Easy, man, it's not a threat. I just don't want you shopping LaWanda around to big shots. I think we're *this* close to getting a deal, with all the talent in this band. Just do me a favor and let me know before you arrange any outside projects. Get approval, man. It's in the best interest of the band. It's got to be all about the band."

"You want me to get approval," I said, and I found myself amused, realizing he had a Napoleon complex. "All right, man, I'll ask your permission to do demos, to tune my guitar, and to wipe myself after I use the bathroom." I stepped inside for my instrument, and left.

I walked in a quick pace, and headed toward the beach, even though my car was in the opposite direction. The ocean was always good for clearing my head.

Saturday afternoon was a peak period for street vendors and musicians along the Venice walkway, and the stroll was packed with people. I wanted to connect with someone new, even for just five minutes, to help get Sam off my mind.

I'm still practically new in town - I need to make some friends!

The light sea breeze hit my face, and I heard a hodgepodge of music as I walked closer to the heart of the district.

A white guy and a young black woman were performing together in front of a t-shirt shop. I stopped and folded my arms to listen as he played guitar while she sang folk songs. She had an average face, but her body was killer, with big breasts in a tight, fringed sweater. Her voice sounded flat, and his guitar playing was nothing special, yet there was a good-sized crowd standing in a semi-circle, enjoying them.

I noticed she was looking right at me as she sang. *Oh my god, am I The Face?*

I smiled, uncrossed my arms and swayed with the music, even though there was hardly a beat to find. She broke off her gaze, but I caught her peeking several times more.

After their third song, the guy spoke to the crowd. "We'll be taking a short break, so don't go too far. I'm Shakey Jake, she's Brenda, and you're you." The people laughed, and sprinkled coins and bills into his open guitar case lying on the ground. Then they wandered away.

"Nice sound," I said, stepping closer.

"Ehh, it beats working for a living, and these tourists don't demand much." he said. He looked at my guitar case. "I see you play."

"A little. I'm in a band. For now." I chuckled.

"I know what you mean."

"Nice smile," the girl said. "I'm Brenda."

We shook hands. "I know. I mean, I heard. I mean, that's what your partner said." We held our glance for a while.

"Jake," she said to him while looking at me, "we already made more than our take for a Saturday. Let's call it a day."

I saw him look back and forth between her and me. He lowered his eyes and shook his head, then he shoveled up the money from his case and closed it with a loud thump. He gave me a final tight-eyed look.

"I'll hook up with you later tonight," she told him, but he was already walking away.

Brenda took my hand. We small-talked as we strolled down winding streets, in the general direction of my car. After a few minutes, we arrived at her small upstairs apartment. She must have known I was watching her behind as we climbed the stairs; she put an extra swivel in her hips.

"Make yourself at home," she said. She went into the bathroom and closed the door. I plopped into a green beanbag chair near a greasy window.

In moments, she opened the bathroom door, and stood naked, shadowy against the bright bathroom light, striking a pose with one arm high and the other arm on her hip. *Yep, she's a singer, a wannabe diva.* I smiled and widened my legs.

I left an hour later. We never exchanged phone numbers, and barely knew each other's names. And I never saw her again. But I *would* see Shakey Jake.

Chapter Fourteen

Morning in America

"All Together Now," Galen Dooley said, looking out his office at the station parking lot. He said it again twice. "Let me run that title past Ann upstairs. I think it could work. Let's schedule the first show for October 23rd. One segment on culture, one on lifestyle, and one on happenings around town. Stephanie and Drake, the news anchors, are available to shoot stand-ups three hours a week. You'll have a film crew available two full days a week."

"Galen," I said, "what do you think of the idea of doing a music segment every once in a while? As a public affairs show we can spotlight big groups along with local bands that are looking for exposure. Right now there's a big punk scene happening in town, and a new wave scene, too. I think we can get some great stories. At least it'll be dynamic, stuff people will want to see."

"Well, l-l-l-let me run that past Ann. You haven't done your first show yet, and you want to make changes already, young man? What corporate's looking for is a more cultured, fine-arts type of thing. I don't think we want to scare people away with kids wearing razor blades and diving off the stage. Let me talk to some people about that one first."

"How about just local people, then, like the Eagles or even the Carpenters, something more mainstream?" I was trying to save my idea. The word "Carpenters" calmed him down. He said he'd talk to Ann, the program manager who apparently had to check all of Galen's major decisions.

I now had two weeks to produce, film and edit our first half-hour show. Luckily, I had the training and confidence to do it. *Thank you, Professor North.*

Producing the first show, under a deadline, was unlike anything I had done before. But pieces fell into place. I did all of the research, writing and editing; then I would take Stephanie or Drake to a park or museum plaza, and have them read introductions to each piece. Later, one of them would read the voice narrations for each segment.

Galen, (or Ann—I suspected she called every shot) approved the idea of doing a pop entertainment profile for the final segment. They said I could cover music, movies or sports for the last six-minute piece.

"I want to turn 'All Together Now' into *Hype Magazine* on the air," I told Linda one night. So I put my heart into producing a killer music segment for the first show, hoping to steer the whole program in that direction down the line. My old files from *Hype Magazine* came in handy.

I found, going through them, the name and contact number for Beverly Franks, a Los Angeles-based singer who had three hit records and a growing following. Her manager and I arranged for the interview at her home. My film crew would be able to shoot her full band rehearsal the same afternoon.

"Come on in, guys. I'm Morty, Miss Franks' manager. Make yourself at home." He scurried off to another room.

Beverly was a velvet-voiced soul singer who was popular on the jazz and pop charts. Her album sales and hit singles enabled her to buy a beautiful house on a steep Hollywood hill above the heart of the city. My film crew set up their camera and positioned the lights.

We killed time by looking out the big picture window. We could see Sunset Boulevard and most of the L.A. basin. Musicians started arriving, going to a far-off garage area.

An hour and ten minutes later, and still no singing star. I could hear the manager off in a room somewhere on the phone. I was about to search for him, when Beverly emerged down a spiral staircase in the center of the large room. She was wearing an all-white evening dress, which looked striking in the daylight against her dark brown skin. She walked right past the sound and cameramen to shake my hand.

"Welcome to my home, dahling."

Her makeup and hair were flawless, but there was a fuzzy white shadow of cocaine powder that sat below her nostril. I suggested she check her makeup one last time before we began. She glided to a mirror over the fireplace, looked at herself, and started laughing. The crewmen and I looked at each other in amazement while she dusted the remnants away.

When I got home from work, I called Jason.

"Who is this?" he asked. "I don't know any Anthony. I *used* to have a friend named Anthony, but he got a TV gig and went all Hollywood on me. In fact, I haven't seen him in weeks."

"Go ahead, get it out of your system, man. I've been running around like crazy with this new job, my band, plus the new apartment..."

"Well, I'm enjoying having *my* space to myself, so I guess we're both happy."

"Okay, Jason, what's with the bitchy new attitude?"

"I don't have an attitude, do you?"

"Look, Jay, I'm tired, and I don't have time for this. Let me call you some other time."

He hung up before I said the word "time."

"Carter against Reagan," I said to Linda. "There's a whole lot riding on this horserace."

The two of us were sitting in the dim light of the production department, watching the election results. I was standing over her shoulder while she sat at her desk. We were bathed in ghostly light from her little black and white TV.

"It's just so hard to believe, they're about to elect this guy," she said. "A rotten-hearted failed actor. I mean, who sees this guy and thinks, 'he should be leader of the free world?'" She looked back at me. "Are you going to pull up a chair?""

"I'm okay. It looks like results will be coming in soon. Don't give up hope. Maybe Carter can pull it off."

I said it but I didn't really mean it. Reagan was heavily favored to win. The big election had created a state of tension around the city. People in television, and show business overall, knew Reagan presented a threat to their way of life. They knew that behind his charismatic character was a conservative with an "every man for himself'" point of view. He was in favor of deregulating every industry in the country, including television and radio. In Hollywood, where fake sincerity and hubris were everywhere, people saw right through Reagan's performance. Yet, he was favored to win.

"Carter is a turkey," Linda said, "and Reagan is about to eat his lunch."

We sat and watched for five minutes until someone came up behind me.

"Do we have an actor for president yet?" It was Galen. He joined us in Linda's cubicle to watch Dan Rather's West Coast election feed. "How's it look so far?"

"Really, really bad," I said. "Reagan won the Midwest, the South and most of the Northeast. But get this: Jimmy Carter just *conceded,* even though the polls aren't even closed in California yet."

"I just don't get it," Galen said. "They're voting for somebody who's against government to run the government?"

"He's a cowboy," Linda said, "and Americans love cowboys. He makes Carter look like a schoolmarm. He's a puppet head whose strings are being pulled by his rich friends. We are so screwed."

We watched another hour and listened to the final results. I learned Galen was an old liberal who knew what Reagan did to California, and feared the worst.

"Good God," he said, "the guy threw crazy people out of mental homes and onto the streets. That's where the whole homeless thing started."

I watched Reagan smile and wave as balloons dropped and a sea of blond people clapped wildly, almost out of control with joy. Reagan would later say it was morning in America, but we feared it was closer to midnight.

Chapter Fifteen

The Breaks

Something was up with Sam. He was full of excitement at band rehearsal the next day. Schoolgirl excitement: nervous energy, smiles and unexplained giggles. It was as if our previous argument never happened. He even gave me a thumbs-up after hearing me warm up my voice.

"Sounds good, brother man," he said.

"Never seen you like this before, Sam. You got some last night, I bet," I said into the mike. "Some brand new stuff, you old dog."

"Naw, blood, it's all about the music. I got a new cat coming in today to try out for keyboards. Wait'll you check this guy out."

I gave a quick scan to see if La Wanda, Don and Chuck were as surprised by the news as I was. They were. Our eyes darted around the garage at each other like pinballs.

Before anyone could respond, I heard four sharp knocks at the door, then it opened. The first thing I saw was a mountain of yellow-gold hair, haloed by the Venice sun behind him, hair so high it barely fit through the open doorway.

"I'm Kevin McGraw."

He was wearing a bright red cardigan sweater, and an even brighter smile after saying his name. We greeted him, then Sam told him to say a few words about his music background. Our leader stepped aside after a few moments, and Kevin moved to the keyboard to play a Peter Frampton song.

The boy could sing *and* play. But even more important, he had the image Sam thought would bring us a big break.

"With your looks," Sam said, seated on the floor, practically at the guy's feet, "you don't even *have* to play. You could just pretend to be playing, and we could get a record deal. You know, like those bad acts that lip synch on "American Bandstand." You *know* they can't play a lick - they can just stand there and look pretty."

I saw Kevin scowl for half a second before he caught himself and grinned, shaking his head.

"I'm not just a pretty face, Sam, don't lay a trip on me like that, dude." Then he flashed a million-watt smile. He knew he was in. This guy was used to winning.

As it turned out, his added synthesizer *did* give the band a richer sound, like hits that were on the radio, but he also changed the chemistry of the band, which was strained to begin with. La Wanda was unhappy about her weight problem. Don's wife was pressuring him about too much time with the band. Me? I was fed up with Sam's iron-fisted control of the group, even though he backed off a little after I stood up to him about the demos. And now there was a new member to get used to, someone who might even be a threat.

Weeks later, at the beginning of our third full rehearsal with Kevin, Sam walked up beside me, and elbowed me to make an announcement into my mike. I pushed him back, then I walked over and leaned against a wall and studied my fingernails.

"Do you all want the good news or the better news first?"

"Drama queen," Don said. "What's the damn news?"

"The news, pinhead, is two things. The good news is we have a high-profile gig in two weeks, at a place in Hollywood you know and love: Odd Todd's. The better news is, to make the new wave transition complete, we are no longer Night Club. Our new name is, are you ready, Modern Man."

Lawanda and I looked at each other in confusion, then she weakly shrugged her shoulders.

"Nice name," I said after thinking, "but do we at least get a say, or get to vote on things happening around here?"

"What *is* the problem *now*, Anthony?"

"Sam, it's like we're all on this train that should be going forward, but instead, we're zigzagging from side to side. Maybe if the process was a little more democratic, we could put our heads together to make this work, instead of just following your dictates." I turned around to look at the band. "I mean, is anybody else willing to speak up here?" Everyone's eyes fell to the ground.

Sam and I were almost shoulder-to-shoulder. He took one step forward and turned around to face me.

"So, I'm a dictator now? Okay, Anthony, let's talk. I didn't want to bring it up, but you're pushing me against the wall, dude. The main reason we switched to New Wave was your singing. You have a fine voice, but rock and soul music are not your thing. When it comes to emotion, intensity, range - I don't know, man, it just wasn't working. We get breaks here and there, but they're just not paying off for us the way they should."

"Hey, Sam, man," Don said, "be cool, bro."

"Motherfucker, how are you going to insult me in front of the band? So, let me get this straight: you hired me for your group even though you didn't like the way I sang? I guess that just goes with the crazy-ass way you've been running this damn band." I was almost nose-to-nose with him.

"I chose you because of your pure voice and your songs, but the temperament just isn't there sometimes, you *know* that. But it's all moot now, 'cause New Wave is a whole new ball game. We tweak the arrangements, put Kevin up front with you, and bam, we're in."

"Hey folks," Kevin said in his lazy surfer drawl, "I may be the new kid, but I came here to play. I say we get started."

Chuck, who looked bored by the drama, quickly yelled out a countdown, and we began our first song. Sam and I gave each other a look, which to me meant, "This isn't over."

Don's wife, Elizabeth, came to pick him up twenty minutes early. She grabbed a folding chair and sat directly in front of La Wanda. Her hands were crossed ladylike in her lap, with a small Bible in one hand. She didn't smile or tap her foot; she just sat statue-like.

When three o'clock came, we all went our separate ways, in unusual quiet.

Sam called each of us the next day, with specific ideas on what to wear for the big show - the colors, style, hair - he even wanted the guys to wear makeup, like the British New Wavers. It was a dramatic change, but, as usual, I was the only one in the band who spoke up with any doubts, any concern that we were going down the wrong road. I was growing tired of being the only dissident, so I went along, and gave it a chance to work.

Two weeks later, on the day of the show, we were finally going to meet Odd Todd, a legend among musicians in Hollywood. His club had given breaks to dozens of bands that got deals, and he was known for treating music people with respect and fairness, which was rare in the business.

I walked up Sunset, and saw the words "Modern Man" on the marquee. It took moments to realize that was *me*: I felt no connection to the name at all. I went inside, and found the narrow little dressing room far in the rear, where the band was filtering in.

La Wanda and I sat together at the mirror, Chuck and Don were off in a corner, and Sam was with Kevin in another area. We were now like every other band: singers, rhythm section and keyboard players separated into little cliques.

"How're you feeling about the show?" I asked La Wanda.

She was putting on too much makeup.

"I don't know, you go first. Actually, you've made it clear how you feel about things. You and Sam need to just quit it and grow up."

"La Wanda, look at us. Is this what music is all about now? Hair, clothes and makeup? I told him on the phone I'm not wearing eyeliner. There's a limit, man."

"Did you see?" she whispered. "Sam and Kevin are wearing eyeliner *and* powder."

I looked over, and she was right. "Oh my God," I said. I wanted to make a joke about them looking like drag queens, or ask how Sam found enough makeup for his fat face. But I wondered if I could even trust La Wanda now. "Let's just do this damn show. These people might love us, Clive Davis could be out there right now - who knows. Let's kill out there."

Odd Todd knocked twice on the door and entered. All six of us turned and looked with amazement as he stood in the doorway. Todd was almost seven feet tall, and probably weighed less than two hundred pounds. His skin was the palest white, contrasted with jet-black hair.

He bent down a few inches to swing his head through the doorway. In a foghorn-deep voice, he said, "I just wanted to say good luck to you guys. You have my support, and I'm looking for big things out of you." He turned, and bent stiffly under the doorframe, walking away as quickly as he came. All of us blankly stared at each other for a few seconds, mouths wide open; when his footsteps were safely gone, we burst out laughing.

Don and I took a short walk out front, then we returned backstage just as the announcer was introducing the opening act. A comedian stood alone in the spotlight, telling twenty minutes of jokes about Reagan, yuppies, the death of disco. We all got ready to go on, and I felt the surge of adrenaline that only comes just before the music starts.

I heard the words "Modern Man." We dashed onto the stage to take our positions, expecting to feel the shockwave of energy you usually get from an audience.

There was no applause. We stood for what seemed like forever, but for ten seconds we were as stunned as the audience seemed to be. Sam eventually counted off the intro to "One Good Love," which sounded dynamic and new, as Kevin and Sam exchanged keyboard licks.

Odd Todd's had an excellent new sound system, with better clarity and separation than the El Rey or anywhere else we'd played. We never sounded better. Don and Chuck were in a definite groove. But the crowd gave us no energy during the song, and there was only polite applause after the opening number.

By the second song, the audience totally lost interest in us. They resumed their conversations and cocktails, with their laughter and self-involved stories. Todd was standing against the wall off to the left, towering over little people, and I saw him shrug his shoulders as if to say, "what happened?" It was like playing at a wedding where no one cares about the band, but it was worse because we were up on a stage, in spotlights.

The band charged ahead with the third number, "Everybody Loves You." In the quiet middle of the song, a guy wandered to the front edge of the stage. *Where have I seen him before?* I sang a few more lines, then it hit me. Shakey Jake! He was the guy at the beach, playing guitar for the chick singer I banged. He came as close as he could, near the footlights, and said, "You guys are clowns."

LaWanda and I looked at each other. I tried to envision what we must have looked like from out there, wearing coordinated clothes in yellow and black, long hair piled atop our heads, men in makeup, jerking and twisting to the staccato beats of the music. We looked around at the guys, who had all heard the man's remark. But the band played on.

Most clubs have a policy of 'free liquor' to performers, and the guys took advantage of it this time. They got wasted. Don and Chuck tried hard to get me to drink, but I had my usual bottled water. We were sitting at a table in the half-empty club.

"That was one big bummer," I said. "It's like we were set up."

"At least it's over now," Chuck said. "Come on, Ant, have a drink." He swilled from a bottle of beer.

"It wasn't so bad, you guys," Sam said. "We sounded great and we're getting exposure. We just have to be patient."

I looked at Sam, and I was ready to explode. I had had enough.

"Sam, if you think tonight was good, you're living in a fucking dream world. They hated us out there. *Hated* us. You could have named us the Modern Bozos." I heard everyone put their drinks down at the same time, looking for a fight, when

Odd Todd appeared out of a shadow like a ghost. He came to our table.

"In truth, guys, I have never booked a black or mixed act here, and I wanted to see if folks would accept something different. Obviously they're not ready for this, and I should probably apologize for tonight. At the same time, I seriously wonder if you people are going in the right direction with your music."

"I know where we're going," Don said, "straight to the circus. Some jerk called us clowns." He lifted his beer. "Cheers."

Todd counted out some hundred-dollar bills into Sam's palm. "Hey, I love you guys," he said walking away, "I just want you to think about your future."

"We were Todd's science experiment," I said.

We had no scheduled performances, so before we left the club we all agreed to cancel rehearsals for a few weeks to think about what direction the band should take.

I looked at all the drunken faces around me. *Nobody else was tripping.*

Was I the only one who was ready to quit the band?

Chapter Sixteen

Christmas Weekend

Linda was standing with four people I didn't know. I walked toward them, wondering why no mention she was inviting a gang of people. They were outside the Small World Theater, on the weekend following Odd Todd's, and we had a date to catch a show there. The line outside on Hollywood Boulevard was long.

Before I reached Linda, I ran into Bill Graham, promoter of the show. He was busy schmoozing with people down the line. I spoke to him.

"Thanks again for the tickets, man." I shook his hand. "I'm a big fan of Earth Wind and Fire."

"And you are?"

"I'm Anthony Adams." His face was blank. "I picked up two tickets from you Thursday, and a backstage pass." Still nothing. "I work at KCBS-TV." His face lit up.

"Anthony! Glad you could make it." Now the handshake was vigorous.

He talked about his big plans for Small World, explaining how the place had closed back in '75, when multiplexes strangled business for single-screen movie houses. He had leased it cheap, and turned it into a concert hall, along with four other places on the coast. He was somebody worth knowing.

But I couldn't leave Linda and her friends waiting too long (since I had her ticket), so I gave him my business card, and moved on up the line.

Linda was standing in tight designer jeans, and I noticed how flat her butt was. She introduced her friends: John and Rose, who seemed like a couple; Katie, whom she called her special friend; and Dana. She saved Dana for last, and introduced her with a wristy flourish.

Dana Thomas had a sweeping brown afro that made her look angelic, and she had Egyptian princess eyes. Best of all, she had a nice, big behind. She smiled at me. *I hope she didn't catch me looking at that boo-tay.*

We walked into the main lobby, which was decorated with white and red Christmas lights. The six of us entered the auditorium and found seats together near the front. I sat on the aisle next to Dana, and I could feel something between us - from our eye contact, the way she played with her hair when we talked. She said she was a teacher, but that she really wanted to be a singer.

"I wish I could stay and talk to you and relax," I said, "but there's something I have to do backstage. If you all will excuse me, I'll be right back."

I was eager to see what Earth Wind and Fire did behind the scenes. I got up to leave, and flashed my pass at the guy standing at the backstage door. I looked around, then I found a place to stand on the side of the stage. Earth, Wind and Fire's equipment was in position behind the curtain. Their name was emblazoned on the only set of drums on the stage.

"Where," I said out loud, "is the opening act's stuff?"

Two young black men walked into the spotlight in front of the curtain, carrying their own microphones. I stood and wondered what was happening. An engineer, six feet from me, started a tape machine, which blared a collection of prerecorded beats into the Small World's powerful sound system. The audience of young people, black and white, clapped wildly when they heard the first strains of a song called "The Breaks." The performers stomped aggressively, joyfully, from one side of the stage to the other. The two men, alone, entertained the crowd with thirty minutes of rhymes and high-energy sounds, and the audience was having fun. Bill, the promoter, was on the opposite side of the stage, bobbing his head to the music and clearly happy with what he was seeing.

Earth, Wind and Fire's show was hot. But somehow, their drums, bass, guitar, piano, vocals, horns and strings were almost matched by the energy and the intensity of two guys alone on a stage.

Before going to join Linda, Dana and the rest, I talked with the promoter.

"You just witnessed the next big thing," Bill said, pointing his finger into my chest. "If these two guys can electrify an audience like I just saw, there's no stopping them. Instead of paying Earth, Wind and Fire with their freaking horns and strings and crap, I can pay a couple of guys to boogie on the mike and get the same result. No tour buses, no high overhead - it's a promoter's dream. What a Christmas present. And just think how cheap their records will be to produce. I'm telling you, kid, the future, in one word, is—rap."

Chapter Seventeen

Where The Smart Money Is

Television City was buzzing. New shows were popping up every week, and business was booming. I was one of 35 new employees hired in the fourth quarter alone. The place was a beehive, and Ann Miller was the queen bee. I'd never met her, but I learned to beware her sting.

I was sitting in a weekly one-on-one meeting with my boss, Galen.

"'All Together Now' is doing better than expected," he said. "Ratings are good, and Ann likes it. Well, she didn't *say* she liked it; I'm going by the lack of criticism. She's not big on praise."

"I'm hearing a lot of things about Ann. Not all of it good."

"She means well, don't get me wrong." He stood up and walked to the window to peek through the blinds. "She's a control freak. But that's how some people survive, by being in charge of every detail around them. Or *trying* to be. I understand her. It's her weakness."

Through his babbling, I was thinking how I should spring the next stage of my plan.

"What do you think, Galen, about making the music segment a weekly feature on the show?"

He turned from the window and looked at me. "As long as you stick to local people and keep it interesting, that shouldn't be a problem, unless I hear otherwise." So far, so good. "Speaking of music people," he said, "check this out."

He reached for a thin manila folder on his desk, and slid it toward me. It was labeled "William Washington." I picked it up.

"The name is vaguely familiar," I said, opening the folder. A single, tiny newspaper article, the size of a credit card, floated into my lap. "Once-Great Producer-Drummer Tries Comeback."

William "Sticks" Washington, the article read, was booked to do a small gig at a North Hollywood club.

"I grew up listening to this guy's music back in Chicago." In my head I hummed some of his classic songs: records that were like three-minute operas, full of intensity, lost love and passion. In his day, he had three top ten records as writer and producer. "And he's a damn good drummer, too."

"Well," Galen said, "he should be good for a five-minute piece in your music segment. Get some good Soul City stories from him. Should be fun." We sat quiet for a few seconds. "Shouldn't you be out there working, son?"

I located Washington's address and phone number. He lived on Common Street in south-central Los Angeles, so I scheduled an interview and a crew.

Two days later, our van was crawling through the south-central part of town, in one of the most blighted parts of Los Angeles. I was in the front passenger seat. Leo, the cameraman, drove slowly and surveyed the landscape.

"Wow," he said, "you'd expect better from a guy who made all those big records."

Mike, the sound man, yelled from the back of the van. "This is gang land, you guys. Look sharp. I hope nobody is wearing red or blue colors." He and Leo knew the streets well, after working twenty years as a team in the field.

I glanced down to see what I was wearing: shades of black and tan. "How in the hell," I said, "does this keep happening over and over? A guy sells three million records, and he ends up living in the poor house. Literally."

Leo nodded his head in agreement, nervously focused on the young men standing idle on street corners we passed.

"I just heard one of his records on the radio yesterday," I said. I was almost angry at the thought of meeting yet another great songwriter who made millions for his company and ended up broke.

"I'll give you ten-to-one this guy's been married at least twice," Leo said. "*That*, son, is how you end up in the poor house." Washington's place was a simple white bungalow, with cement where a lawn should be, and bars on every window and door.

The men unloaded their bulky equipment. I wanted to help, but according to union rules, only certain people could touch certain things. The guys slogged their gear up a few steps to the door, while I carried my notepad and pen.

A young woman answered. "You here for the interview? Willie!!!" she screamed. She had one large pink roller above her forehead, and she was wearing matching pink house slippers, even though it was one in the afternoon. "Willie be out in a minute. Come on in, y'all can sit down if you want to." Leo started wrestling with his tripod while Mike focused on microphones, cables and lights. He tapped me on my shoulder.

"Where's the guy going to sit?" he asked. "Where do you want lights? This place is a disaster."

The shades and curtains were closed in the small dark living room. There was a short, ugly sofa with flowers and stains on it. It was covered with clothes, towels, and a young child's toys. A stained shag carpet blanketed the floor; the walls were hard to see in the dim light, but they seemed to be wood paneling that had been painted gray or brown. There was no place where we could have him sit with a complimentary background.

"Maybe," I said, "there's a patio or backyard where he can sit."

"Oh, you don't like my house?" said the young woman, who returned to the room. "Why y'all want to talk to Willie anyway? It ain't like he on top of the world or nothing. What station you from?"

"We have a tight schedule," I said. "Do you think Mr. Washington will be long, ma'am?"

"*Mr. Washington*?" she said with a sneer. "Where the hell you from? Willie!!!!"

She left again, toward the hall, and bumped shoulders with the great William Washington, who entered the room. "Excuse you," the woman said. She slid her feet like sandpaper down the hardwood floor of the hall, and closed a door behind her.

"I see you've met my wife," he said. He was wearing a suit that must have been ten years old, but still looked sharp and clean. His processed hair was slicked back.

"Hello, Mr. Washington," I said.

He smiled and shook all our hands, and said we should call him Sticks.

He told us to follow him to the back of the house. We entered a neatly decorated room, which must have been his den. On the walls were gold records with the big blue Soul City "SC", and there were dozens of photographs and awards on the walls. A leather chair was in a corner, with a plant on one side and awards on the other, and I told the guys to set up there.

"You a young man for this kind a work," he said. "Where you from, schoolboy? It's good to finally see a brother doing his thing like this. You a brother, right?"

"Of course I'm a brother, man. And I'm from Chicago."

Leo and Mike were almost ready.

"Cool as ice," Sticks said. We were standing in the doorway, watching the setup. "I been kind of low key for a few years. A lawsuit against my record company, divorce, rehab, teenagers, bankruptcy—man, I'm glad the seventies are gone. But it's a new day now. I got a new band, and it's time to make music again." He pulled a toothpick from his coat pocket, and clamped down on it with his teeth.

"You must have some horror stories to tell about the business," I said.

"Horror is too nice a word," he said. "Everybody I worked with at the company had to sue to get their money, or to get out of bad contracts. Fans think just because you got a hit record or you're on TV, you must be rich. But most cats were making less than you could get working in a factory at Ford or GM."

Sticks took a step back to let Mike through the doorway. The soundman mumbled something about needing a different battery pack from the van.

"But, Sticks, you had a good run of hit records for a while," I said. "You made a lot of money for *somebody*."

"I'm going to tell you this, between me and you," he said. "The record companies make good money. Distributors make even more. But creative people? Writers and performers? We get pennies and crumbs. The real money goes to - are you ready?"

I was anxious to hear his revelation, and I had no idea what he was about to say. His voice was now a whisper, even though Leo was occupied and out of earshot.

"Get this. Radio stations make the real money. How in the world do think "Rapture" gets to be number one for two weeks like it is now? Think about the garbage that goes to the top of the charts. "Bette Davis Eyes," "American Pie," "My Sharona." Did you buy them songs, man?"

"Not a single one," I said.

"So how do you think some of the worst music ever made goes straight to the top?"

I shrugged my shoulders.

"Damn it, boy, it's because radio stations are making major bank in return for stuffing that crap down kids' throats. I heard of program directors getting thousands of dollars for playing a song. Cash money. That FCC license is just a license to print money. They used to say FCC meant "For Cash and Cocaine."

He was rolling the toothpick quickly from one side of his mouth to the other. "And don't talk to me about blow. Hell, there's a white trail of cocaine from the record companies to the radio stations to the retailers. So, where's the smart money in this game? I'll tell you. It's with cats working at the radio stations."

"...payola," I said, almost under my breath. "I thought that was in the '50s."

"I had a song that was kept from number one because of a so-called hit named "Ballad of the Green Berets." Now you can't tell me kids were calling up stations requesting a song that *supported* the Vietnam War, can you? In the sixties? What I'm saying is all true, brother. But you didn't hear it from me."

"But Sticks, why can't we talk about this in our interview? That explains part of the reason pop music and radio are so bad."

Sticks came even closer toward me and spoke directly in my ear.

"Don't ask questions that'll get us both hurt, schoolboy. It's not just radio and record people running the game, but some things you just don't discuss."

Mike yelled "ready," and the interview came and went. But Sticks' last comments gave me a chill as I thought about them in bed that night. I didn't want to end up like him: bitter, broken and broke. *A life of music, but nothing to show for it except tall tales and guys who got rich off of me. Waking up to a poisonous wife every morning*. Maybe it was time to rethink the whole music thing. I drifted to sleep, and woke up hours later to the ringing alarm. It was like a wake-up call.

The Sticks interview fit nicely at the end of a show that also featured an Asian Art exhibit and a restaurant review. "All Together Now" was up and running, and I got an opportunity to also work in the newsroom as a freelance writer and producer, sometimes doing news, but mostly doing sports. I liked editing sports highlights and writing scripts for the sports anchors. The work was time-consuming and intense; from time to time I would lose track of the days of the week and holidays. Someone in the sports office casually asked what I was doing for the holiday, and I realized it was New Year's Eve. When that day's broadcast ended, I quickly called Jason, whom I hadn't spoken to in a while.

"I totally had no idea it was New Year's," I told him. "I can't believe another year's passed me by. Anyway, where's the party tonight, man?"

"I have a date, but what did you have in mind?" Jason asked.

"Man, it's this warm weather out here making me lose track of seasons and holidays. Back east, they're probably under three feet of snow. Jason, it's 78 degrees outside. I don't know if I even *feel* holidays anymore."

"Believe me, you get used to it. And you can't go home again. You're one of us."

"Dude, this is my third New Year's out here already. Unbelievable. So, let's celebrate. I'll call a few people, and we can ring it in at my place. How about nine, nine thirty?"

"Let me check with my date, and we'll try to stop by for a minute," Jason said.

Linda was also planning to celebrate at a party with her friend, but said she'd rather get together at a small gathering at my place. She agreed to bring her friend.

Dana also agreed to bring in the eighties at my apartment, and said it could be a kind of housewarming. She and I had been talking on the phone regularly, and had a nice dinner once. She wanted to spend more time together, but my job and my hours made that difficult.

I left the studios, and drove to a big supermarket to buy some food for the party. At the checkout counter, my eye caught the latest *Hype Magazine*. "Best and Worst of 1979" was the cover article. I opened to a short interview of Steely Dan, written by Charlene Sweet, with photographs by Tom Robinson. What a lovely team, I thought - a team of vicious, backstabbing vipers.

The line was long, and the store was packed with people buying party food and supplies. I stared at the cover of *Hype*, and wondered if I should buy it or not, but I decided not to support them. I put it back in the magazine rack—backward, so no one else would buy it.

Jason, Linda and Dana all arrived at nearly the same time, after nine. Jason and Linda, though, were without their dates.

"The fool decided to work tonight," Jason said. "He said he could make a fortune on New Year's Eve—he said drunks give big tips and he couldn't pass up the money. That's what I get for messing with another cab driver."

"At least you didn't get stood up," Linda said as we all stood in the living room. "My girl wanted to go to this big party in Beverly Hills. I never wanted to be with a bunch of show biz phonies in the first place. So we agreed to disagree. I like the intimate thing, you know."

I put some records on the stereo, and turned on the television with the sound all the way down. Dick Clark was already celebrating the New Year at Times Square, on East Coast time, and somehow it seemed wrong to be showing that in California, three hours before our midnight.

The next three hours went by fast; we made a comfortable quartet. It was nice to be surrounded by friends, old and new, as midnight approached. Jason and Linda both loved traveling, and warmed up to each other sharing road stories. Dana really liked me, I could tell, and she took over the role of host as the night went on.

"I would like to make a toast," Jason said from his seat. "In a few minutes it'll be 1980, and I think this will be the dawn of some great things for all of us. I'd rather be surrounded by sweaty men right now, but what can I do. I appreciate my old friend, Anthony, who helped me rediscover my music, and I hope I'm making some new friends here tonight, with you two fabulous ladies. So, out with the old, and in with the new. It's a wrap, seventies. I just know the eighties are going to be good to us all."

A west coast countdown began, and I kissed Dana, our first kiss, at midnight.

Chapter Eighteen

Lessons to Learn

"She's not a typical L.A. chick," I told Jason on the phone. It was the last day of March, and he was shocked to hear I was seeing the same girl for over three months now. "She's not a clingy psycho wannabe actress. Least I don't think so."

"Yeah, but she's a church girl. And that's a whole issue itself. I played for my choir for years. If you want to find some devilish folks, just look in the nearest church."

I was at my desk, scheduling interviews. Jason told me to pencil him in for lunch soon, and after I hung up, the phone rang again. It was Dana.

"Speak of the devil," I said. "Jason and I were just talking about you."

"Good things, I hope," then she giggled. We chatted for a minute until she said, "Look, Anthony, I need to talk to you. There's something about me you need to know. Sort of like a secret."

My mind started racing, wondering what it could be. Did she have a young child? A criminal past? Fatal disease? I imagined the worst. Herpes!

"All right, Dana. There's an Italian place in West Hollywood called Carlos. Meet me at seven. Can't wait!"

It was hard to focus through the rest of the workday. I thought about the band, which was on indefinite hiatus since Odd Todd's. I wanted to at least check in with La Wanda or Don, but maybe some time apart was best. Seven o'clock rolled around, and I walked into the darkly lit restaurant on Melrose. She was sitting at a table in the rear.

"Okay, what's the big surprise?" I asked after I settled in my seat and we ordered.

"Anthony, we've been dating for three months now, and there's just a little something about me you don't know."

"Well, spill it, babe, why the suspense?" I took a nervous sip of water, sucked an ice cube into my month, and shattered it to pieces.

"It's about something that I really want to do with my life." She clasped her hands and put them on the table softly. "I want to be - a singer."

I stared at her for a few seconds, expecting her to say more, relieved at the mildness of her secret and slightly disappointed that the news was what I considered trivial. I fumbled for a response.

"Uhh, okay, how long have you wanted to sing?"

"The truth is, I'm already singing. Sort of. I'm in the choir at church."

"You are? You never mentioned that. Maybe we need to share more about each other. What else you holding back from me, babe?" I winked at her and smiled.

"I never told you, or any of my friends, because I don't know if I'm any good. At my church, anybody can get into the choir, so that's not a big accomplishment. I'm still working on my confidence before I really step out there. And, you, being a musician, I didn't want to compete with you."

"Compete?" I said with a chuckle.

"What are you laughing about, Anthony? See, that's why I didn't want to tell you." Her back stiffened.

"I'm sorry. Maybe 'compete' isn't what you mean. Baby, I've been surrounded by music people all my life. It's not important what I or anybody else thinks about your music. What matters is that you develop your talent and take it as far as you can. Whether you're going to sing for twenty thousand people, or just sing at a best friend's wedding, just do what you can do, and don't be afraid."

"You're right," she said, relaxing back in her chair.

"Fear can hold you back, Dana. It's powerful. My father was afraid of success - he drank his talent away. My best friend Jason is the most talented guy I've ever known, but something is holding *him* back. Fear of failure, or fear of success. Either way, his music ends up in the same place - nowhere."

"So, what about me? Can you help me? I'm singing a solo Sunday." She leaned forward with a sexy smile. "I've heard you sing and play. Can I get a few lessons? Anything?"

"Sure, girl, what's there to lose? I haven't set foot in a church in ten years, but I would love to check you out." She looked at me with anticipation. I was hoping she'd forget the whole idea.

The next morning was April Fool's Day. At work, Galen had scheduled his weekly production meeting, which was just a quick, no-nonsense update. I walked down the main hallway, past the lunchroom full of people - they were all chugging coffee and sucking on cigarettes. At a minute to nine, the staff made their way, zombie-like, into the conference room, taking seats at the long table, three people on each side, and me next to Linda, with Galen at the head. The other head of the table was usually empty.

Galen cleared his throat and began. He talked for ten minutes about ratings, and the tight budget. Then the operations manager, Kurt, talked about scheduling. He stood up.

"Mobile 14, Leo and Mike, are going on vacation in two weeks…"

"And not a moment too soon," Leo said, followed by a chorus of giggles.

"…so we have to hire a freelance team..." Kurt stopped suddenly and looked toward the door, his eyes widening.

The room silenced as everyone's head turned to see Ann Miller, Galen's boss, who never came to meetings. She walked in, and sat at the empty seat opposite Galen. Everyone sat up straight, except Galen, who seemed to shrink down into his chair about two inches. Ann plopped her heavy leather briefcase onto the table. She twirled her finger, signaling Kurt to continue. He stuttered through a quick summation, finished, then pointed at Galen.

"Well," Galen said, "Ann is with us from upstairs—good morning, Ann—and I'm just guessing, but I bet she'd like to say a few words to the department."

"Thank you, Galen," she said in her proper New England accent, "and good morning." She stood up and folded her arms. "The theme of what I have to say is 'productive change.' As you know, there's a new man in the White House—a great man, if I may say. Our station manager just returned from Washington. He, and others like him, was told that the White House plans to free stations from a long list of rules, regulations and red tape that have been holding us back for years. You're going to hear the word 'deregulation,' or as I like to call it, liberation. There's a lot more I could say, but know this: television, as you know it, is about to change. It will be a productive change, and you will all have to be on your toes to keep up with things."

"One man's liberation," Leo said "is another man's oppression."

Her red lips made a tight smile like a crack in the ice. She sat down, and Galen called the meeting to an end. There was a stampede to get out of the room, but Galen and Ann stayed behind, at their opposite sides of the stretched-out table, Ann talking, and Galen listening.

I walked down the hall, between Linda and Leo.

"What was *that* all about?" I asked.

"I don't know," Linda said in a quiet voice, "but something stinks. The dragon lady is definitely up to something."

"It's all politics and money," Leo said. "Those fat cats in Washington don't care about people or public affairs or local programming. Our ass is grass."

"Look around this place," I said. "Everybody's whispering." The department was usually full of voices and activity in the morning; but now, there was a funeral parlor atmosphere. "Watch your back around here, folks."

The three of us split up. I sat at my desk and tried to work, but I needed to walk off some nervous energy. I passed through accounting, the art department, and the sales office, where I saw Ann Miller talking to the suited salesmen, this time with hand motions added to her routine.

This is crazy. What have I gotten myself into?

Since the band had been inactive, I was making extra money working weekends in the TV sports department. Saturday morning rolled around, and when I arrived at the station, I found a memo in my box. It said the regular sports anchorman was off; Joe Morgan, baseball Hall of Famer, would be replacing him. Joe had only recently retired, and never anchored a sports highlight show before. Today's show would be an audition for him to do more work for the station. My job was to watch all the network games of the day, edit the highlights, and write Joe's script—to make him look good. Joe was always a favorite player and hero of mine. At the very least, I'd be good for an autograph after the show.

Alone in the sports department, I watched and logged the baseball, basketball and golf broadcasts, monitoring up to five TV sets at once. That was the easy part. Around four o'clock, it was time to start the hard part: editing and writing. I was surprised Joe hadn't shown up yet; I had expected him to come in early for his first time on TV.

I ran back and forth between the editor's booth and my typewriter, matching and timing each play with corresponding words for Joe. Show time was approaching fast, and he still wasn't there. At five o'clock, the highlights and the script were done. I stood in the editing room with Alan, who had helped me condense twelve hours of sports into three minutes of action.

"The tapes are locked and loaded," he said. "All we need now is a talking head."

"Damn, man," I said, "what happens if an anchorman doesn't show up?"

"I've been here sixteen years, and it's only happened twice. Once, the news anchor read the sports. The other time, we went to DEFCON One and let a producer sit in and do the show. Hey, this could be your big break. If you want to go on the air, ask the producer. But hurry. It's almost show time."

I was deciding what to do, looking up at Alan's TV monitors, when there he was: Joe Morgan casually stepped onto the news set and took a seat. He was the ultimate in relaxed cool—with an Italian suit and a fresh haircut. He picked up the script I had left at his seat, and he read it through. Ten minutes later, the opening music began, and the newscast went on the air without a hitch.

Joe was flawless. He read the script with confidence, and my highlights were timed with his delivery. His four-minute segment flowed like he had been doing it for years. Maybe he had been practicing, or got coaching somewhere. Perhaps he had enough ego to make him think he could do anything.

I went to the main lobby after the show, and headed for the control room to introduce myself and congratulate Joe on his performance. As I walked across the long room, the doors to the studio burst open, and Joe walked out. He went right past me, greeting two young blonde women who were seated in the plush red chairs of the lobby. The women were bubbly in their praise for Joe. I was expecting a handshake at least, or some acknowledgment. But Joe walked out of the building, a blonde on each arm.

Allan stepped into the lobby and stood beside me.

"Where is he? Is he still here?" He sounded frantic, looking around the empty area.

"Gone, man," I said.

"I wanted to get his autograph," he said. "Son of a bitch. The show just ended two minutes ago."

"Does he have any idea," I said, "where those highlights came from? Or who wrote his script and worked all day to make him look good? He walked right past me and didn't care who I was. I mean, I realize star athletes are pampered and think they're above it all, but that was cold-blooded."

I made a deal with myself that evening at home. When my music took off, and I became famous, I would never take for granted, or disrespect, people who worked with me or admired me. When that day came, I vowed, I would try never to make anyone feel as small and used as I felt then.

Chapter Nineteen

Either You Can Sing or You Can't

I got home from work and plopped down on the bed. I picked up the phone and dialed.

"What's up, Sam?"

"What's happening, Anthony? Long time, no hear."

"Well, you could have called anytime."

"Three weeks turned into three months pretty quick, huh, buddy? What are *you* doing home on a Saturday night?"

"I'm thinking about the music, man. It's time we give it another shot," I said.

"You might be right. I'm ready to play some music again my damn self. How's next Saturday at three sound? I'll call the rest of the guys."

"I'll be there on time as always."

A week later, the stinger from the Joe Morgan episode was still in my back as I drove to rehearsal in Venice. Being brushed off by him made me want to be a star now more than ever. Three years in Hollywood had taught me there were two sets of rules: one for the rich and famous, and one for everybody else. When I became a star, no one would ever snub me like that again.

I could feel myself, for the first time ever, craving stardom. *It's time for a change.* I took in a deep breath, like I was taking on a new obsession. I wanted to embrace it and wear it like a second skin. I had become a musician for love of the music and because of my father - not just to be a star, like most people in show business. But I was ready for a new attitude, and this band was the ticket. Now all I needed was to get these damn people into shape.

My car crawled down the crowded Hollywood Freeway, and I was late for rehearsal, the last one to arrive. Everyone else was plugged in and ready. I dropped my bag in a chair, hooked up my guitar, and stepped to my microphone.

"Well, now," Sam said dryly, "the gang's all here, so let's get started."

Something was wrong. Sam usually had news or something to say before every rehearsal. We hadn't been together for months, and I expected something - anything. But Don, Chuck, La Wanda, Sam, and Kevin were barreling ahead into "One Good Love" as if nothing had ever happened.

I noticed a pink purse on a chair near the wall, and a bible on top of it. *La Wanda carries a backpack, not a purse.* Midway through the song, Don's wife, Elizabeth, came down the stairs from Sam's home. She sat in the chair, and put the purse and bible in her lap.

She sat there for the entire rehearsal, sometimes reading, sometimes staring blankly into space, massaging her temples or stroking her hair. This is not a good thing, I thought. We ran through our set of music once, then Sam said, "Not sounding our best, people. Truthfully, that kind of sucked."

"Yeah? I wonder why," La Wanda snapped back.

"Don and Chuck, you guys are not holding the rhythm down tight," Sam said, "the harmonies are off and everyone is dragging—nervous or something."

"I don't want to offend anyone," I said, "but don't we have a 'No girlfriends or wives' rule? We might suck because we've been off for so long, or maybe because we have an audience. It's hard to find the groove when we're being watched."

"Either you can *sing,* or you *can't,*" Don said sharply. "Watch yourself, son."

"This is crazy, you guys," Kevin said. "All I can focus on is Don's lovely wife not digging the music. It's a little distracting."

Elizabeth quietly got up from her chair and went back up the stairs, purse and bible in her hands.

"You guys are assholes," Don said. He put his bass into a stand, and rushed up the stairs.

"What's happening here, folks?" Chuck said from behind his drums.

"Maybe we need a permanent break," La Wanda said. Things just aren't working out. Sam, you *did* say no girlfriends, boyfriends or wives, you know."

"I know what I said, La Wanda. It was a compromise. It was either the wife, or no Don today."

"I think we'd better start looking for a bass player," Kevin said. The rest of us looked at Kevin, then we looked at Sam. *Did Kevin know Sam and Don were brothers?* Awkward silence was broken when Don came back down the stairs.

"I can't do this, you guys. I've been thinking about it for a long time. I need to be playing my music for the Lord. I have to move on." He took his bass off the stand and put it into its case. "This has nothing to do with Elizabeth, by the way, so don't blame her." He grabbed his bag, and walked back toward the stairs. "I'm wishing you guys all the best. Y'all be cool." He darted up the steps, and he was gone.

I waited a few seconds, but no one moved or spoke, until I found some words to say.

"Come on, you guys, this band is worth saving. I *don't* want it to fall apart, and I want us to do whatever we can to make it work. Sam, can we try and find another bass player and stay together? Hell, *I* can play bass and Kevin can be the front man. This room is full of talent; we just need to find our voice, the right formula. I really hope we give ourselves a chance. I *don't* want to go through another band breakup."

My eyes welled up, but I fought back tears. I knew this was a crucial point for the band. But no one else spoke up.

"Bernard Edwards, the man from Chic himself, told me his secret. Just stay together! Sometimes it's not just about talent, it's about giving ourselves a chance to succeed. Don't we all want to be stars? I'm not giving up on this band."

La Wanda was shaking her head, slow at first, then faster. Everyone else seemed to be avoiding eye contact. Sam quietly started switching off equipment. The guys followed his lead and began to pack. In my heart, I knew it was the end of the band. Modern Man was history.

My father wanted me to learn clarinet. I hated clarinet, preferring the much cooler guitar, which I already played so well at 13. Yet he forced me to carry that thing to lessons after school. Man, how I hated it - how it sounded, how it looked, how I must have looked playing it. One day I was walking home, a few minutes of light left in the sky. Up the street, coming toward me, I saw three guys. I only recognized one: Willie, a bad kid from my school. I shoved the clarinet in the left side of my jacket. What's that in your pocket, yellow freak?

Gimme your money, now. Willie did all the talking. I must not have moved fast enough. First a powdery flash, then a popping sound, as I fell to the ground. I heard their footsteps trail off, like chickens scattering. But I was okay. I ran home, and found a bullet lodged deep in that clarinet. Music saved my life.

But how was I going to save my music?

When I got home from rehearsal, I had a phone message from Dana. She wanted to go out, but I called her back and told her about my horrible day. *I lost my band.* I climbed into bed and pulled the covers up to my chin.

On the TV, there was a rock group performing on "Saturday Night Live." The horrible front man was singing flat, and the band was either sharp or in a different key. Their lyrics sounded like an eight-year old had written them. The audience clapped wildly for them after one song. "No-talent fucks," I said out loud.

Maybe it was time for *me* to move on—away from the music game, as Don had moved on from secular music. Disillusionment was bitter in my mouth as I drifted off to sleep, too tired to get up and turn off the set. I remembered what Sticks Washington had told me, and I wondered how much it cost this crappy band to get a spot on national television.

In the morning, I picked up Dana for church. She lived in south-central Los Angeles, in a neighborhood pockmarked by churches and liquor stores. I rang the doorbell to her apartment. She opened the door wearing a beautiful flowered spring dress, with sunlight soaking into the whiteness between blossoms.

"You look good," I said in the doorway, eyeing her up and down. "I mean, really good."

"Thank you," she said. "I won't say I'm not a little nervous about singing my first lead today."

"You'll do fine. Just go with God, as you Jesus people say."

"Don't blaspheme, Anthony Adams, do not blaspheme," she said with a smile. We walked down some steps, and got into the car. "If this is what it takes to get you into church, then I'll sing every week."

"Well, I don't think *I'll* be singing any time soon," I said.

"Oh, that's right, your band broke up. I'm really sorry to hear that." She rubbed my back with her left hand. "I'm dedicating my song to you, baby. Just wish me luck. The church is at Crenshaw and Adams, we're almost there."

We passed a few more blocks, and I heard music pouring out of several smaller churches that were close to the sidewalk with their doors open. Dana's church had first service at nine, and we were early as I pulled into the parking lot. She kissed me at the door of the church, then she disappeared down the aisle amid the people who were lingering, arriving and finding seats.

I sat next to a grandmotherly woman who was sitting alone in the middle section. "Good morning," I said to her.

"How you doing, young man? I ain't never seen you here before."

"I'm here with a friend. I haven't been to church in a really long time."

The organist began playing music.

"You need to be in church every week, child. God is good."

A teenager read some announcements, then the choir rose from their seats on the stage to sing one song. I tried to make eye contact with Dana, but she was singing with her eyes closed. The choir sat down again, and there was more sermonizing. Twenty minutes later, I looked at my watch as the choir stepped up again. An usher passed out fans, and the old woman next to me started fanning herself furiously.

For their third song, Dana stepped to the front and grabbed the mike. The church was quiet, as everyone seemed interested in hearing the new girl sing. After an eight bar intro, Dana sang.

"What a friend we have in Jesus..."

Her eyes were closed, and her voice quivered, wrapped in nervousness.

"What a friend we have in the Lord..."

The old woman next to me said, "Bless her heart." Dana was having trouble finding the key; she cupped her hand to her ear. The organist was too loud, and Dana probably couldn't hear herself.

"What a friend we have in Jesus..."

"Mmmm, mmmm, mmmm," the old woman said, "she can't sing, bless her heart. She need to just sit down."

Someone in the crowd yelled "take your time, sister," but the song seemed endless and agonizing as Dana worked her way through it. Eventually it came to a painful end. She stepped back into the line. The drummer started playing a fast tempo beat that brought everyone to their feet, clapping. "Lord," the old woman said leaning close to my ear, "some people not meant to sing."

"I know," I said loudly. "That's my girlfriend."

She stopped clapping, looked at me, then she grabbed my upper arm and smiled as if to say "you poor thing." The choir did a last song, and the service wore on for another ninety minutes.

I thought of what Don had said the day before: *either you can sing or you can't.* He was right, and there was no in-between. Of course, he said it in defense of his wife, and in anger. But it was clear: Dana could not sing.

Church audiences, and black people in general, are especially critical of singers. Organists, drummers and other musicians might play like they just picked up the instrument yesterday and still get by, but a singer has to have the voice of a soulful angel.

Maybe there was a way to help Dana develop her voice, to sing on key, or to learn confidence. Then I remembered how she put her hand up to one ear, which is a sign that a singer can't distinguish her voice from the music and can't hold her own melody line. That can't be taught. *"Either you can sing or you can't."* Dana's voice was a lost cause. But how was I supposed to tell her?

When the service was over, she came up the aisle to me, still wearing her deep blue choir robe.

"I need a hug."

The old woman next to me smiled and patted my back, then walked away.

"It was awful. I never, ever, want to sing again."

Chapter Twenty

Black Friday

FEBRUARY 1982

"You forgot your mother's birthday."

My father sounded sad. But he couldn't have been as disappointed as I was – in myself. I *never* forgot mom's birthday.

"You're changing, boy. Letting California go to your head. What is it – almost five years out in that place? Hmmph. My son going Hollywood."

Same old Dad. We hadn't spoken in months, and I thought the call would make me homesick. But now I was glad to be two thousand miles away.

"I'll call back when she gets home, maybe send some flowers. You're making me feel crappy."

Silence. I looked at the clock in my kitchen. It was 7 PM – 9 in Chicago.

"I guess I *am* changing, Dad. I'm not a kid; I'm 27 years old. And 'this place' feels like my home now. My TV career is going smooth, I got some dollars in the bank, and I got a steady girlfriend."

"What are you going on about? Boy, just call your mother this evening."

I *wanted* to tell him my band broke up; that I had lost touch with all the members. I *wanted* to say we thought it was best to let it die instead of chasing the rainbow. But I felt attacked enough, so I just said goodbye and hung up the phone.

February, I learned, is the rainy season in southern California, and there would be no rainbow at work either. I was at my desk, pants soaking wet from running across the parking lot. It was storming outside when Galen called an impromptu staff meeting. His announcement? He was leaving KCBS, and dropping out of the business altogether.

"It's been a fun ride, people," he told the conference room crowd. "But I'm old, and it's time for me to grow up and do something real. I'm going to divinity school, *so* far away from here. In more ways than one."

"Fifty is not old, man," said a male voice in the crowd; a chorus of agreement followed.

"Things are changing, you guys," Galen said, "and when you get a big five in front of your age, you realize it's time to play for keeps, to get real."

"Notice that Ann's not here," I said quietly to Linda. "Do you think she's forcing him out?"

"I have no doubt," she said. "She wants to run the whole game. That woman would screw her grandmother to make herself look better."

Galen's resignation destroyed morale in the department. He had been the perfect boss: open to new ideas, understanding of your concerns, and he actually listened. I thought back to the conversation with my dad.

Galen would have made a great father.

He cleared out right away. He heaved some papers, plaques and pictures into a box, and headed for the elevator. When I saw he was walking alone, I sprinted to his side and walked with him. I was surprised no one else was there to see him off, even though I was one of the newer employees. I gave him a quick hug; we wished each other luck, and the elevator door closed.

I got back to my desk, setting up meetings with Drake and Stephanie down in the newsroom. When I stood and looked out the window, Galen was crossing the lot with his cardboard box full of nine years of memories. The rain surged. His box had gotten heavy and wet, and it slipped from his hands, spreading a zigzag of white papers at his feet. He dropped to his knees and scooped the soggy mess into what was left of the box.

By October of 1982, eight months later, Galen was a forgotten memory around the station. Ann was in charge, but surprisingly she didn't care what stories we covered. Her office was on a higher floor, and her focus seemed to be even higher.

That allowed producers to do a wider range of stories. Drake suggested we do a feature on L.A.'s punk music scene. He was a closeted fan of punk music, and the subculture was threatening to bubble up from underground status and break into the mainstream, like disco had done five years before.

I decided to cover the story, since the music was the talk of the town. I met Drake one night in front of the city's biggest punk clubs, the Vise. He was wearing a sport coat and tie.

"Leo and Mike are on their way," I told him.

"I hope this works out," he said nervously. "I want to reveal the power of punk music to the world, but I'm not quite ready to come out of the closet as a punker myself, at least not all the way. I don't want it to affect my job."

"It will definitely affect your image," I said, "from a young, stuffy newsman to a weekend punk freak. You'll have to walk a tightrope and not come across as a cheerleader in the report. But don't worry; you're working with the best here. I'll help you." I convinced him to take off the tie so he'd look more natural in the scenes inside the club.

Leo and Mike arrived, and parked their big white news van in a bus stop right in front of the club. Leo slid his press parking pass onto the dashboard. He grabbed his camera, got out, and looked around at the people.

"Have you ever seen a bigger bunch of freaks in your life?" he said to Mike too loudly.

The two of them walked toward me and Drake, and I told them all what I had in mind for the night: the shots I needed, the people to interview, and the questions to ask.

"Sounds good," Leo said, "but if just one of these weirdoes so much as touches me, I'll break their friggin' arm off."

I looked at him and tried to figure out the reason for his sudden rage, then it hit me.

"Leo, it's not a gay club, it's a punk club. Most of the guys in here *hate* gays, and they're not too fond of blacks, Jews or anybody else."

"Oh," he said, "then no problem. Let's do it."

I had Drake shoot a short standup outside the club, then we went inside. An opening act was on stage, playing to a rat-a-tat beat that sounded like a machine gun. The mostly male patrons were either standing still or gyrating to the furious beat.

I asked a waitress where I could find the owner. She led me through the shadowy crowd to a side wall, where two big men were sitting menacingly at a round cafe table. Light from a small white candle made them look like witches over a cauldron. The club owner was sitting with the manager of the headlining act, the Ruptures.

"Have a seat, young man," the club owner said. "You guys are right on time. Dave, this is Anthony from the TV station. They're doing the piece on the Ruptures I promised you."

"It's not about the Ruptures," I said, "it's about the whole punk scene. Your band will just be a part of the piece."

"Hey, wait a minute," the group's manager said, "I thought you were doing a piece on my guys. That's what I've been telling everybody."

"It all depends on the interviews. Whatever's most compelling, whatever tells the story best. I made that clear on the phone."

"Well, let me tell you something, Andrew," the manager said. "This band is for real. The Ruptures are about to have a breakthrough with their second album. Everybody who hears them says they're the next big thing. If you want a story, focus on my guys. Jim, Rip and Joey are the future of punk music."

"We'll just have to see how everything goes. Like I said, the focus will depend on how good the interviews are, along with other elements we get tonight. I'll go get my reporter now, and we can get started."

I wound my way back to the entrance to get my crew. The crowd had grown thicker, and the music was louder. The nameless opening act was chanting a call-and-response of "Go back where you came from," and they were working the audience into a rage. It was harder to push my way through the people, and I realized I was inside a tight circle of young men who were looking and chanting directly at me.

The music got louder. I tried to push my way past the shoulders of two men who were tightly locked together. Their stink hit my nostrils; they smelled like cigarettes, vomit and beer. "Go back where you came from," the band said one last time, and the circle of men repeated the phrase, looking directly at me.

One of the men grabbed his empty beer bottle by the neck.

Then the music stopped. The audience began to hoot and clap, the circle of men loosened, like a rope letting go, and I pushed my way free.

I was shaken; looking into the eyes of crazed fools who wanted to hurt me. I thought back to the music, with lyrics of only those six words. The hypnotic, robotic beat of the drums, the angry pull of the electric guitar and its single screaming chord. It was the first time I saw music being used for evil, for inciting rage.

Woozy—smelling body odors, feeling body heat, confused about the sudden circle episode and the rotten-flavored music—I stumbled toward the entrance. I threw up in the corner of the club, not able to make it to a bathroom on time, even if I wanted to.

Looking down and stomach empty, I was happy to leave my mark in this place. I caught my breath and found the crew, and we interviewed the Ruptures before they took the stage. I thought back to how Galen said television was powerful. But *I* knew the power of music. It had the force to turn a bunch of powerless losers into potential killers.

On Friday, three days later, Ann held her monthly staff meeting. She was firmly in place as the director of programming, production and promotion—the third most-powerful person at the station after the general manager and the head of operations. Her memo said for everyone to meet in the cavernous lunchroom rather than the conference room.

Everyone from the three departments, all 48 of us, waited ten minutes past the scheduled time. Then Ann entered the room, followed closely by the top gun—John Cooper, the president of the company who had flown in from New York. Ann wore a blood-red business dress and a plaid blazer, and Cooper was wearing a gunmetal gray business suit, with a red tie.

Ann first complimented everyone on their hard work and patience. She explained how Cooper had been spending a lot of time in Washington, and how the television business was about to see a big period of growth and profitability. John slyly winked at Ann. He was sitting in a chair behind her, with his elbows on his knees and his back hunched. He was staring down at the floor.

Then Ann dropped the bombshell. All of our local programs, with the exception of the news, were canceled, effective immediately. "All Together Now," "Pacific Currents," and "Evening Magazine" were being replaced with "Jeopardy," "Wheel of Fortune," and "Family Feud." The children's show was canceled, (to make way for "The Smurfs"), along with the live morning talk show. The FCC, Ann said, had relaxed rules for local stations to carry public interest programs, and the result meant the loss of 23 jobs, including mine and Linda's.

I heard a gasp in the room when Ann announced the layoffs. She continued to talk - about generous severance pay and how the cuts were effective right away - but everything after "loss of 23 jobs" was meaningless. John Cooper said nothing. Two women on either side of the room cried softly. Ann talked about the great times and changes ahead for the company, and she even smiled once or twice as she went on.

Her words were now background noise, like traffic or refrigerator hum. Her blood red lips were moving, but all I thought was *two great jobs, lost within two years*. Being fired from

Hype had been a genuine shock. But this news made me feel numb, like it was all part of doing business in corporate America. *Welcome to the real world.*

Four-dozen people around me looked frozen in time as Ann wrapped up her statement. She was almost giddy describing how the station would benefit by becoming "leaner but not meaner." (Three weeks later, she was rewarded with stock options and the title of vice president of programming.) But now we all sat, in the thick air of the lunchroom, knowing things would never be as they were. Linda's face was bloodless white. I searched my feelings, but I couldn't find any. Instead of sadness or shock, I still felt nothing, and it felt good not to hurt.

The lunchroom emptied slowly, like the end of a funeral. People who still had their jobs rushed back to their desks, knowing they'd be working twice as hard. "The living will envy the dead," I said to Linda as we walked back to our desks together.

"Vampires," she said. "The world is full of vampires. We're all walking dead, just waiting for someone to throw dirt on us when we stumble." She was talking through tears, said she was thinking of moving back to Texas. Her mother was old and she'd be able to live rent-free. We hugged. I thanked her for making my job possible and for being a good friend. I cleaned out my desk. With no band and no job, it was truly Black Friday.

Chapter Twenty-One

Talent

THE NEXT DAY, OCTOBER 1982

"You should come home, baby," my mother said when I phoned her with the news in the morning. "Get out of that crazy place and come back to the people who love you, your family."

She was right. And wrong. Los Angeles *was* a crazy place, full of competition, nepotism and racism. But she was wrong about the baby-thing. I wasn't a baby or a kid; I was a grown-ass man. When I heard her call me "baby" —like she always did—it erased any thoughts about returning home. I was 27 years old, determined to make it on my own. *No, Ma, I'll be okay. I can find something else to do somewhere out here.*

I called everyone with the bad news. Dana was shocked to hear about my layoff; she agreed to come over later that night. Jason was surprised to hear from me. We had been out of touch for a few weeks, so I asked him to stop by in the afternoon. We both had a lot of stuff to catch up on.

I looked around the apartment after a flurry of phone calls, and realized how little time I had spent there, being caught up with a job and a working band—well, a band until exactly a week ago.

I went down to the lobby to check for Saturday morning mail. A paper flier above the mailboxes advertised "the Annual El Dorado Apartments Block Party" for later in the day. I read the flier, and heard a voice coming from behind me.

"It's our yearly potluck get-together. You coming?" the man asked.

"This is the first I've heard about it," I said. "I've been so busy and spaced out lately, I never noticed this until right now."

We introduced ourselves. He was David Nelson, one of my next-door neighbors. We had never met, and barely even seen each other, in the two and a half years I lived there. I thought of how my mother called this city a "crazy place" minutes ago, and she hadn't even been to California. It was *totally* crazy to go that long living next door to a stranger.

"Well," David said, "this is a great chance to meet some of your neighbors. Everybody is so busy and spread out these days. You should come. Bring a friend. And a dish. Or a friend who *is* a dish," he said and laughed.

"I just might do that. I certainly got time now. Man, I must have missed the fliers and parties from the last two years. So, you work in the business?"

"I used to be a band leader and arranger for Capitol Records."

"Oh, are you the guy who used to work for Frank Sinatra?"

"You've been talking to Mina, I see. That woman. Yeah, I was Mr. Sinatra's arranger for a few years, and I was his musical director for a short while. They don't make 'em like that anymore. But I was put out of business by four certain longhaired punks from England."

"Is *everybody* in the building a musician?"

"As a matter of fact, most of us did either work in the movies or music. A lot of us are retired or semi. You'll meet all the heavy hitters at the potluck up in 210. It'll be good to have some young blood around. Not that we're vampires or anything."

How, I asked myself, how could you live next door to someone for over two years and never see him? That was just one of the questions making me wonder again if Los Angeles was the place for me. Neighbor Dave seemed like a good guy, and as a fellow musician, he could have been a needed friend all this time. But in L.A., no one said hello as you passed them by; people didn't sit on their porch or front stoop and chat with neighbors like back in Chicago. Hell, no one even *walked* down the street: cars were the one and only means of getting around. A city of loners. But I wasn't a recluse, and I didn't want the city to make me one.

Jason arrived at three, just as I began cooking some rice for the potluck. He looked different, and it took me a few seconds to realize he had shaven off his mustache. He looked like he had been working out, and he proudly sported a pierced ear with a small diamond in it.

"That's not all," he said as he followed me to the kitchen. He rolled up his shirtsleeve and revealed an eagle tattoo on his left upper shoulder. "I figured if I got my wings, I'd have a better chance to get into heaven."

"Sounds good," I said, "but you'd better get the same wings on your right side, or you'll just be flying around in circles."

We laughed, and I started chopping an onion, hoping it wouldn't make me teary-eyed, though I probably could have used a good cry.

"How are you taking the job thing, the layoff? Are you okay?"

"I've been cool about it so far. I didn't come to California to work in television anyway— the money seduced me. I'm supposed to be a writer. Getting fired from *Hype* was harder, 'cause that was my passion. Man, I loved that job. The TV thing helped me save some money and meet people, and it was fun. But I want to find another writing gig. *Real* writing, not third-grade writing for retards sitting on their sofas."

I dumped the rice, chicken broth, stewed tomatoes and shrimp into a pot of hot onions and garlic. Jason was staring at me.

"Negro, I have never seen you cook before. What's this all about? Your new girlfriend? Are you having a breakdown?"

"Everybody in the building is having a potluck dinner this evening. I just found out about it. I meant to tell you. Hey, you should come. This place is full of talented people, turns out. Starts in an hour."

"That sounds mildly appealing. So, besides the job thing, what's new in your world? Wait, I'll go first. Anthony, I've given up on ethnic men. I'm giving my classical music career another try, and I'm meeting all the right people now. But if I'm going to get to the next level, I need to take a step up in class. The brothers just can't be counted on, I'm afraid. And don't ask what that Arab cabdriver thing was all about."

"So, what, you're dating white men now?"

"Look, what do these women all have in common? Pearl Bailey, Lena Horne, Leslie Uggams, Diana Ross, and Donna Summer. They all married white men, and their music careers absolutely took off. You need somebody who can introduce you to the right people and take you to the right parties, and Leroy from Long Beach may be good in bed, but he can't stroke your career the right way. If I'm going to be the next Andre Watts, I need a man with some wattage, baby."

"That all sounds totally ridiculous, Jason, and please don't call me baby."

Apartment 210 belonged to Helen Bernstein, who had been a jazz singer during the Big Band era. The first thing Jason and I saw as we entered Helen's open door was a white baby grand piano in the middle of the living room. It was an odd place for a piano: everyone had to walk around it to enter the apartment. The piano was clearly the focal point of the room, more than the grand fireplace or the wide sunset view overlooking the courtyard.

There were about a dozen people in the room. Everyone smiled and continued their conversations as we searched for the kitchen to drop off my pot of red rice. I wanted to find David, Mina, or the host, so I could introduce myself. We found the kitchen.

"Will you look at this spread? Amazing," I said to Jason. "Is this catered? Everything looks perfect. Let me put my little pot of rice out of the way over here."

"I wasn't hungry before," Jason said, "but I am now. Ribs, fried chicken - somebody here must own a restaurant." We stood in the kitchen looking out at the people. "And you were worried we'd be underdressed coming here. These Californians always dress like they're ready to go to a baseball game."

Someone clanged on a water glass for attention. Jason and I stepped into the living room. A woman was sitting, barefoot, on the piano.

"People, people, hello everyone. It's just after five o'clock, so let's go ahead and get started. I see some new faces out there, so let's do introductions. I'm Helen: singer, host, and attention whore, otherwise why would I be up on this piano. We try to do this every year, to help make the El Dorado seem more like a family, and I want to thank everyone for coming. If we could quickly go around and have everyone say a few words, before you know it, we can eat." She looked around, and her eyes stopped at me. "Here's a cute couple."

I looked at Jason, gave him a smirk, and shrugged my shoulders.

"Let's start with the new kid on the block."

I was caught off-guard, but I answered my cue.

"My name is Anthony Adams, and I..."

And I froze.

What do I say? Am I a musician, a newswriter, a songwriter, TV guy - what do I tell these people? Okay, I'm not nervous; I just can't find the words to summarize my short life in a few clever sentences. And I don't know who I am or what I do.

It seemed as if I was standing there for five minutes with my mouth open, but Jason later said it was closer to five seconds, uncomfortable nonetheless.

"My name is Anthony Adams, and I'm really happy to be here. Thank you." I blurted it out.

Jason spoke next, then it quickly went around the circle, since most of them knew each other.

Helen put up her hands and said, "Before we eat, how about some music? With this much talent in the room, we could put on our own show. I'll start - surprise, right? David, you play, I'll sing."

"What happened to you, brother?" Jason said quietly.

"I don't know, my mind just went blank. I *never* did that before. It was like I couldn't verbalize who I am or what I do. And that "cute couple" remark threw me for a loop. They must all think I'm gay. But I'm cool, now."

But I wasn't cool. I was embarrassed. I even thought about having a drink. Some of these people used to be big shots and might even have contacts. But I blew it by freezing before they even learned my name.

Helen was singing "The Man That Got Away" to David's accompaniment. Next, Zachary played a short solo piece by Duke Ellington. Then Mario pulled out his saxophone and played a duet with my downstairs neighbor Teresa, who played piano. I didn't know everyone's name, but the talent and confidence, the experience and joy of people who lived and loved music, was uplifting to me.

"Let's play something," I said to Jason as we stood around the piano listening with everyone else. The short February sun had set. Air in the room was warm and sweet with the smell of something baking. Helen lit a fire that put a warm orange glow on everyone's face.

"Are you up to it?" he asked. "You might pass out or faint or something. Stage fright *does* come out of nowhere sometimes, you know." He was challenging me, so I asked if he knew "Piano Man."

I wanted to sing well, to redeem myself after looking foolish during my introduction. I felt strong positive energy in the room when I hit the first words of the song, and I fed off of it. I *did* sing well. Conversations stopped as people were curious to see if I had the goods - this light-skinned cross between Al Jarreau and Johnny Mathis. I jumped an octave during the last verse, and hit all the high notes perfectly. They applauded at the end. Jason stood and took a bow, but my mind was somewhere else.

The song.

The words and the message of the song hit my heart, and when I thought back to the lyric *"Man, what are you doing here?"* I realized, like a bolt of lightning, it was time for me to leave Los

Angeles and my broken dreams. Before the clapping stopped, I knew I had to split away from California. I wanted to get out before the crushing disappointments made me speechless forever, or caused me to lose whatever talent I had.

Chapter Twenty-Two

The Message

DECEMBER 1982

If I wanted to leave town in December, I had to work fast to get things in order. And there were three people I needed to deal with before I hit the road.

Gordon.

My first college roommate. Last I heard, he still lived and worked in Manhattan.

"Sure thing, buddy, you can stay with me as long as you like."

Jason.

I needed him to watch my apartment for a while. I still had a lease on the place, but I trusted him to handle things during my…my whatever. If I came back to California, my apartment would still be here. If I decided to stay in New York, I could simply give thirty days notice.

"Show those New York bitches who's running things, Ant."

Dana.

This one should be as easy as the first two. I picked her up and drove to the Hollywood Hills, parked the car, and told her the news.

"Anthony. I can't believe you're leaving me. I mean, wow. I know I'm not the most exciting girl in town, but I thought we had a good thing going. I can't believe you're leaving me." Then she grew quiet; I looked over and saw she was crying.

I was sad and felt guilty to see her cry, but it also made me realize I wasn't in love with her. It was like watching a TV character in a soap opera. I felt detached, like a heartless dog. It was my first time breaking someone's heart, but then I remembered all the times I had been dropped by girls in college. It was better to dump than be dumped.

Two days after Christmas, I boarded a plane, with two big suitcases and a guitar. Six hours later, I was in New York.

On the cab ride from the airport to Manhattan, I tried to convince myself I was making the right move. Okay, I had gone from America's third largest city, to its second, and now to the biggest. That sounded good. I had a lot of money saved up. I knew a few decent people in New York, and there were hundreds of job opportunities just waiting for someone like me. All I needed was a little luck.

The first thing I noticed from the cab was two tall buildings, miles away but still imposing. They were the World Trade Center. I remembered how people in New York were disappointed to lose the "World's Tallest Building" status when the Sears Tower went up in my hometown.

The towers were far away in the winter fog, but even from a ghostly distance, they said, "*This* is like no place else. *This* is New York City."

The cabbie let me off at a big train station, and I stepped into a sea of people unlike anything I'd seen in Chicago or Los Angeles. Thousands of worker bees, sprinting and hurrying by, anxious and intense. *They would crush me if they could.* With my bags and guitar awkward under my shoulders, I caught a train to midtown. I climbed the dark stairs from the subway, and more towers greeted me: the sparkling Rockefeller Center, where Gordon worked.

I entered his building, and got on an elevator. The doors opened onto the eighteenth floor, and he was standing there with a sheet of white paper in each hand. He looked as frantic and busy as everyone else in this city.

"Well, look who's here. Anthony Adams, you old dog, you," Gordon said. He gave me a big hug, which I couldn't return, since dropping my bags might have made my guitar case fall to the ground.

"Look at you," I said, "big time producer, shirt and tie, mister yuppie. How long's it been, five years since college? You look good."

"Well, the blond hair is going, and the gut is bigger, but it's a good life. Follow me to my office where you can put your shit down."

I followed him through a maze of hallways, trying to keep up. The wide corridors were full of workers; they scurried by, as if their underwear was on fire.

Gordon's office was a small room with no windows and barely space for a second person. I squeezed into a chair, and I noticed a picture on the wall from our college days.

"That's from our radio show, 'Saturday Graffiti,'" I said.

"Look at us, Anthony. Can you believe we were ever that young?"

"You have all this great old stuff," I said. "I don't have anything from back then. I never saved a goddamned thing." He had an amazing collection of photographs and clippings on the wall beside his desk. The only memento *I* had from school was a college diploma.

"I have to get back to work right now, buddy. Here's a key to my place. Very easy to find, right on Second Avenue. I'm taping an interview with this really cool guy, Grandmaster Flash, the rapper. You're welcome to stay if you want, but I have to jet. It's so great to see you, Ant."

He slapped my back after handing me a set of keys and a yellow piece of paper with his address. Then he picked up his white papers and dashed out of the office, sheets rustling in his wake.

I was curious to see him interview the rapper, but I was exhausted: jet-lagged, hungry, sleepy and needing a shower, trying not to be overwhelmed by my first time in New York City. I reluctantly passed on seeing his interview.

I rode the eighteen floors back down, and stepped out onto the street. Now it was nearly dark, and I noticed the brilliant Christmas lights and decorations that gave the plaza a dreamlike shimmer.

Then it hit me: *Anthony, you must look like the biggest rube in the world, staring up at skyscrapers and lights, bags in hand.* New York had a way of making you feel like a bumpkin if you were new in town and didn't match their energy and indifference to everything. Even being from Chicago and Los Angeles, I knew I looked like Cousin Gus from Bugtussle. I lowered my head and hailed a cab. It took me to Gordon's place, where I found his guest room in the back, and collapsed on the soft white bed.

Hours later, I woke up and stood at the fifteenth floor window, looking at the East River. It flowed by like slow black oil. Gordon's keys rattled in the door to his apartment, which he flung open.

"You should have stayed. What happened to you?" he said. It was nine o'clock at night.

"Man, I was so tired and funky. How did the interview go?"

"Grandmaster Flash is awesome," he said. "He's the voice of the people, a genius." Gordon slammed his briefcase on the dining room table, and got a beer from the refrigerator. He started leafing through his mail.

"Voice of the people?" I said. "Gordo, what do you know about the *people*? Son of a rich doctor from the Hamptons."

"I'm telling you, Ant, this song, 'The Message,' is opening a whole new side of life that no one's seen before. It's raw, real, like an open vein."

"No one's seen before? What are you talking about?"

Gordon shook his head, then pulled a 12-inch vinyl record from his case, and put it onto his turntable. He dropped the needle, and I listened to the opening bars of the song: it had a catchy beat, and trippy space-age sound effects. After a long intro, two rappers lyrically rode the beat, describing a grim urban nightmare of poverty and desperation.

Two minutes later, the record was still going, now adding violence and prostitution to the landscape. The beat, which was catchy at first, now sounded repetitive, with no chord changes or dynamics. The message of the song was that ghetto life was inescapable, and hustling, prison and death were inevitable.

Many minutes later, the record was finally ending. Gordon was nodding his head throughout the song. He had a satisfied look on his face as if he had discovered a dark and dangerous world, like the first white man sailing up the Hudson. It reminded me of our sophomore year in college, when he and his friends at the radio station discovered the records of Robert Johnson, Jelly Roll Morton, and other ancient bluesmen. The black kids I knew *hated* the blues, but white kids sucked it up with a passion only anthropologists knew. The white kids had no black friends, but they embraced the blues like it was their own.

"Are you digging this, or what?" Gordon asked when the music stopped.

"I can't say I'm exactly liking it," I said. "I'm glad it's over. It went on forever. In fact, it makes me want to kill myself," I said with a laugh.

Gordon looked at me with his eyes and mouth wide open. "Anthony, you're kidding me. This song is real. It's visceral, like a knife cutting through all the bullshit. What happened to you out in California?"

I thought about the song again, in the dual contexts of music and racism.

"As a musician," I said, "I'm not sure why anybody would want to listen to that more than once. It's sonically harsh, the music goes nowhere, and it makes me feel sad."

"That's it!" Gordon screamed. "It makes you *feel* something. And that's what great art is supposed to do. Make you feel." He crushed the empty beer can in his hands, and went for another one.

"Yeah," I said, "maybe 'sad' is the wrong word. It *would* make me feel angry and hopeless if I were living in those conditions. You know I'm biracial, and as a black man, it makes me angry that my people are living like that. As a white man, I'm thinking: it's like a jungle - okay, and…? What are you doing to lift yourself out of the jungle, selling dope and hooking?"

"I'm shocked, Anthony. You sound like my father."

"Man, look back at disco. They said disco was repetitive, soulless, robotic—all the things I just heard on 'The Message.' For pure music, I'd put any Bee Gees song up against what you just played. The only message I got from 'The Message' is I want to stick sharp pencils in my ears."

We both laughed, but Gordon was still dumbfounded by my reaction to the song.

"Great art *should* make you feel something, it's true. But who wants to feel miserable? I always thought music should at least make you feel good, man. Remember, I *am* a musician."

Gordon looked at me and shook his head again. "I thought you, of all people, would be able to relate to this song."

"Why, Gordon, because I'm black? Where does it say all black people have to love all black music?" I caught myself, and changed the tone of the conversation. "You haven't changed much in all these years, you know. Somehow it all leads back to your father, rebelling against authority. That's what this is all about, you know."

"You got it all figured out, huh, old man?" he said.

"Not all of it. I just know you guys think black music is cool - from a safe distance."

We argued into the night, like we did as roommates our first two years in college. It was the kind of stimulation I missed, and never got, during my years in Los Angeles.

Contrary to what I told Gordon, I *did* think I had him figured out. Black music gave him a distant connection with people he never knew and would never know - people he only saw from the back of a cab or an NBC town car. It gave him a way to acknowledge racism without feeling culpable for it.

But I never shared that with him. He was a good friend, and I didn't want to cross the line. I knew how uncomfortable some people got when racism was the topic. And I was in *his* home.

Gordon gave me the names of several people to contact for jobs in the city. Most interesting was a man who had just started a new television network, the first national black cable network in the country. Gordon had met him around town, and said the guy might be looking for producers. I climbed into bed, still tired and jet-lagged, staring at the slightly torn business card Gordon had given me. Beneath a BET logo, it said "Black Entertainment Television."

Chapter Twenty-Three

Betting On A Dream

I always had trouble waking up in a strange place. I needed three or four seconds of disorientation before remembering where I was, and how I got there. For a few seconds, I dreamed I was on a cloud. Then I woke up.

Gordon's guest room was simple and tasteful, and all white. White curtains, white carpet, and thick white down comforter. Everything was white except the TV and clock radio. The clock said seven AM, and I looked out at the cold cityscape, wondering how to make the best of my first morning in New York.

I planned my day while I was in the shower. I knew about a music conference at nine, where I could meet radio and record people. I also wanted to contact the guy who just started Black Entertainment Television.

Gordon was gone for the day, and I got dressed quickly so I could join the slipstreams of people on the sidewalks, running around, looking for their dreams. I loaded my bag with resumes and cassette tapes of my best songs. I was shocked when my phone call got through to Robert Johnson's office, setting up a two o'clock appointment with him, the president of BET. It was a long shot to get him on short notice, but maybe it was a good sign.

A short cab ride took me to my first stop, the Essex Hotel, where "The Radio and Record Maker Convention of 1982" was being held at a ballroom. Forty-five dollars seemed like a lot of money to get in for just a few hours, but it would be worth it if I connected with someone who could get one of my songs recorded by a star, or get me a production deal.

The program listed several panel discussions and workshops for the day. One that stood out was a panel called "The Right Singer, The Right Song." One of my favorite singers, Cheryl Lynn, was listed as a panelist. The problem was that it began at nine AM, and it was already after ten o'clock.

I rushed down the hall to find the Atlantic Room, hoping to catch the end of the discussion, but busboys were cleaning the empty room, preparing for the next presentation.

"You're late, fella," said one of the men. "They all headed down toward the food area."

I walked farther down the hall, turned a corner, and came face-to-face with Cheryl Lynn. She had scored a big hit, "Got To Be Real," during the disco years, but I knew she was trying to redirect her career after disco died with a thud.

Wow, she's fine.

I wasn't expecting her to be so pretty, so I was tongue-tied.

"Hi, you're Cheryl Lynn, right?" It was the dumbest thing I could say.

"That's right," she said with a look of exasperation.

She was busy preparing a plate of food, but this was a rare opportunity, and I forced myself to be aggressive.

"Hi, my name is Anthony Adams, and I'm a songwriter."

"That's nice, Anthony. Good luck to you." She flashed a beautiful smile, and continued loading her plate with ham and cheese. It was a classic Hollywood brush-off, but I didn't back off.

"I have all your albums. I was wondering—which one is your personal favorite so far? I thought your second album was great." I was using the "true flattery" routine I developed at *Hype Magazine*, where you pour on the compliments, as long as they're sincere.

"That's my favorite, too. I was able to be more creative on that one. It didn't sell as well, but that speaks to the artistry of it." Her articulation was perfect on every word; she spoke in a soft, feathery voice.

"Miss Lynn, I have several songs that are just right for you." I reached into my bag and brought out a cassette tape. "All my contact info is on the case, and I think you'll be pleased. The first one was written just for you."

That wasn't true, but it didn't matter anyway. Her plate was heavy with food as she looked at my tape like it was a piece of moldy Brie. "I really can't accept that or even listen to it. You'll have to send it to my manager, for legal reasons. I really have to go now."

I stood in the alcove of food, dead meat everywhere. For a moment, I thought of dumping my tape into the bowl of mayonnaise. You try to be assertive, I thought, and you get smacked down; but if you're mousy and go through channels, you get no attention. Her manager would just toss my tape on a pile with a thousand others. That would be a waste of time.

I walked over to Broadway, and I made a bet with myself that I could get a job at BET. I'd impress the guy with that job I had back in L.A. But I desperately needed to find an approach that would pay off. A New York style. And I needed to think of it quick.

Black Entertainment Television. I'd only seen snippets of the channel, but I liked the sound of the name. They probably do lots of black-related news, culture, sports and public affairs, I thought as I walked. Surely the people there were full of pride and good intentions, willing to give a break to a young black man with great qualifications. What a joy to work for a black network. I was betting on a dream.

BET's New York offices were located, oddly enough, in a building where Church's Fried Chicken and Colt 45 Malt Liquor also had corporate headquarters. A ride to the third floor took me to a small suite of offices. The secretary told me to have a seat, and wait for Mr. Johnson.

One small television set was playing in the reception room, and it was tuned to BET. The screen showed a music video, with black women dancing to a song called "Doin' the Butt." The camera swung, swiveled, and zoomed in and out on the ample behinds of the young women in the video. What the hell is this, I thought. It was my first time seeing BET.

The secretary told me to follow her, and she took me to an office where Robert Johnson was sitting behind a long, wide desk that was covered with papers, and had three red telephones on it.

"Good morning," I said with a smile.

"Have a seat, young man." He didn't make a move to shake hands, so neither did I. He just peered at me from over his glasses, like a laser scans the bar code on a can of corn. He looked me up and down. "What can I do for you?"

"My name is Anthony Adams, and I understand you're looking for producers and creative people to work at your new cable channel. Here's my resume." I handed it to him.

"Where the heck did you hear that?" He pushed the glasses high on his nose, and briefly glanced at my life story. Then he let the paper float down to his desk.

"Let me tell you a little about BET, because you look like you may not be in the know. I'll tell you what BET is. It's me. You're looking at it. Robert Johnson started this company three years ago with $15,000 and a dream. A dream to become the first black network in the USA. So, now, tell me what you can do for me—what ideas do you have that can help Robert Johnson?"

His attitude was surprising. I couldn't figure why he was being adversarial. I suspected he didn't like the way I looked when he glared at me over his glasses. Maybe my hair was too long or my skin was too light. All I wanted was a job as a show producer, but now, I felt like a ten-year old in the principal's office.

"Well, I produced a public affairs show in Los Angeles for two years, and I also did a lot of production work at the public TV station at college in Chicago. I can help you create a news or public affairs show, weekly or nightly, covering New York and the country."

Johnson's shoulders dropped with disappointment. He stood up. *This is not going well,* I thought. *How quickly can I get out of here*?

"Public affairs? Look, young man. I'm competing with the big boys for viewers. Every minute of the day, people can choose between me, or some glossy, high-budget network show. So, I have to compete on a different level. I keep my budgets low, and I keep costs down. That's the only way BET will survive." He pointed to his television. "*This* is how we survive." A group of black women were grinding their breasts into the wet windshield of a car, as a song called "Put 'Em on the Glass" played. The video was cartoonish and freaky, and the music was horrible, but I tried to ignore it.

How can I get a show from this guy, and do I even want one?

I spoke up, trying to find a median between aggressive and appeasable. "How about a weekly news show that also covers music, sports and entertainment?"

He thought about it, and seemed to like the idea. "I might need that, one day soon," he said as he sat back in his leather chair. "But right now it's survival time. This is what I've got: gospel music, infomercials, and videos, because I've found a market that seems to enjoy that mix. If I try putting on "60 Minutes" or something, before I'm ready, I'll be out of business. On the other side of this desk. With you."

I tried not to be discouraged as I walked to Gordon's apartment. But it was hard. Cold wind was blowing down Fifth Avenue. I buried my face in my warm coat as light snow began to fall. The rejection, the cold weather, the general pace of life made me miss California.

There was still time to let New York love me. I just didn't know how anybody could stand out among the millions of people here, looking for their time in the sun.

Gordon's apartment was warm and comfortable, and I relaxed in the quiet solitude. I was watching the six o'clock news, comparing it with the L.A. news, when he came home. But he wasn't alone - he was with a friend. I turned and saw Gordon's white face in the dim hallway, and only saw the dark, tall shadow of his hulking guest.

"Yo, yo, Anthony, what's happening, man?" It was Gordon's voice, but I had never heard him talk that way. He seemed to be imitating a black man.

"I'm in here watching the news."

They walked in, and I clearly saw a big, dark-skinned man with an angry look on his face.

"This is my friend Norman Washington, but we all call him 'Black Ice.'"

I hopped up off of the sofa to greet them; Black Ice began a complicated handshake, which I followed.

"What's going on, Ice?" I said.

"Yo, not Ice, not Black, it's Black Ice. Don't get it twisted, yo," he said.

"Black Ice and I went to Catholic high school together. He's a rapper now."

"Really? I'd like to come see one of your shows sometime."

"Check it," Black Ice said. "We got a show tomorrow in the Bronx. I hook you up."

"I'm leaving town, yo," Gordon said, "so I won't be able to make it, kid. But, you should go, Anthony."

The two of them sat at the dining room table, and Black Ice got a plastic bag out of his thick coat, unfurling the bag onto the table. It was full of marijuana.

"Come on, Ant, let's get stoned," Gordon said.

"None for me, thanks."

I walked over to the TV set and started flipping channels. I landed on MTV, which was a new cable channel airing music videos all day and night. A group of blond-haired men were singing and playing guitar, and one of them was familiar. I looked closer, and the camera cut to a tight shot of the person I knew. It was Kevin McGraw, who used to be in my last band.

Kevin!

Kevin from my group Modern Man - was fronting a successful band on national TV. The video ended; the announcer came on and said it was the number one video of the week across the country.

That made me think seriously about getting high with the guys, to help get over the entire fruitless day. From the egg I laid with Cheryl Lynn, to the busted job interview at BET, and now to an ex-band member with a number one song. I wanted to get high for the first time, but I glanced over at Gordo and Black Ice, and saw how they looked, sucking in smoke. They looked pathetic, trying to escape reality, the way my parents used alcohol out of weakness. I wanted to be stronger than that. I turned off the TV and walked over to them.

"I think I'll check out your show tomorrow, Black Ice. I just need some directions."

Black Ice took a strong puff of smoke, and let it out smoothly. "If you think you can handle it, son. You *know* it'll be off the hook, tomorrow being New Year's Eve and all."

New Year's Eve? Once again, a holiday snuck up on me. I was used to spending New Year's Eve safe at home, away from the drunk drivers and flying bullets. *Damn, I'm going to be in a strange town, on New Year's Eve, with a bunch of pot-smoking, rap-loving, gun-shooting, wild New Yorkers.*

Chapter Twenty-Four

New Year's Eve in New York City

I fell in love in New York - in love with Gordon's cloud-white guest room. I slept better than I'd ever slept in my life while I was in that room. It was the most peaceful sensation: waking to the total absence of color, which seemed to whiteout all the city noise and job pressure.

Again I wondered where Gordon found white doorknobs, white lighting fixtures and white curtain rods as I woke and looked around. The peacefulness of the room made me forget, for a short time, the pains and little failures from the day before. Seeing Kevin on TV was a fitting end to a fruitless day, and the white room was a perfect antidote to it all.

I got up and walked around the place; Gordon was gone. He had left a note reaffirming the fact he was spending a few days upstate with a lady friend. He left the address to a ten o'clock party he thought I might like; some people from our college class would be there, so I planned to go later. I remembered today was the last day of December.

Within a few hours, I was ready to explore the city, and soon I was walking down dirty snow-lined Second Avenue. I saw a crowd lined up, waiting to get into an art exhibit. Thirty or forty people, well dressed and some in fur, were eager to get into the Blackstone Gallery. I was standing toward the end of the line when, at exactly one o'clock, the doors opened and the people flooded into the place.

"What's all the commotion?" someone said behind me. It was a rich-looking middle-aged woman who walked up to my side.

"I don't know. It looks like some kind of art exhibit."

"Well, *I* want to see what's causing such a stir," she said, clutching her beaded purse as we walked to the front windows. We stared quietly at two paintings, one on each side of the door, as more people rushed past us.

On the left was a piece of red canvas, with the words "Cassius Clay" printed in capital letters. Beneath the words was a line drawing of a person who was probably supposed to be Clay, but looked nothing like him; it resembled Frankenstein or some robot creature.

On the right was a painting filled with chaotic symbols and words: body parts, banana peels, animals and kitchen appliances were spread over the canvas.

"This is what they're rushing to see?" I said to the lady.

"I've never seen anything so ugly in all my days. What do you think, young man?"

I looked closer, then stepped back to see if I could find any merit in the drawings.

"I'd say ugly, along with unstructured, violent, cartoonish and childlike. You're from New York, ma'am, I'm guessing. Is this part of the New York art scene, because I don't get it."

Just then, an older married couple walked up beside us. Their cold breath made fog on the gallery window as they looked lovingly at the paintings, cooing like doves.

"Doris, is that you?" the man said. "We haven't seen you in ages." The three of them exchanged hugs as I stood back and watched. "I promised to get Arlene a Basquiat for Christmas, so here we are. We'd better get inside before they're all gone." The couple hurried inside.

"Basquiat?" the first woman said to me with her mouth hanging open. "I had no idea. What was I thinking?" She went through the door, and I watched as she now admired the paintings with her friends in the gallery. She put her tiny white hands on her cheeks, and nodded her head as she examined the modern art on display. Soon the windows were fogged up from the breath of the people inside. All I could see was their shadows, and the blurred red painting that now looked like the scene of a crime.

There was a lot more I wanted to see in the city, so I wandered around until seven, when I called Black Ice. He was on his way out, so he quickly told me how to get to his show by subway. I drifted a while longer, then I went down into a dark, smelly station.

The train to South Bronx was noisy and crowded, and covered with bright, illegible graffiti. I sat in an empty seat near the door, remembering how you weren't supposed to make eye contact with New Yorkers. As with dogs, a stare was an aggressive act. I slouched down into my torn seat, and put an angry scowl on my face. The ride was long, until finally I heard the words, "South Bronx Station, The Bronx."

I followed Black Ice's directions, pausing under dim streetlights to read my handwriting. Each step I took, I asked myself what I was getting into. I wanted to see the young rap scene firsthand, since hearing Gordon play "The Message;" since catching the music on an L.A. street, and having a promoter rave about it. But these New York streets were cold and crackling with danger and despair. Whole city blocks were burned out and vacant; groups of young men stood shadowy in front of liquor stores, talking loud, I guessed, to scare away their enemies in the night - real and ghostly ones.

A line of people were standing in front of the Disco Fever lounge, waiting to get in. The club's name was an obvious carryover from a Donna Summer past; the "Disco" half of the neon sign was partially destroyed. Disco had become a bad word.

I joined the quick-moving line to get in. Two mammoth-sized bouncers were frisking people as they entered, taking an occasional knife or bottle of liquor from patrons, and giving out claim checks so people could later recover their stuff. I reached the front of the line; one of the big guys just looked at me, and pointed me toward the cashier without a frisking.

The hall was filled with young people. I guessed they were mostly from 18 to 23 years old. There were no white people in the club. Black and Puerto Rican kids were intermixed in groups that were defined by the colors of their clothes.

I headed toward the front, where a DJ was on stage, flanked by an MC on each side. One of the MCs was Black Ice, finishing his performance. I squeezed my way to the side of the stage, watched and listened to him.

"Five hundred years of slavery
and then one day, they say, "you're free"
but slavery is a state of mind
it kills your soul over time
our history, our language, our family system
have been destroyed, and now we miss 'em
Now we're trapped here in the ghetto

I said, now I'm trapped here in the ghetto
Cops are crawling everywhere
They'll bust ya head 'cause they don't care
The white man thinks they still own me
But I believe in Marcus Garvey
I'm going back to Africa
I said, I'm going back to Africa..."

When Black Ice finished, two men started fighting in the middle of the crowd, and two other men began a separate fight in a back corner of the club. Bouncers appeared and stopped the fights almost as quickly as they began.

The DJ played a James Brown cut, and people started dancing. The music was loud and vibrated right through me. I smelled body heat rising from the crowd - musk, deodorant and perfume swirled in the thick air. An old disco ball hovered overhead, not spinning or lit, and probably broken. I was overwhelmed by the contradictions: the club felt comforting and dangerous; the crowd seemed hostile and inviting; the rap music sounded earnest and stupid, all at the same time.

I greeted them as they left the stage.

"What's up Ice - uh, Black Ice."

"Yo, I know you, kid? Wait, you that writer dude friend of Gordon's. What's happening, kid?" We slapped hands and bumped shoulders.

"Just checking out the show, man. You all were rippin' it up out there."

"Rockin' the crowd, keeping it real," Black Ice said. "What you got up for this New Year's Eve? You gonna stay and party?"

"No, man. I've seen what I came to see, which is you. I'm heading back to Gordon's place. I'm a little bit out of my game here."

"Yeah, look at you. Not exactly fitting in, like you from Kansas or something. But you cool. I'm gonna chill here for a few hours with my girl over there, but let me walk you out, so you don't get jumped or something. I'm surprised you ain't get jumped yet."

Black Ice walked me toward the door. I was ready to leave, and he must have sensed my alienation. We walked past a circle of dancers, half wearing red and half wearing blue. A member of one group challenged an opponent, but instead of fighting, they danced - aggressively and competitively, like peacocks scratching the dirt to show their dominance. I caught up with Black Ice, who was nearly at the door.

"What you think, kid," he said, "this all new to you, huh?" We stepped into the frigid Bronx air.

"This is something different, man, definitely something I won't forget. How long have you been rapping?"

"Couple years. Since high school. You should try it, man, you might have some talent."

"Talent?" I laughed to myself, and blew some warm air into my hands. "You never know, man. You never know."

"This is the voice of the people you hearing tonight. Have you seen this city, man? It's like they dropped a bomb in the Bronx and left us to live in the ruins. Ain't no jobs, can't afford college. And they put a actor in the White House. So you know it's all a joke. If I ain't rapping, I'm robbing somebody's house. I'm rapping to save my life, son."

"Graffiti is a big deal out here," I said, "which helps *make* it look like ruins." We were standing in the doorway; two couples pushed past us leaving the club.

"That's all part of the game. Graffiti, breakdancing - it's a whole world. I don't dance, but I do my share of tagging. My brother got me into it. House was always full of spray cans. He started by painting our jackets, shirts. Then he started painting buildings. I'm better than him now. Got my own tagging crew."

"School me on this, Black Ice. If you're unhappy with the way your hood looks - broken windows, abandoned buildings - then how does it help to have everything covered with spray paint? If you owned a building, would you want it covered with bright paint like that?"

"See, you wouldn't understand. It's like being the invisible man living here. So what better way to make a name for yourself than to put up a piece that's original, that says something, right in the neighborhood where your boys can see it? Everybody be talking about *you*. Believe this: if I wanted to display in a fancy gallery downtown, I could. But I'm keeping it real, 'cause this is the streets, and this is where I'm from. I gotta go, homie." He banged his chest with his right fist.

I said goodbye to Black Ice, then he darted back into the club. I jogged to the subway station, all the while looking at the graffiti-covered buildings that lined the street. I thought I saw Black Ice's name at the bottom of one piece, in red, green and black, but I couldn't make out the words as I ran. The building had boarded-up windows, and looked a hundred years old.

Minutes later, I stepped into a train that was nearly empty, then I walked toward the front where about a dozen people were seated. I was hoping to reach Manhattan before midnight, maybe to see the big Times Square celebration.

It was an eye-opening night. I had seen Black Ice's real side, and I realized he over-performed when he was around Gordon. The popularity of the rap show caught me by surprise. The mass media had not yet discovered the depth of the music among young people, in spite of a few hit records around the country. I was glad to witness it firsthand.

Most of all, I was intrigued by what Ice – Black Ice - said about talent. *You should try to rap. You might have some talent.*

I had zero interest in rapping. I was sure it was another fad that would fade as quickly as disco. I had none of the anger that fueled rappers, or that they pretended to have. I knew that the best rapper in the city would pale next to my musical ability on five instruments. I had considered saying all this to Black Ice, but he probably would have knocked me out. Biting my tongue might have seemed cowardly, but I wasn't a fool, and this was *his* turf.

It was after midnight when the train reached midtown. The streets were full of cars and people, and I heard a noisy celebration a few blocks away. 1982, and I was in New York, jobless and alone.

The city was slightly warmer than the Bronx, so I walked to Gordon's building, taking in the odd sights that made up New York. A gleaming new black limousine was stalled at Broadway and 44th, with steam coming from the manhole under it. It looked like the devil's ride. Dark, empty skyscrapers loomed over me, and I imagined what they would look like as ruins one day.

Then I remembered the party Gordon had told me about. It was a ten o'clock party on Broadway, not far. But I figured it was too late now, unaware that the party was probably just beginning. I was tired from the long train rides, so I continued to Gordon's.

I had wanted to go to that party, but then I would have missed the rap thing. My head was full of images and emotions when I finally reached Gordon's apartment, so I decided to write a song. I hadn't written a new song in months.

I'll write about New York, and how it feels being here, like a fish out of water. Then I remembered how Joni Mitchell wrote "Woodstock" even though she didn't attend the festival. I focused on the party I missed on Broadway. I turned on all the lights in the white room, and wrote.

New Year's Eve in New York City

Cold wind is blowing down Fifth Avenue
Heading to Broadway, I'm here without you
What will I do
On New Year's Eve in New York City
Skyscrapers cold and black as the night
Shiny black limo is stalled at the light
What a sight
New Year's Eve in New York City
Well, I can't find a bar to step out of the cold
But then there's a party near 14th, I'm told
I'll play it bold
My first time in New York City

Now, they know how to do it
And everyone looks fine
I'll try to forget you and have a good time
Out of my mind
On New Year's Eve in New York City

Man on piano, play me the blues
'bout the guy who had true love, only to lose
Put on my walking shoes
And hit the streets of New York City

Old man in a doorway turns up his collar
Says "Button up your coat, the wind will make you holla"
And can you spare a dolla
'Cause a dime won't do in New York City

Don't know if I'll ever find my way home
What's a child doing here all alone
On my own
New Year's Eve in New York City

Without warning your life will up and change
Got no one to love and everything's strange
Been rearranged
And I'm in New York City.

But I'll be home soon to start it all new
To find a new lover, a new point of view
And I'll always love you
New York City.

Chapter Twenty-Five

Attitude

NEW YEAR'S WEEK 1983

I stayed in bed most of New Year's Day, except for a lunchtime run to a Chinese restaurant. Football and game shows took my mind off the cold weather and the fact that Gordon left me alone in the city.

His electric typewriter came in handy for typing the final draft of my new song. Reading it in the light of day made me realize three things: I missed California, I didn't actually love New York (in spite of the lyric), and I might, just might, have been in love with Dana. I remembered how she made me feel, how she was always there for me, and wanted to be together every chance we could. I didn't appreciate her when we were together, and it must have hurt when I broke us up.

I got out my guitar, and ran through the song several times. After some work, I settled on a 12-bar blues arrangement, and I was proud of the finished product. But the melancholy tone of the piece made me ache to find a place to call home. It made me want to talk to Dana.

I called her Los Angeles number, but her phone was disconnected. *What could have happened in four weeks?* I had no other way to contact her, so I made other "Happy New Year" calls. My parents were doing well in Chicago, frozen under three feet of snow. My other friends in L.A. were enjoying the hazy sun, and I wished even more to be there. More football and game shows, and soon the day was gone.

The second of January was a business day, and I was happy to be able to beat the streets again. I got out early and found a coffee shop on Fifth and Broadway that seemed to be full of creative people.

I was standing in line to order, when someone tapped my shoulder and a deep voice said, "Aren't you that music writer from L.A.?" The voice was unmistakable. I turned around to see it was Harvey, Sylvester's manager.

"That's me," I said. "What's happening, Harvey. What are you doing here?"

"I'm about to ask you the same question," he said. "Me, I'm producing some tracks for my new group. Hey, weren't you a songwriter? You were supposed to send me some songs."

"Harvey, man, I did. I brought you three songs personally. You were supposed to get back to me. I figured they weren't what you were looking for. But I *do* have some new material you need to hear."

"That'll be right on time, young brother, 'cause I'm looking for one more song, a solid hit. If you can do it, you'll be set for life. We're doing our last session today at five at ABC Studios in the Brill Building. Come check it out. And bring your New York attitude."

At noon, I picked up lunch and headed to Gordon's to get my music and guitar for Harvey's session. The phone was ringing as I put the key in the door.

"Hello?"

"Hi, Anthony, this is Jason. You got some mail that looks important. I thought I better call you."

"Open it up, man."

The phone was silent for a few moments, then he began to read.

"Dear Mr. Adams, we are contacting you on the recommendation of Wendy Robinson, former publisher of *Hype Magazine*. As you may know, *Hype* has been sold to our company, Warner Publishing Group. Blah, blah blah..."

"Jason, don't blah blah blah me! What does it say?"

"It goes on. We would like to meet with you regarding future opportunities at *Hype Magazine*. Please contact our New York headquarters at 511 Fifth Avenue, signed, David Freeman, blah blah blah."

"*Hype Magazine* was sold? Who the hell knew? And Wendy recommended me to them. This is too much."

"Boy, you better call these people," Jason said. "You wanted to work in New York, didn't you? And they're right there."

"I need to sit and figure this out, Jay. Let me get back to you later."

I spent the next few hours gathering my tapes, and going over songs to present to Harvey. But half my mind was on the letter from Hype.

I picked up my guitar, and sang, "We Go Back and Forth," thinking of how my career was a tug-of-war between music and journalism. I played "Don't Let Me Go," which could have been about being fired from Hype and KCBS. I slowly realized how every song had a subtext relating to my personal life.

At four-thirty, I took a deep breath, and headed to the studio to meet Harvey.

He was seated alone in the control room when I got to ABC.

"I'm always the first one to get here," he said, "cause I'm the one paying the bills."

I got out of my old Chicago winter coat, and sat in the chair next to Harvey, putting my guitar to the side. An engineer was setting up in the recording studio.

"If you have time," I said, "I got two songs for you that'll be perfect for your girls - with the right arrangement."

I was excited just to be inside the world-famous Brill Building, where hundreds of hit records were born. And now, I had a chance to pitch *my* songs to a hit-making producer.

"I'm just looking for one - *one* smash record with this new act. I may go broke paying for these sessions if I don't get a hit. It's a rough business, son."

"When I met with you in L.A., you said things were getting funky in the music business - and not the *good* kind of funky."

"I could tell you some stories. But I won't. Young man should learn the game on his own. I'll tell you one thing though. Black music is in real trouble. Started with the whole crossover thing a few years ago. Once you cross over, you can't cross back. To span that river, man, you have to drop a lot of what makes you special. Before long, there's nobody left on the black side of the river, and soul music dies. That's what's happening today."

"Exactly what's happening, Harvey?"

"Giant corporations are taking over the independent companies that developed the music. At a big company, every song you put out has to be a hit, because of high overhead. When an album flops, that singer is dropped. Disappears faster than holiday music on the day after Christmas."

"I haven't dealt with any record labels yet. Can't keep a band together long enough to get to that level."

"In a few years, you won't even be able to buy any good soul music. After Aretha and James Brown are done, it's over, baby."

I was eager to play my songs, but Harvey was giving me a history lesson. It was interesting stuff, but I wanted to put the focus back on my material and me. *My New York attitude*.

A man in a suit opened the door of the studio; seven musicians went in. They got out their instruments and took positions. Harvey jumped up, dashed out of the control room and into the studio. The engineer came into the control room, and sat at the mixing board.

I watched as Harvey orchestrated the session. He knew what he wanted, and worked hard to get the singers and musicians to duplicate what he was hearing in his head. Big beads of sweat were on his forehead. I watched for nearly three hours, until I decided Harvey would never have time or energy to listen to my songs. I grabbed my stuff, and when I caught his eye, I waved goodbye and left.

I walked down the hall toward the elevator, and peeked into the studio next door. I couldn't hear a sound, but through a double glass window I saw a solitary man standing at a microphone. He looked like Black Ice, but younger. I opened the door to the control room and stepped in.

"What you want?" A second man, in a backwards baseball cap, was seated alone at the mixing board.

"I'm just checking it out, kid," I said with my best Bronx attitude.

He looked me over, eyes stopping at my guitar. "Okay, that's cool."

I watched as he ran the board, while the rapper performed at the mike. The young man flowed fearlessly with his rhymes, without looking at notes, like he was making it up as he went along. The man at the controls started a prerecorded tape, and together they made a song. I watched for a few minutes, then left the room.

I imagined Harvey pulling out his hair right about now: working with high-strung musicians, writing a lot of checks.

I called Warner Publishing at 9:01 the next morning, still lying in bed. A secretary put me through to David Freeman's assistant.

"Oh, Mr. Adams, David Freeman has been trying to get in touch with you."

"Yes, ma'am. I'm right here in New York."

"Well, that's wonderful," she said, "because Mr. Freeman is interviewing people to work at the new *Hype Magazine*, and he said you're highly recommended."

"Awesome. I'm right here in midtown; I can come in anytime."

"Excellent. Can you come in this morning at 10:45? Mr. Freeman has a small window for a short first interview."

"I'll be there. Thanks, ma'am."

The thought of going back to *Hype Magazine* had never crossed my mind. But I assumed it was a New York job and Wendy was gone, so maybe things would be better.

I heard someone walking down the hall. It was Gordon. He peeked his head in the doorway and stepped into the room, dripping wet, toweling himself.

"You up?" he asked.

"Man, where in the world have you been? How was your getaway?"

"It was beautiful," he said. "A lot of skiing, lots of good food and wine, lots and lots of sex." He dried his head, and shook out the thick, dark hair. He had no problem standing naked before me, just like in college. It creeped me out now like it did then. "But it's back to work today. How's New York treating you?"

"Well, for starters, I met one of my favorite singers, went to a scary rap show in the Bronx, wrote a new song, met a producer I know at the Brill Building, saw a crazy art exhibit - it's been like three months of L.A. life packed into three New York days."

"Things happen here, Ant."

"And...and," I said excitedly, saving the best for last, "I just got off the phone with the magazine where I used to work over three years ago. They want me back." I looked at the clock. "Hey, I better get in the shower. I have to be there in two hours."

"Well, good luck, pal. I'll be at the network till late if you want to call me." He left to get dressed, and I got up to shower and begin my day.

David Freeman's assistant looked nothing like her voice. On the phone she sounded like a petite, pretty young lady. In fact, she was six feet tall and built like an East German athlete. She told me to be seated in a chair under a huge Warner Publishing logo, and at exactly 10:45, Freeman opened his office door and told me to come in. I grabbed my briefcase full of writing samples and resumes. His large wood-paneled office had a spectacular view of the city. We shook hands, and I sat down.

"I only have a few minutes," he said, "but thanks for coming in on such short notice. We're looking for some creative people to help run *Hype Magazine*. I understand you're a crackerjack writer."

"I am, sir. I brought some samples and clippings for you to see."

"Tell me how you ended your relationship when you worked for *Hype*."

"Well," I said, thinking fast, "I'm a musician, and I needed some time to try the rock business while I was still young. That didn't quite work out as I hoped. I left on good terms with the publisher, though, and it was a great place to work."

"Yes," he said, "I've spoken to Miss Robinson about you, and she thinks you'd make a fine member of the new team, maybe managing editor. Here's what's happening: Warner is going to pump about a million into taking *Hype* to the next level. So, let me take a quick look at your material."

I handed him my portfolio. *Managing editor?* That was something I wasn't prepared for. It sounded like a high-paying gig, which would be important for living in New York. But I just wanted to be a writer, and I didn't want my career sidetracked again like it was in L.A. I watched Freeman rifle through my samples, nodding his head along the way.

"This is all fine and good. I have a meeting at eleven, but I want to bring you in again in a few days to meet some other people. I'll have Miss Haas call you."

She called that afternoon, and two days later, at 4 PM, I was again sitting under the Warner name, this time wearing a new suit, watching the burly assistant at her desk. Two minutes after I sat down, another man entered the office. He checked in with Miss Haas, and chatted with her. Then he sat across from me. I introduced myself.

"What's happening, bro?" he said. "I'm Ricky Sharp."

Chapter Twenty-Six

Theater of the Moment

I sized up this Ricky Sharp character. Firm, dry handshake: confident—or at least trying to project confidence. Accent, but not from New York; the few words I heard were more Californian. Wearing a light tan suit—stylish, but not something you'd sport in January, so he wasn't up on his fashion. Lingered at Miss Haas' desk—joking and making small talk, almost flirting. Dark skin, about my height of six feet two.

I finally pegged him to be my age, a ladies' man, popular in high school, college frat boy, from California, not a great student, but got by on his looks. Of course, all those things could have been wrong; I was just trying to occupy my mind. The one thing I knew was that we were competing for the same job, and I didn't like to lose.

We waited in David Freeman's outer office for ten minutes that seemed like thirty.

The big man's door opened. He called for us to come in together. Sharp and I looked at each other with surprise, then we stood up and walked in. Two chairs were opposite Freeman's desk, where there had only been a single chair two days ago. We sat, and I wondered what this was all about.

"Good afternoon. I assume you two have already met." Sharp and I both nodded, though we barely said five words to each other. "Good. Here's what's happening. I have two jobs open at *Hype Magazine*. One for Managing Editor and another for Contributing Editor. I've interviewed you both, and looked at your material, references. I want to hire you both, but the question is, which job for whom? That's what I have to decide here today."

He paused, as if waiting for one of us to speak, but I was stunned by the theater of the moment. Did Freeman expect us to fight for these positions, like Roman slaves—could he be that dramatic? I spoke up after a few awkward seconds of silence.

"Maybe you could clarify how the jobs are different, and we could see which one is a better fit for which man."

"For me," Sharp said, "I'd say *my* experience managing a crew at KCAL would make me a natural for the Managing Editor slot. I'm just saying."

"Good, good," Freeman said, pressing his palms together at his mouth, in a prayer position. "Tell me more."

I cut off Sharp before he could speak again. "Well, I managed crews for years at KCBS, in the studio *and* in the field. It's part of my versatility, as a manager and a reporter."

My opponent said, "Ricky Sharp was responsible for day-to-day publication of the college newspaper - at age nineteen. Chief Editor."

I didn't know which was more amazing, that Sharp was falling for Freeman's tactic, or that he referred to himself in the third person. He had said "Chief Editor" emphatically, like he had been head of NASA or something. I didn't yet know which position I wanted - the manager job or the writer/editor job. But

I got caught up in the competition and the dramatics, so I played along.

"Mr. Freeman, I worked at *Hype* for two solid years. I have contacts in the music business, I know their system, and I know how to improve the magazine to make it more current. Personally, I think they're still caught in a seventies groove. In fact, I'm working on a proposal for change that I'd like to send you."

"Interesting—do that," Freeman said. He looked at Sharp. "Richard?"

"Wait," Sharp said, "I subscribe to *Hype*, and it's not just music. It's movies, TV, all kind of shi.....stuff. My background puts me in a position to manage a team that can cover all of show business from the Oscars to, I don't know, the MTV Awards."

"Okay, guys," Freeman said, "in all fairness, Anthony is right that the person and the job need to be a good fit. What's happening is that you two are equally skilled to do either job out there. The contributing editor job is half writer/reporter and half editor. The managing editor job directly supervises all eleven staff writers. Let me think for a second." He paused, and said, "I've got it."

Freeman swiveled his chair around to look out the window, his back to us. Sharp used two fingers on each hand to massage his temples. I looked up at the plaques and photographs on Freeman's walls. He turned back around in less than a minute.

"Here's what's happening. The two of you will share equal responsibilities as *Hype's* co-executive editors. It couldn't be more simple. You will both write articles occasionally, edit whatever the staff generates, get the magazine produced every two weeks. For problems or disagreements, the publisher will be out there to break any ties. It's a genius move: instead of getting half of both of you, I'll be getting two hundred per cent of you both."

I was dizzy at how fast things were developing. But I needed a job.

The plan would depend on forming a good relationship with some unseen publisher, and especially with Sharp. I looked over at him; he was staring straight ahead.

Freeman told us what the salary would be, and it was good. But somehow I'd have to fabricate the "proposal for change" I told him I developed.

"You can think about it if you want," he said, "but I'm ready to get things flying out there."

"Mr. Freeman," I said, "you keep saying 'out there,' and I'm not sure what that means. Where are the jobs based?"

"I'm sorry," he said, "I thought I told you guys. "Warner Publishing is here in this building, but we decided to keep *Hype* headquartered out in Hollywood, where the action is. If you want the job, or jobs, you'll be relocating to L.A. And just to make it interesting, the first person who shows up out there can choose his own office."

"I accept," Sharp said. "I don't know about your man here, but I'm ready to go to work."

"I'm there, too," I said. I had to force the words out.

So now I'm job-sharing with a stranger, returning to *Hype Magazine*, and heading back to Los Angeles.

I had felt pressed to accept the offer after Sharp did, but I knew I could back out after thinking about it if I wanted to.

"Good deal, men," Freeman said. "Miss Haas will type up contracts by tomorrow." He stood up; Sharp and I bounced up after him. "Welcome aboard, captains." He smiled. "*Co*-captains."

Chapter Twenty-Seven

Happy Hour

I left the Warner Building at rush hour, and entered a stampede of workers running from their jobs. I caught a few of their faces. You know: that beaten-down look you get after a day on a nine-to-five job. *Was I ready to join their ranks again, in a weird job situation with a stranger, at Hype?*

There were human bodies for as far as I could see, up and down Third Avenue - cold, foggy breath hanging in the air above them - like sad marching penguins. What a way to live, I thought.

I found a pay phone, and called Gordon.

"Man, that's radical," he said after I told him about Freeman's offer. "It sounds like just what you want."

"It may *sound* good, but help walk me through this thing, Gordo. The pay is decent, even better considering the lower cost of living in L.A. I'll get to report and write, and also manage and edit other writers."

"That's great stuff for your resume, Ant."

"The bad news is that I'll be paired with a guy who might be cool, or might turn out to be a jerk. The good news is that I'll be moving back out west. Man, I miss California—I had no idea how much it feels like home out there. Here in the city, I never found that 'New York state of mind.' And plus, my feet have been *freezing* since I got here."

"Hopefully the guy gave you some time to think about the deal, right?"

"Time? He wants us to come in tomorrow to sign contracts!"

"Look, when they want you to sign a contract, that means they really want you. *I'm* just a schmucky salaried guy who can be fired anytime. A contract is the big leagues. So, here's what I suggest: think about it tonight. Have some dinner, sleep on it, and in the morning maybe your head'll be clear. I'll see you at home, buddy."

Maybe I can relax and think if I explore the city.

I let the living currents of the streets carry me. We flowed up an avenue here, turned down a street there, stopped at red lights, and charged like a herd of cattle at green. Waves of people disappeared down subway stairs, and sometimes I had to fight their undertow just to stay above ground.

I looked for a rhythm in the way the people moved—distinctive beats. White men walked with their backs stiff and their arms tight, even young ones. *I'm half white. Why don't I walk like that? Or do I?* White women led with their swaying shoulders; their hair bounced like staccato sixteenth notes. Black women tried to lead the way of every herd, hips swaying, perfume in their trails. Black men glided smoothly, with a slick but measured swing, like a linear dance.

I walked and watched the crowd for an hour. Not a soul made eye contact with me. And if I dropped dead, they would walk right over my body.

The crowd and I stopped at a light, and I heard faint music nearby. I looked over to a sign above a barroom door; it said "Blue Lizard Lounge." A man stepped out of the club, and through the open door I heard a live band playing the blues. I broke from the frozen pack, and went inside.

"If I didn't have bad luck...
I'd have no luck at allllllll."

A man in a suit was finishing a song. As the door closed behind me, he was leaving the stage, waving to the twenty or thirty shadowy people applauding his show. I walked closer to sit at the bar, and I recognized Joe Williams, the famous jazz-blues singer. He stepped to the bar, and I heard him order black coffee. I wanted to meet him. *What should I say? Remember Cheryl Lynn!*

"Can I buy that for you, Mr. Williams," I said from three seats away, "I love your music."

"You do? I haven't seen you in the audience until right now. Where the hell you been, hiding?"

The bartender put a cup of coffee in front of him, and I realized he was getting it for free, like when I was in a band. Joe took a sip, then he grimaced as if the drink was bitter. He let out a deep, weary breath.

"I heard the music when I was passing by, decided to check it out."

"Yeah, you what we call a duck: people who duck in from the cold. There's a couple more of your kind in here." He swiveled his chair around to face the small crowd, and said, "Quack, quack."

A guy sitting next to him laughed. I shook my head, and asked the bartender if he had hot chocolate, like bars back in Chicago.

"Hot chocolate?" he said loudly. "Man, this ain't no Chucky Cheese. Now, I do got some milk, though, if you want me to warm some up for you."

More laughter; the smirking bartender pointed at Joe Williams as if to say, "That was for you, Joe," then he walked to the far end of the bar.

Like synchronized swimmers, the men at the bar picked up their drinks at the same time and swilled. Then they clanged their cups and glasses on the counter, staring blankly into the mirror behind the bar. Some looked up at the silent TV overhead.

A music video was playing on the screen. Three rappers dressed in black were posing and parading back and forth on a stage. They wore black Stetson hats and thick chains around their necks. The two main guys were working hard to look menacing. None of them was playing an instrument.

The men at the bar said nothing; one of them picked up the guitar case beside him, and slowly walked back toward the stage. I tried to make eye contact with Joe Williams, and when I finally did, I opened my mouth to say something, but he quickly spun his stool to put his back toward me. Whatever words I planned to improvise were stuck in my throat; they evaporated when I exhaled.

I stood up to leave. I smelled food, and toward the back of the club I saw a handful of people standing at a single buffet table. Two men got into a shoving match over who was next in line, until one of their women broke it up. My first time witnessing "Happy Hour," but no one was happy.

As I wrapped my scarf and got ready for the cold, I thought of the things I considered saying to Joe earlier. What was it like singing with Count Basie's Orchestra? How do you keep a band together and make a living with music? Do you still get nervous before you go on? And how do you maintain your voice after all these years?

But now I wanted to ask a different set of questions. Why are you singing at Happy Hour in a midtown dump? And how can I avoid becoming mean and bitter like you?

I turned and hit the door. It was colder and windier now, and dark. I've had enough of New York, I told myself. Now there was no doubt. Time to move on.

Gordon and his girlfriend were watching television when I got home.

"Hey, Ant," he said. "I was starting to worry about you out there. I don't think you've met my girl, Sheila. Sheila, this is my best friend, Anthony."

I was still locking the door behind me; we greeted each other, waving from across the room. In the dim light, I saw Gordon quickly remove his hand from the front of Sheila's pants. She had red hair and big breasts, like so many of Gordon's other girlfriends. I sat in the chair opposite them.

"Gordon, you're good with music trivia. Here's one for you. What's the second to the last song on Led Zeppelin Four?"

"Out of nowhere with the questions," he said. He sniffed his fingers. "Let me think. Is it...is it 'Going to California?"

I didn't respond, giving him time to think. "Oh, man, you decided to take the job, and it's out west!" He stood up to give me a hug, and I stood for him. "It'll be fantastic, believe me. A great job for you. When do you make the move?"

"I'm going in tomorrow to sign a contract, then I'm heading to the airport to try and get a flight. I'm ready to make that move, man. But I'll leave you kids alone and go pack. Treat him right, Sheila. He's a good friend. And a good kisser, too."

Gordon threw a pillow at me as I ducked into the hallway.

"Just kidding," I yelled as I entered my room.

I gathered all my stuff, mostly clothes, underwear, and tapes. In my papers I found a copy of "New Year's Eve in New York City." I looked over it, and thought of what a great way it summarized my time here. I signed my name on the bottom, and left it on the dresser for Gordon to find. *One day, buddy, this will be worth money.*

Chapter Twenty-Eight

The Game

If you've ever flown into Los Angeles at night, you'll remember what it's like. One minute, the airplane windows are filled with darkness—you're either cruising over the cold Pacific Ocean, or over some lonely black mountains. The next minute, the ground is covered with lights.

The lights go on for miles. They could be streetlights, billboard signs, headlights, or house lights. Often they're just searchlights down in Hollywood, trumpeting the latest disposable record album or movie. From high up, they look like stars on the ground. They made me think of a giant Monopoly board—an illuminated game, waiting for you to claim your prize, or go broke.

The lights grew clearer as we glided into the airport. My plane landed, and I finally felt like my New York experience was over. I was home again.

Jason met me at the gate.

"Thanks for picking me up, man." He was dressed in an all-white tennis outfit, and he looked like he'd lost a few pounds.

"Welcome home, bro. I was starting to wonder if you were coming back or staying out there. You made the right choice."

"Well, New York is a great place to visit and all that. And I was ready to stay out there. But they made the choice for me when they said the job was out here." We pushed our way through the slow-moving crowd. "It would have been interesting to be a New Yorker, though, even for just a while. But I'm really glad to be back."

I claimed my guitar and bags after a long walk through the airport, then we stepped into the January night. We walked past a long line of yellow cabs, crossed the street, and went into the parking lot. A lone taxi was waiting among the regular cars. Jason stopped and opened the door of the cab.

"Here, get in," he said. "This is my friend, handsome Hassan."

"What's up, man," I said, peeking my head into the cab to see the guy's face. He was a young Arabic man with a dark grizzly beard and mustache. He nodded, and started the cab. Jason got into the back seat, and I slid in beside him. I looked at him; he just smiled and looked away. Soon we were speeding up the Harbor Freeway.

The night sky was clear, and I could see a few stars high in the open darkness.

I thought back to New York and the way it bore down on me—the soulless skyscrapers, the traffic, and especially the people, with their neurotic energy rushing up and down the avenues. The endless hunt of the workday, and the starless nights. I remembered my brief contacts with Cheryl Lynn, Joe Williams and the guy from BET—how each one left a bad taste in my mouth.

Then I looked up at the L.A. sky from the speeding cab window. I had only been gone from California for two weeks, but everything about it looked new again. The city made me think of possibilities and freedom. I was happy to see stars again. They gave me hope.

The cab stopped in front of my apartment building, the El Dorado. Jason and I got out and walked around to the trunk, where he handed me my keys.

"Aren't you coming up?" I asked.

"Nah. I've had a long day, but I'll catch you tomorrow."

"What happened to the white men thing you talked about?"

"It's simple, Ant. Once you go black. Or brown. That's all I can say. And as far as your apartment goes, it's all in order up there. I stopped by every other day and watered your plants. Welcome back, boy."

I thanked him, got my things and carried them up the stairs, through the lobby, and into to my apartment.

It was midnight on the kitchen clock. I was ready for bed, ready to get in the ring tomorrow at *Hype Magazine* and play the game. Ready to face whatever I needed to do, to reestablish myself and find a home there. But I needed to do one important thing before crashing in the bed.

I went to my stereo system and started flipping through the albums. *H, I, J, K, L....* There they were. Three Cheryl Lynn albums. I pulled them out of the stack. I didn't want to destroy them, but I also didn't want them in my collection anymore, after the way she blew me off back in New York. I looked around, bleary-eyed and tired, and found the front closet, where I stuffed the albums behind some boxes on the floor. I brushed my teeth humming "Got To Be Real," and went to bed.

The next morning, after showering and dressing, I walked down to my old Dodge in the basement garage. The car was dusty, but luckily it started, after a few coughs and wheezes. *Sorry to leave you sitting so long, Blue.*

I drove down the Santa Monica Freeway, searching for *Hype*'s new office. David Freeman had given me the publisher's business card, which had an address of 17000 Jupiter Lane, city of Santa Monica. The name *Timothy Wilson*, Publisher, was above the address.

Hype's funky little Hollywood office was gone. In its place was the glass and steel of one of Warner's sprawling corporate developments in the suburbs. It took thirty minutes of rush hour traffic to get there, until I finally saw the giant "Warner" sign on a twelve-story building. I parked, and walked to the front lobby.

"Good morning, can I help you?" the receptionist said without looking up.

"Hi, I'm Anthony Adams, a new employee."

"One moment please." She looked at a sheet of white paper, flipped the page, then looked at me and said, "I don't find your name here. Are you sure you're at the right building?" Other employees whisked by, flashing their ID cards at the nearby guard.

"Here, call him," I said, showing her Timothy Wilson's card. She made a brief phone call, then pointed toward the elevator.

I rode to the seventh floor. The door opened to a brilliant sign with "Hype" spelled out in faux-computerized metallic letters. Wendy would *hate* that, I thought.

Another receptionist pointed me toward Wilson's office, where I saw Ricky Sharp sitting and talking to the man who must have been our new boss. I knocked on the floor-length glass door, and Wilson waved me in.

"Hi, I'm Anthony Adams," I said.

"Come on in. We're just getting started," Wilson said, walking toward me, shaking my hand.

He was an average-looking midwestern type, with glasses and brown hair. He pulled another chair to his desk. I sat after shaking hands with Sharp.

Wilson answered his ringing phone, and got into an animated discussion with someone he called "David," which I guessed was David Freeman back in New York. I looked over at my co-executive editor.

"How in the hell did you get here so fast, man?" I asked.

"I got wings, son, I got wings. Nah, seriously, I got on the plane soon as I left Freeman's office. You need to move fast in this game, junior."

"So, it looks like we'll be working together," I said. Awkward silence. "What do you get into, outside of work?"

"I got to tell you up front, I'm not trying to make friends or get to know people. I'm just here to make my money and handle my business. But we can be cool."

"I'm not trying to be your *friend*, but, damn, we do have to work together."

"Yeah, yeah."

Wilson was still on the phone, but he gave us a look.

"When I was here before," I said, "it was a low-key place. Everybody knew each other. We were up in Hollywood back then. This is a whole different game, this corporate thing."

"Yeah, but it's still just a job. I worked at big companies before. Once you learn the game, you'll see the rules are all the same. Just different players. Just have to watch your back at all times."

Wilson hung up the phone, and turned his attention to us.

"Okay, where were we? Right. This is the new *Hype*. Short history: small rock magazine, bought out by Warner's, new headquarters, lots of money going into it, new redesign being unveiled in September, lots of work to do. That's where you two come in."

"I worked here before," I said, "so I know a lot of the history."

"And I'm the fresh new blood," Sharp said, "with new ideas to take us forward instead of backward."

"Well, you have to know where you've been before you know where you're going."

Wilson looked at Sharp, then looked back at me, arching his brow.

"Okay," he said, "I don't know what's up with you two so far, but there's a lot at stake here. This isn't a basketball game. We're on the same team. For whatever reason, corporate is making you *both* in charge of day-to-day creative operations. Over the next few weeks, the three of us can hash out the details of who does what around here. But we still have a magazine to put out, with a deadline coming. First thing, you guys need offices."

"According to Mr. Freeman," Sharp said, leaning forward, "the first one here got to choose his office."

Wilson looked at Sharp, then squinted his eyes as if unsure of what he had heard.

"I don't know what that's all about, you guys, so screw that crap. Freeman is in New York and I'm out here. I've assigned Adams to 712 and Sharp to 713. And anyway, you'll be spending most of your time in the pit, with writers and graphics people. I'll let you two get settled in. Question: can I get a story from each of you for next month?" We both nodded our heads. "Meet with me here around two. Good deal, guys."

I walked to my office. It was huge, compared to what I expected. The desk was close to the window, and a conference table for six people was on the far side of the room. It could have been the office of an accountant or a banker; there was no sign of music or entertainment anywhere in the decor or on the blank walls. I wanted to change that soon.

I walked the short distance to Sharp's office next door. He was on the phone, feet up on his desk. He waved me in, still talking.

"...no, no, damn it. My deadline is in three days. I need to interview him sooner than that. Get back to me quick as you can. You owe me. Later." He hung up the phone. "What's up, Adams?"

"Nothing. Just stopping by to check out your digs." His office was exactly the same as mine, down to the dark green chairs around the conference table. "I'm going down to personnel, then I'm going to order some supplies. Since we're a *team*, as Wilson said, I thought you might want to go—put up a united front, you know, walk among the troops."

"Look, son, I don't know how many ways to tell you this. I *don't* want to be friends. You and me can work together, and everything can be cool. But I don't want to hang out, and I *don't* care about making a statement for these fools."

"You know what? You're being a straight asshole. It's pretty rare for *one* black man to be management in this town, much less two. I'm planning to be in this job for a long time, and I thought we could get a good start. But if *this* is how you want to play it, fine with me."

I waited a few seconds for him to respond, but he seemed lost for words, so I turned and left the room. That felt good, I told myself, really good. I remembered something Jason used to say: *Sometimes, being a bitch is all you have left*. If Sharp wanted to be cold, then I'd have to play his game. I just had to make sure I kept Wilson in my corner.

I headed down the hallway and toured the offices. The pit, as Wilson called it, was an open area of desks in the center of the main work space. The area was recessed into the floor, and you had to walk down two steps to enter. About a dozen people were working, among the sounds of phones ringing and typewriters clicking.

I saw several familiar faces that had come over from the Hollywood days. Phoebe was now the graphics director; we laughed and hugged.

New faces were here, too. The friendliest was Kenny, the young mailroom clerk. He was red-haired and had pale white skin, but he sounded like he was from the darkest part of Brooklyn. We chatted for a while as he filed letters into the mail cubbies, then he nervously said, "Can I ask you a personal question?"

"Go ahead."

"Are you black?"

"Yes, Sherlock. I haven't had that question in a long time. Dad is black; mom is white. Almost as white as you. That's a forward question to be asking your new boss, you think?" I changed the subject. "So, are you in college?"

"I go nights at Santa Monica City College. My moms moved out here last year, and I'm just getting settled. I'm planning to be a rapper one day - working on my MC skills, know what I'm saying? Yo, if you want to meet some honeys, just let me know, boss, I hook you up."

"No, that's cool, Kenny, I'm good. But I *might* ask you to fill me in on a thing or two around here."

"Sure thing, boss, you got it."

One thing I'd learned from previous jobs was to make friends with secretaries, security guards, and mail clerks—the bloodstream of an organization.

I loaded a box full of supplies, and headed to my office.

On the way there, I passed Wilson's glass office, and there was Sharp, again sitting with our boss. The door was closed. I saw them nod their heads in agreement. *What are they talking about in there? Maybe I should join them.*

I knew they were probably just talking about a story idea or some business. But I didn't know Ricky Sharp, and I didn't trust him. We weren't supposed to meet with Wilson until two. I walked past the office. Sharp noticed me, then cut his eyes away quickly. I had a deep suspicion something was happening, and I felt left out.

So this is how you play the game.

Chapter Twenty-Nine

I'd Be Lost Without You

"Anthony, this is Jason."

"What's happening, man. You're getting an early start. What's up?" It was Friday morning, my second day back home. I was still wet from the shower.

"I had to catch you before you left. How are your songwriting chops? I have a friend who has a cousin whose friend just got a record deal. Her name is Whitney-something. He wants me to write some songs for her debut album. You're the first person I thought of. What do you think?"

"What do I think about what? Are you writing her songs, or you want me to do it?"

"Let's collaborate! Let's do it as a team!"

"Jason, do you honestly think we could work together?" I was wrestling to put my clothes on while holding the phone, and wrestling with the idea of working with Jason, knowing his temperament—and mine.

"Let's see if we can write one song - maybe two, and see how it goes. Just think about it, boy. Call me tonight."

I had only co-written a song with someone once before: "One Good Love," with Sam Stone. I preferred to write on my own, and couldn't imagine fighting over words and chords with Jason. We would either make a great song, or end up hating each other.

I finished getting dressed, and headed through light Friday traffic to *Hype*'s offices.

Phoebe was alone in the pit. She stood scratching her head, staring at a collection of layouts and drawings spread across her desk.

"Three weeks of work," she said when she looked up at me.

"Problem, Febe?" I asked.

"Wilson called me last night. Everything's on hold. The redesign for September is up in the air. Didn't you hear about it?"

"Uh, pretty much. Everything will fall into place soon." I could see, from her desk, Wilson wasn't in yet to explain what the hell was happening.

I headed down the hall, straight to Sharp's office, suspecting he might be behind something, but his door was closed and his room was empty, too. I went into my office and waited for the boss to get in.

After ten minutes of busy work, I walked back to Wilson's office just as he was picking up a phone.

"The redesign," I said, "is there a change?"

"Maybe yes, maybe no," he said, hanging up. "Several things are happening. We've got some research that says rock music is sagging. Not just sales, but everything: radio play, concert attendance, customer loyalty. The future for pop in general does not look bright." We were both still standing.

"What does this mean for the magazine?" I asked.

"Well, it coincides with the sale to Warner and the redesign. There's an idea afoot to change formats and direction entirely - to focus on rap music."

I had to sit down.

"You look like you're in shock, Anthony," he said chuckling. "We do have some time to work with. But New York definitely wants to consider a drastic change. They feel rap is new, vibrant, of the streets." He made quotation marks in the air when he said "of the streets." He went on. "And we're always looking for growth points and new markets. Rap is not *my* thing, but a change might be worth considering. Hey, it's not my decision. I'm just the damn publisher."

My head was swirling with the idea of working at a rap magazine, being surrounded by rap music, immersed in a world of rappers.

"Are you going to be okay, buddy?" Wilson asked. "David Freeman is flying out Monday to feel things out, and he'll decide. So everything's on hold till then. Just keep doing what you're doing, Anthony, and we'll be fine. Take half the day off if you want."

He put his arm around my shoulder and led me to the door. He closed it, and through the glass I saw him get back on the phone as I walked to my office.

Ricky Sharp.

Everything would have been fine—things would be normal if there were no Ricky Sharp suddenly in my life. Wilson didn't say it—he didn't have to—but I knew the whole rap magazine concept came from Sharp. He was probably a rapper himself. Come to think of it, he reminded me of Black Ice, just less friendly and with a college degree. I looked again to see if he had come in yet; I wanted to see if he was behind this so I could rap him in his head, but he was still out.

Now rap music seemed like a runaway train, rolling over everything in its path, and in mine. I thought of the way music, commercials, fashion, and movies were all showing more rap attitude and influence. But was there anything I could do to affect what was happening at *Hype*?

I had the weekend to think about it.

I decided to contact old friends, and Dana was on top of my list. Her number was disconnected when I called from New York. But I knew the school where she worked, so I called there.

"Fremont Middle School," the secretary said, "can I help you?"

"Yes, I'm trying to contact a teacher who works there. Miss Dana Thomas. Is she there, or can I leave a message."

"Dana Thomas?"

"She teaches seventh grade, tall brown-skinned woman with lots of hair?"

"Oh, Miss Thomas. I'm sorry. This is a big school, and we have lots of teachers. She's in class now, but I can leave a note in her box."

I left a message for her to call. I was eager to hear from her, but after the way we broke up, I didn't know if she'd even call me back.

I didn't see Sharp all morning, and he may not have even come into the office. The energy in the pit was especially low key after lunch as word spread about the possible format change. *Hype*'s employees were mostly white, and I never had the feeling rap was popular among the staff. The workers probably felt threatened by the news. Surely they were already unsettled about going from den mother Wendy, to Warner's corporate grip. Production came to a standstill, so I took Wilson's advice and left early for home.

Friday night came; still no call from Dana.

I woke up early Saturday morning with a snippet of a melody in my head. I tried to catch it, but it got away. It was replaced with thoughts of Dana and everything that was happening at the magazine. *This is a good mood to write a sad song.*

I called Jason, and said we could try writing one song together to see what happened. He came over in the afternoon.

"How's it feel to be back again?" he asked. "Sounds like you had a wild time in New York."

"I'm just settling in," I said, "and I discovered I'm not an east coast person. Important to learn. A lot of guys our age are bouncing around the country, trying to find a place to call home."

Jason sat down, while I got my electric keyboard from the front closet. I blew away the dust.

"Anthony, why were you so hesitant to write a song together?"

"I just know we'll probably end up killing each other. Remember at the guitar store, competing for attention, or at least *you* were."

"That was totally you, Anthony, just showing off. Guitar players get to stand up and be all cool. Piano players have to act crazy to get attention. Little Richard, Jerry Lee Lewis, Elton John, acting a damn fool. So, I just had to show who was the boss. Like Miss Ross."

"That's just sad you can't let the music speak for itself. Oh well, let's do this. Tell me more about this Whitney girl you're writing songs for." I finished putting the keyboard on its stand, and plugged it in.

"I haven't heard her yet," Jason said, "but they say she's a phenomenal singer. She's a pretty church girl with lots of soul, but they want her to do pop stuff. The record company wants commercial crossover."

"Yeah, doesn't everybody. Man, this should be easy." I picked up my guitar, and Jason sat behind the keyboard. "So let's write a song, Jason. We need to decide on a process - who writes the words, who writes the music, or a little of each."

"Why don't we start by brainstorming some ideas," he said. "What are we going to write about? Just another love song?" We thought quietly for a few seconds. "Anthony, what's it like, for you, falling in love with a woman?"

"Wow, that's a damn good question. Let me think." I strummed on the guitar strings. "The first few times, if I really like her, it's like she takes my breath away, and after a while I feel like I'd be lost without her. After a few weeks or months, it feels like my heart will burst open if we haven't been together for a while."

"Mmmm, okay, okay." He was writing on a piece of paper.

"All right, Jason, your turn. What's it like with a man? Any different?"

"Being in love with another man? It's not for the weak of heart, honey. You think you've found somebody to save the day—your hero, your angel from heaven. But when things get rough, that angel turns into a devil, a damn shark in the water, smelling blood. Love is like blood." He laughed.

"Really?" I said, "I guess it's all the same. People break your heart, and they don't care. Except for Dana, every girl I've been with turns into the devil's daughter after they see I'm in love. Man. I thought being with dudes would be easy for you all. Men just want to screw. Seems like that would be easy. An endless party."

"It *is* a party," Jason said, "if you're a slut! I could find five hundred men to have sex with tonight if I wanted to. But it's not a party when you finally want to settle down."

I jotted some of his phrases. He continued. "It's not a party when you're a romantic at heart, like me. I have met *so many men* who run off like a thief in the night when commitment becomes a topic. Our problem is, men are so damn easy, and there's always a better looking guy around the corner, so being a whore becomes a way of life. Until you get old and wrinkled—then nobody wants you!"

"Jason, you guys are having a picnic compared to dating these crazy-ass L.A. women. Give me a break."

He put one hand on his hip. "You wouldn't last two weeks trying to deal with these man-hoes, trying to find one good love, like that song of yours."

We continued to talk for a while, both taking notes, both sharing the frustration of our dating worlds. After an hour, we cobbled our notes and our best lines together, and came up with a song for a young woman.

Once we were satisfied with the lyrics, we hammered out the music: a simple pop/R&B chord progression. I was happy and surprised by the final product.

I was also shocked to hear the things Jason said about dating men. I'd always assumed he was having a ball, with a different guy every month. But he made it clear that male relationships were often fragile. His stories made me appreciate the relative ease of being with a woman, even though I hadn't been on a date in weeks. It was Saturday evening, and I still hadn't heard from Dana.

Dana.

For the first time, I was feeling lost without her.

I'd Be Lost Without You

First you took my breath away
Now you've got to save my day
I'd be lost, lost without you

I'm alone and I can't wait
Till you open up my gate
I'd be lost, lost without you

You came like a shark in the water
Treated me like the devil's daughter
But it wasn't long before I knew
The angel in you
I'd be lost without you

Never been in love before
Till you opened up my door
I'd be lost, lost without you

You came by and swept me up
Now you've got to fill my cup
I'd be lost, lost without you

I've lost my concentration
Thinkin' bout my situation
Hoping that you'll come to see
The angel in me - I'd be lost without you

Feels like my poor heart will burst
Tell me you love me and I'll dive feet first
I'd be lost without you

You hit me like a thief in the night
Stole my heart and it feels all right
I'd be lost without you.

Chapter Thirty

Brave New World

MONDAY MORNING

I couldn't see his face.

David Freeman, the Warner CEO from New York, was seated at the head of the conference room table, a foot from the window. Monday morning sun was coming through the glass, and it lit Freeman from behind, making it impossible to make out his face.

Ten men, including me, were settling in, waiting for the big man to speak.

Tim Wilson was gulping coffee, opposite Freeman, down the long table.

Sharp and I had entered the room at the same time, and sat in the only two chairs left, right across from each other, at the table's midsection. We didn't speak—we just exchanged head nods.

Freeman opened the meeting by introducing everyone—various Warner lawyers and marketing men. Only two people in the room were writers: me and Sharp.

"So, let's get to it," Freeman said. "The company bought *Hype Magazine* with one main goal—to make money. But all our research shows that mainstream rock and roll may have peaked—zero growth potential. That news, plus new ownership, makes this the perfect time to consider a format change. Your man here, Richard Sharp, has a proposal to change Hype into an urban rap magazine. And this rap thing may be huge. Sharp, tell us your idea."

Sharp bolted out of his seat with a smile, and walked a few steps toward the window, where a flip chart was waiting.

"Next year is 1984," he said. "There's no 'Big Brother' yet, but it *is* a brave new world. That means new music, and new opportunities to make money—with a new magazine. You all have heard rap music, probably from your kids or their friends or on TV. Believe me, rap is going to be huge one day, bigger than it is now, and I propose we make *Hype* the magazine of record for the rap revolution."

He showed three charts illustrating sagging sales of rock, pop and R&B records. Then he went on about the power and potential of rap music, and how white kids were buying more and more of it. The suits watched him like he was describing a secret land of silk and money.

"If you want growth," Sharp concluded, "if you want to take it to the top, then rap is definitely the way to go."

He sat down, and a buzz went through the room, until Freeman spoke.

"Good job, Richard. Now here's the secret for you and Anthony. And for you, also, Wilson. I actually had something like this in mind when I hired you two young men. Not specifically rap, but I knew it was time for a change at this old dinosaur, time for something younger. So I like the idea. Now I want to hear from Wilson and Anthony."

He was looking at his publisher, Tim Wilson, so Tim spoke up, though he looked skeptical and unprepared to speak.

"I don't know," he said. "I've thought hard about it, and it seems drastic to me. You know, we saw disco come and go. And God forbid if you had put a million dollars into a disco magazine when dance was hot. But it's gone! And there's no way to know if rap is going down the same chute—tomorrow, next month, or next year. It's a big risk to take."

"I disagree." One of the marketing men spoke up. "Mr. Freeman asked us to do some research on this last week, and we found that rap has the potential to be explosive, in terms of sales, demographics and user loyalty. Rock fans are over twenty-five and getting older, and kids are not getting into rock. All the corporate money that went into rock five years ago, for lack of a better term, killed its spirit. *Rap* fans, however, are generally under 18, and we think it will be a long, long cycle. At least twenty years of growth potential."

"Wow, twenty years," Freeman said. "That's a new boat for all of us." The men laughed and nodded their heads. "Anthony?"

Their heads whipped around to look at me.

When he called my name, my mind flashed for a second—back to the stories my father used to tell about being a musician on the road. How hard it was to travel and hustle for gigs. Horror stories, like going to towns that had a history of lynchings and the Klan. Club owners who would stiff him on his pay. But he played anyway. Not for fame or money, but because the music was his life, and it represented his soul.

And now my job wanted me to write about rappers: "musicians" who didn't play instruments, and used other people's music. I hadn't thought about it much until now, standing up to speak.

"Looks like I'm in the minority here—in more ways than one. Personally, I have no interest in listening to rap, writing about rap or learning about it. Last week when I signed up here, I thought we'd be doing what made *Hype* great to begin with: rock music and entertainment. I had no idea this was happening. So, I'm with Mr. Wilson, but for a different reason. I know rap is getting big, but it's big for the wrong reasons. It's the emperor's new music. Unoriginal, stolen and sampled beats. On top of the sex, the attitude, the narcissism and commercialism. The posturing—it's all nonsense and fake. It's a bunch of schoolyard bullies running the school, on braggadocio instead of talent. And the music—for anybody over twelve with an ear—it's unlistenable."

"But you know what, Anthony?" Freeman said. "It's for those very reasons that it *will* work. Look at what you just said. Youth, sex, attitude, commercialism. Loyalty. Energy! It all adds up to one thing: sales. To kids without mortgages or debt, with money to burn and lots of hormones running through their smelly little bodies. The music itself is almost beside the point."

The lawyers nodded their heads, and the marketing men whispered to each other while Freeman paused. His face was still hard to see, with the sunlight glaring from behind him. He was like a shadowy wraith, powerful and quiet, while we waited. I was intrigued by what he said, so I spoke.

"Rap is a legitimate outlet for black anger. I saw it with my own eyes in New York. But when corporations—us—get a hold of it and suck it dry, it dies the same death as rock, disco and R&B. And if the music is 'beside the point,' then how do we sustain a magazine, long-term, with inconsequential disposable music? Then you'd have to get off into other stuff just to fill up space."

"Exactly." A different marketing man spoke. "There'll be rap jewelry, clothes, cologne, headwear, shoes, movies. You create a whole celebrity-based world of, well, as you said, stuff. Shiny stuff. Think of the most ridiculous thing in the world, like, I don't know, metal teeth—and if a cool rapper wears it, kids will go for it. I guarantee in three years we'll be able to sell these kids anything. And rap will be the soundtrack to it all - the next big thing—and we believe *Hype Magazine* will be bursting with the ads to sell it all."

A third suit spoke up. "If there's one thing kids want to do, it's break away from their parents and carve their own identities. We did it with rock; these kids are doing it with rap. No better way to scare your parents than bring home an album by a big, angry, pot-smoking black guy. We did it with peace and love, they're doing it with attitude and anger."

Another buzz went through the room; the guy smirked.

I felt like a vegetarian at a jackals' feast.

I looked down at Sharp, but he avoided my eyes. I wanted to give him a head nod for how he was playing the game—manipulating these greedy men, working behind the scenes to get his way. The idea of *Hype* going rap made me sick to my stomach. And it never would have happened without Sharp. I sat.

"Stein," Freeman said, looking at one of his men, "what did you learn from the ad agencies?"

"We're in good shape. Ninety per cent said they'd be on board if we make the switch—mostly the fast foods and movie studios, and of course the record companies. There's work to do, but all I see out there is growth."

"Let's do it," Freeman said. My heart sank. "Let's make it happen. Anthony and Wilson—I see your points. But the numbers don't lie. Richard Sharp and Anthony Adams, I like the dichotomy of you two. I'm looking for you guys to balance each other out, so we don't go hardcore, over the top. And remember, you're equals here."

Freeman leaned back in his chair and went on. "The redesign will take place in October, and the word of the day is *new*—new look, new graphics. Newly-focused on the new world of rap music. Wilson, we need to meet, flesh out the big picture." He took a deep breath and looked down both sides of the table. "Well, we've got work to do. That's all, men."

Everyone stood up. Sharp reached his arm across the table to shake hands with me; he was wearing a triumphant smile.

"Welcome to the brave new world, son."

I nodded my head once.

We headed for the door, when I heard, "Adams, I need to see you."

Freeman was looking at me. Wilson was still in his seat. The three of us were all that remained. I walked closer to Freeman, and I could see his face clearly now.

"Anthony, I just want to make sure you're on board with this. You've got some strong feelings there. Opposite and equal Sharp's. But right now, we *are* a rap magazine. Like I said, I need you here to balance this thing."

"Yes sir."

"Your writing and editing skill, your mainstream mentality, your sense of what's commercial. That's why I hired you. Sharp can't do this alone. I need your word. Can you put your heart and mind into this?"

I told him yes, but I was telling a half-truth. I knew I could put my mind into it. My heart was up for grabs.

News spread through the offices that *Hype* was becoming a rap magazine, abandoning its coverage of rock and movies.

Most people had heard the news by the time I reached my desk. Kenny was delivering mail to my office when I walked in.

"So, have you heard the latest, Kenny?" I asked.

"Oh, word. I knew yesterday. How was the meeting?"

"They made it official," I said. "We *are* a rap magazine now. I may or may not be around to see it happen, though."

"Wow, that's serious, chief. Hope things work out. Dude wants to change the name, too. Did that come up?"

"No," I said. "Change it to what?"

"Word. Word Magazine."

I said it to myself— "Word Magazine" —and it was no sillier a name than *Hype*. "Word" had a vaguely religious connotation. But maybe that was appropriate—rap seemed to be developing its own system of beliefs, practices and attitudes—sacred and conformist as any religion. From what I remembered Black Ice saying in New York, rap was now a whole subculture of its own.

"Mr. Sharp's got a lot of ideas," Kenny said as he left. "They should change it to 'Sharp Magazine' with all the things *he* wants to do."

I shuffled some papers around my desk, and left the office to see what was happening in the pit. Phoebe was looking at a collection of rap albums, studying their graphics and designs. Small groups of two or three people were quietly huddled over tables or desks talking. A stream of five executives were just leaving the conference room and heading for the elevator. I got the feeling a lot of people were updating their resumes, and making calls, to move on, away from America's first big magazine dedicated to rap music. I wondered if I should be among them. Until I remembered—my contract.

I made some calls, and headed for lunch just as the phone rang. It was Dana. I had to sit down when I heard her voice. She was in class at her school about ten miles away, and she invited me to stop by. I checked my briefcase to make sure I had a copy of my new song to give her.

I drove to her campus, in one of L.A.'s roughest neighborhoods. Graffiti was splattered on stop signs and the walls of liquor stores and nearby apartment buildings. The school loomed more like a prison than a place of learning, with grates on the windows, and a cement-covered playground.

She met me in the school office. "It's so good seeing you, Anthony," she said, reaching out her hand.

"I was wondering if I'd hear from you." I wanted to hug her, but the handshake was a clear signal.

"I've been busy, Anthony. I'm dating someone now, and this school is a handful. Things are a little bit crazy, but I'm taking it one day at a time."

"Can we get away for a minute, or do we need to stand here in the office?"

She punched my shoulder lightly, and I followed her to the teacher's lunchroom. Several other people were inside; we sat at an empty table.

"My question is, when did you find time to meet a man and start dating? We've only been apart a hot minute."

"Anthony, I don't know if we were ever *really* together. Between your band and all your jobs, I was lucky to see you twice a month. I wanted a family, and a man I could depend on. To *be* there. But Mr. Aloof was always about the work first." She stopped, and shook her head. "Hey, I don't want to beat up on you. Are *you* happy now?"

"I'm glad to be back home. I wouldn't say happy. Little kids and retarded people are happy. Me, I just signed a long-term contract to edit a new magazine, and now they're going rap."

"Rap?" she said loud enough for the teachers to look our way. Dana shook her head, then she took a sandwich out of her purse. She ate a small bite.

"Come with me." She stood up, and I followed her from the lunchroom, into the long, dimly lit hall.

She had gotten over me, I could tell, but I was still surprised she had found someone else so quickly. Maybe it was just boredom or loneliness that put her on my mind anyway. At least she seemed happy, and it was my turn now to move on. I decided not to show her my new song.

We reached the end of the hall, and I heard a thumping sound of music coming from outside. She took another bite of the sandwich, then opened a door. We stepped out onto a courtyard. Dozens of teenagers were outside at lunch, but no one was eating.

In the center of the courtyard was a boombox tape player. It was turned up loud, providing the soundtrack for the lunchtime activities. The box was the size of three car batteries, and I wondered how many batteries it actually took to power it. The sound was mostly just bass, with a rapper babbling about how other rappers were "suckers."

We stood and watched for a minute, until the school bell rang, barely audible over the music. But the students did not rush back to class, or grab their book bags as I expected. In fact, the students didn't move at all, and there were no books or bags in sight.

"Doesn't that bell mean it's time to get back to class?" I asked Dana.

"Yeah, but they'll take their own sweet time."

"How can you teach in the afternoon when they've sat through all this?"

"In a word—barely. They're hyped up, full of sugar, and they've been rubbing all over each other." She folded her arms.

"Dana, come on. How does the school allow this to happen? During the day, on campus?"

"Parents. The parents say it's part of black culture; it's their voice and their expression. The white administration tried to outlaw music at lunch, but a few vocal parents said children have a right to show their black identity, through the music of the streets. It became a whole black versus white thing. And you know what happens when race is an issue. People retreat to their corners and stop listening. *This* is the result. A wasteland. It's a whole new world, and I don't know if we can ever get them back."

She took an angry last bite of her sandwich.

I looked at the scene, soaking in all the sounds, summarizing what I saw happening.

"I think there's a bigger issue. There was a time parents weren't afraid of their own kids."

"Amen to that."

I got home after dark, and I didn't turn any lights on. I tossed my briefcase into a corner. Grabbed my guitar, raised the strap over my head and let it settle on my shoulders. I sat in the middle of the floor. The blues were always a good way to get started, especially after a day like today. I ran through some easy chords. After a few minutes, I took an off ramp from the blues and added some jazz and pop flavor to the chords I was playing.

I needed words. I cleared my mind and opened myself up. Took a razor blade to my chest, to look inside my heart. Where were the words I was feeling?

Dana, Sharp, Freeman, *Hype*—all the personal failures. My new job was a joke and a mistake. All the wild school kids with no future, and no music; with only rap—the whole rap thing: was I missing something?

Step back, I told myself, and look at the big picture. You need words.

Then they came to me.
Walk like a lion, humble and proud
Walk like a lion through any crowd

I could hear myself singing, but it wasn't me. I was hovering just overhead, listening, watching. The voice had lifted me up. I could feel wetness from tears on my face, but I didn't want to wipe them away—that would mean I'd have to stop playing, and I didn't want to stop. Like my father, I was playing for my life, singing to save my soul.

Maybe there's a way to find it.

Two weeks later I was sitting, with my guitar, in Shady Ackerman's office. Like a scene from an old movie, I was going to do three songs for a Hollywood agent. He was a top man with William Morris, and I used my *Hype* connections to get an audition. *Bill Withers.* I was either going to start a solo career, or make a massive fool of myself. *Richie Havens.* I was ready to take that chance. *Jon Lucien.* I tried to think of other black men who had careers singing and playing a simple guitar. There weren't many.

Ackerman was on the phone, standing behind his desk. He hung up, and cocked a finger at me, the way you signal someone it's their time at bat. I told him what I had done in previous bands, and what I wanted to do: start a recording career as a singer-songwriter in the vein of James Taylor and Stevie Wonder. Then I sang and played "New Year's Eve in New York City" and "One Good Love." I was about to finish up with "Walk Like A Lion." But I only made it through the first verse.

He cut me off.

He said I had a great voice, and if this were 1970, maybe we could do business, but nobody's buying that sensitive shit these days.

His lips kept moving, but I wasn't listening anymore. I unstrapped my guitar and put it in its case. I think I heard the words "new wave" and "marketable" coming from his direction. I wanted to take my guitar and smash it over his fat head, like the Three Stooges, and this *was* a scene from an old comedy after all, wasn't it? But Mrs. Adams didn't raise me with bad manners. So I shook his hand and said thanks for his time. He grunted. I headed for the door, and almost made it, before he put a cap on the scene.

"Now, can you *rap*?"

Chapter Thirty-One

Every Picture Tells A Story

1987

Trends and girlfriends came and went for the next four years. And hairstyles. I wore a high top fade for the year with Trina, a jheri curl for my time with April, and a short natural for the few months I spent with Monique. L.A. women had one thing in common: they'd cut and run fast if a relationship didn't give them everything they wanted. And I was becoming the same way.

For those four years at my job, Sharp and I worked together—uncomfortably, but successfully—and made Hype the country's biggest-selling magazine of its kind. Rap wasn't a worldwide phenomenon yet—it was still young—but we found a lucrative niche among loyal readers and advertisers.

I was stuck in a job I didn't like, but needed to keep, working with someone I needed, but didn't like. That was my situation. Tension between me and Sharp kept the tightrope tight. He was on one end pulling toward underground rap. I was on the other grappling for the mainstream.

I had to give credit to David Freeman for creating the dynamics that made *Hype* edgy and commercial at the same time. They needed my writing and editing skills, as well as Sharp's knowledge and connections in the rap world. They were lucky to have us together, but I didn't know how much longer the team could last.

It was June, and I wrote an editorial that caused a stir. The piece, called "Crossroads," asked whether rap was heading in a negative direction, promoting a culture of drugs, drive-bys, and gang activity. "The soundtrack of inner city hell" was what I called the music. Sharp had issues with the article, and I confronted him about it after a weekly staff meeting in the conference room.

"It's just you and me," I told him after Phoebe finally left the room. "Now what's on your mind?"

"What makes you think something's on my mind?"

"Your little comments, remarks during the meeting. What's up?"

He picked up a copy of the latest edition and tossed it on the table toward me.

"I don't know, man," he said, "you're looking for trouble. You don't go naming names and calling people out like this. 'Untalented and mediocre?' Man, you're looking for trouble. I *told* you that, before we went to press."

"Yeah, but it's all true. Silly people in a silly culture add up to silly music, plain and simple. That's what I wrote and it's how I feel. We're getting paid to cover it, not to be in love with it."

"Adams, if you hate the music so much, why don't you just quit?"

"Little thing called a contract we signed in New York way back, remember? You don't know this, but I spent good money on a lawyer trying to get out of it. Freeman wouldn't let me go. He must like the way we keep each other in check or something. But one more year, and I'm out of here, Sharp. Then you can *really* build your rap dynasty."

He reached for the magazine, opened it, and started reading from my editorial.

"'Right now, rap music is at a crossroads, between the fun party music represented by the Fresh Prince, and the hardcore street music of Public Enemy. Which way will it go, no one knows. A better question is, will rap ever evolve from stolen samples, bad rhymes and school boy posturing.'"

"Man, that's some cold shit. You need to lighten up—making me look bad. Some people out there don't take too well to criticism. These brothers carry guns. I know some of them. Watch yourself."

I left the conference room and went to my office.

The phone rang. It was Jason.

"Anthony," he said, "what are you doing tonight? I have someone I want you to meet." He sounded excited.

"I'm free, but I'm tired. What's this all about?"

"A friend of mine is starting a record company, and he's looking for a business partner. I told him about you. He's serious and he really wants to talk to you."

"A record company?"

Kenny appeared in my office doorway with a small package. "Who in their right mind starts a record company in 1987?"

"I don't know," Jason said, "people that haven't given up on their music yet?"

Kenny held up the package. I remembered Sharp's veiled warning. I put up a finger for him to wait, but then realized how much Kenny gossiped.

"Hold on a minute, Jason." I motioned for Kenny. "What *is* that?"

"I just deliver them, chief, I don't x-ray 'em."

He handed me the mail and left the office in a hurry.

"A record company," I said. "Let's see my track record so far. We wrote some songs together that went nowhere, I could never keep a band together or sell any songs in New York, why don't I start a record company!"

"Anthony, don't be a little bitch. Be at my place tonight at eight and just meet the guy. Do it as a favor."

We hung up. I examined the package. I couldn't remember ordering anything, and I wasn't expecting a delivery. I put the brown cube-shaped package to my ear. No ticking sound. The handwriting on the label looked familiar, then I peered at the smudged postmark, which faintly read "Chicago."

I ripped it open. It was a collection of old photographs from my mother. Three or four-dozen pictures of me as a child, and of her and my father when they were younger. What possessed her to send me these now, at my office, I wondered. Most of them were pictures I had never seen before, and I was full of questions. I put the pictures in my briefcase, and finished my workday.

I got to Jason's apartment minutes before eight. A man and a woman were sitting in his living room. She looked nervous, and he was watching television, yelling answers to a game show. "Wheel of Fortune."

"Anthony, this is my friend Cedric and his sister, Denise. They're starting a record company."

"What's happening, my man," Cedric said. He got out of his chair and turned off the TV.

"It's been a rough day and I'm beat," I said, "I just wanted to hear what's up. Jason sounded excited on the phone."

"What's up," Cedric said, "is that we're about to bring the world something very special. The record business is poised for a breakthrough, my man."

He reached into his briefcase for some papers, and handed me a three-page packet labeled "Business Plan."

"I can read this later," I said, "but just give me an idea why you think your record company can succeed. And I'm assuming you're looking for someone to invest money."

"What we're looking for is somebody who can dream, and dream big. Berry Gordy did it, and we can do it, too. I'm starting a record company that'll take music to the next level, where talent is king, where songs and lyrics mean something like they used to. People are ready to hear *real* music again."

"Come on, Cedric, it's been a long day. How much money are you looking for? I've been in this game a while. What's the bottom line?"

"Good question. My family is already in for twenty grand, and I'm putting up the same personally. We just need twenty thousand more. If we can raise that, we can get a distribution deal easy. We just need to show them we have funding to stay afloat for a few years."

I opened the business plan. The first two pages were filled with words, but the last page had pictures of three women under the heading "Future Stars." The women were smiling and sexy. I wondered if they could sing; maybe I could hear them sing my songs, which had been sitting dormant for so many years.

"That's a lot of money to invest in somebody I don't even know," I said.

"You know me," Jason yelled. He was now in the kitchen.

"Jason is a part of this, too," Cedric said. "Between all of us, I think we can start something really big. Take the plan, and give it some thought." He handed me a business card. I said goodbye to everyone, peeked my head in the kitchen and waved bye to Jason, who was making spaghetti.

"Make a good choice," he said, and I headed home.

I turned on the car radio for the drive home. Maybe music could turn around the sad and tired mood of a strange day. "Get Outta My Dreams, Get Into My Car" was the first song I heard. I listened to the lyrics, trying to make sense of them, then I changed the station. "Da Butt" was playing, about a dance where you rotate your behind. I turned off the radio. *My God, will somebody, anybody put out some decent pop songs for the radio? Or do I have to be the one?* Maybe Cedric had the right idea.

I called my mother as soon as I got home.

"Do you know what time it is here?" she said.

"Mom, aren't you guys still night owls? I thought you'd just be happy to hear from me. You say I don't call enough. I can't win," I said with a laugh. "Seriously, this is the first chance I've had to call. I *just* got home for the day."

"Did you get the pictures yet?"

"They came today. And sorry for calling so late. But I have a hundred questions, Mom. Why did you send them to my office? I was freaked out."

"I figured you're at your job more than home. I got your work address from that magazine you send all the time. I hope it wasn't a problem. I was just cleaning out a closet and found a whole box full of dusty pictures you might like."

I spread the photos across my bed, noticing the only people in the pictures were me, and my parents.

"That's what happens," she said, "when your parents are both only-children. I was an only child, and your father was an only child. And that meant no cousins or uncles for you. It just happened that you were an only child, too, Anthony. You were a very lonely boy. For that, I apologize."

"You don't need to apologize, Mom. I *was* lonely a lot, but I wouldn't have become a musician or a writer without all the attention I got from you guys. Sometimes it was a blessing."

Looking at the pictures, I noticed that instruments and music were a theme in most of the pictures. My mother would be at the piano, dad at saxophone, or me at any of five different instruments, playing and cheesing for the camera.

"Music filled our world," she said. "Between the fights and the drinking, there were beautiful periods where we'd play and dance and sing. It was my only joy. After you, of course."

I asked her more questions, as the eleven o'clock news played in the background, making me realize just how late it was, Chicago time. We said goodnight, after she made me promise to call more often.

I leaned back on the bed pillows. The business plan from Jason's friend was peeking out of the briefcase near my head. I picked it up, leafed through the pages, and stopped at the last page. There were the three women singers again. This time my eye was drawn to the third girl.

She had a friendly inviting smile. Her name said Ebony Angel, and she looked like one. *Maybe, just maybe*. With better make-up, a decent voice, and a less corny name, I could do something for her.

I tried, tried to sleep, but I had to take one last look at the girl's picture. She was beautiful, but now something wasn't right. *Ebony Angel*. I tried to imagine her singing "I'd Be Lost,"

"One Good Love," or "Heartbreak Fever." If she could sing, even just a little, we could make something happen.

I was coming to realize that looks were more important in the music business than talent, something I should have learned back when Kevin, from my old band, ended up on TV. This girl had the look. I stared at the picture, and wondered if all the pieces could fall into place: could Jason's friend possibly know enough to run a record company? I called Jason. I didn't care about the time, and this was all his idea anyway.

"Boy, why are you waking me up?" he asked. "It's late."

"Two quick questions. Why were you hiding in the kitchen when I was there, and how come you're not putting any money into this thing?"

"I wasn't hiding in the kitchen, boy. I wanted you and Cedric to get to know each other. He said you're cool. And as far as money goes, I'm broke. I'll be on board as a staff arranger and piano player, so I'm down in my own way. What do you think, are you open to the idea of a record company?"

"Man, I'm sitting here looking at pictures of these babes. What do you know about Ebony Angel?"

"Is that the young chocolate one?" he asked. "Girl can sang. Not sing, sang. I heard her once in Cedric's studio. All of them can sing. You should meet with him again and give it some thought. You have too many great songs sitting around collecting dust."

I ran my finger across her picture. "I *will* think about it," I said.

A week later I was in Cedric's Compton studio. We had arranged a night session to run the girl through some songs. She arrived late, and came into the control room with a guy who could have been her brother or her boyfriend. The guy sat down,

Cedric sat at the mixing board, and I led Ebony into the adjoining studio.

She was tall and dark, with long black hair tied back in a ponytail. We talked for a minute or two. I could tell she had a strong personality—and a confidence that bordered on arrogance. She handed me a headshot of herself.

"Nice picture," I said. "You photograph well, but you look even better in person. Who's the guy in there? Your brother, I hope."

She opened her mouth to talk, just as Cedric's voice came through a small loudspeaker.

"Let's get started, kids," he said. "Anthony has a bunch of songs to show you, Ebony. So, let's have some fun."

"Sounds good," I said. I reached in my bag for a lyric sheet. "This one is called 'Heartbreak Fever'." She looked it over, and crinkled her nose as she got to the end of the words.

"I'll try it, but I don't know..."

I sat at the electric keyboard, started playing, and cued her when to begin. Her voice was not bad, and she sang on key. Her sound just wasn't as strong or dynamic as I was hoping. Yet, she had a quality and an attitude that you can't teach and you can't learn. She reminded me of stories I'd heard of a young Diana Ross, whose high school friends said she carried herself like a proud superstar, even as a poor girl living in the projects.

Ebony could be made into a star, in the age of the music video, and with the help from a skilled recording engineer.

"So, what do you think?" I asked her. "You sounded good."

"I know," she said, "I just don't think it's right for me." She handed me the lyrics back.

"Ummm, okay." Stunned, I slid the paper into my backpack and pulled out another song.

"This one is called 'I'd Be Lost Without You.' It's a pop song, midtempo. Let's give it a run through."

"Wow," she said, looking over the words, "are all your songs about heartbreak and loss?" She giggled.

"Okay, Ebony," I closed my eyes for a second and took a breath, "let me play it, and just see how it sounds. Maybe you'll surprise yourself. Let's just make it through to the first chorus."

I played, and she sang, but I could tell she wasn't liking this song any more than the first one. I motioned for Cedric to join us. He dashed out of the control room and into the studio, smiling like a used car salesman.

"It's sounding good in there, folks, really good. That's two hit records so far, my man."

"You guys, I don't know," Ebony said. She was talking slowly—lethargic and bored. "Maybe it's me, but I'm just not feeling these songs. They sound kind of…white or something." She put a stick of gum in her mouth.

"They sound *white*?" I said. "What the..."

Cedric flew toward me and put his hand on my shoulder; he led me to a far corner of the studio, and spoke in a whispered tone.

"It's cool, baby, it's cool. What she *means* is, she's going for more of an R&B sound. Kind of soulful and bluesy. Show her something on that tip. We can *do* this."

"Cedric, I'm not trying to waste anybody's time here, yours or mine. I thought this broad had the look. But this attitude is killing me, man. I mean, damn." I paused, and tried to decide if I should stay or go. Finally, I calmed myself down and said, "I'll try one last song, then I'm out."

I looked over at Ebony. She was looking at her fingernails and flicking them; she seemed to be in her own world. I walked to my bag and reached for a lyric sheet.

"This one, Miss Ebony, is called 'New Year's Eve in New York City.' I hear it with a lot of horns and strings - the chords are a traditional twelve-bar blues progression. So you can put some soul in it."

"Blues?" Ebony said. "Cedric, what the hell am I going to look like singing the blues? I'm 23 years old. I mean, what is this?"

Cedric looked back and forth between Ebony and me. He must have been trying to figure what to say: how to save the session, how to get my involvement in a record company, while soothing his crazy singer.

"I tell you what," he said, "let's call it a night. Everybody's tired and on-edge. Let's hook up again on the weekend, a morning when we all fresh."

I stuffed the lyrics into my backpack. Ebony was already in the control room, summoning her brother-or-lover, who followed her out like a puppy. I picked up the backpack, and, under it, I noticed the headshot she had given me. Now I realized what it was about her pictures. Her mouth was smiling, but her eyes were not. The lovely Hollywood smile couldn't mask the coldness in her eyes.

Cedric tried to calm me down, but I left the studio steaming.

She's used to guy's kissing her ass because of her looks. And she thinks she can talk crazy to somebody she doesn't even know. I'm done, through, finished with this game.

I was in my car, winding through Compton's dark, dangerous streets, trying to find the freeway home. In my anger, I made a right turn at a stop light - without stopping. Just then, I heard a police siren, and saw a cop's red lights on my tail in the rear view mirror. I was more afraid of L.A. cops than I was of street gangs. But the cop didn't beat me; he gave me a $200 ticket. It was the price I had to pay for getting away from Ebony Angel.

In the days that followed, I seriously thought about what Cedric had said at our first meeting—about making real music. I'd look at the pictures my mom sent, with my nine-year-old face smiling while playing guitar. I had given up performing, but as time went by, I couldn't give up the urge to write songs and get them heard.

So a year later, I was still co-editor of a successful rap music magazine, and co-owner of a fledgling record company: True Blue Records—without Miss Ebony Angel.

Chapter Thirty-Two

Don't Believe the Hype

OCTOBER 1988

The new *Hype Magazine* turned five years old, and the company went all out celebrating the anniversary. One Friday night, just before Halloween, Tim Wilson rented the entire Blue Iris Restaurant and Nightclub on Hollywood Boulevard. He invited every top rapper and record person in town.

At seven o'clock, I pulled my Dodge to the front of the club, where two black men were getting out of a beautiful new red BMW. They flashed a wad of money at the valet driver, and peeled some off for him. The valet smiled, and promised to take extra care of the car.

Then another valet driver walked back to me as I sat and waited.

"There's a free lot around the corner," he said, "if you want to park this yourself." I gave him three dollars, and he hopped into the car, shaking his head as he drove away.

I saw Tim standing near the front door, giving a check to the caterer.

"This is Hollywood, Anthony," he said. "You might want to invest in a nice car, or a new muffler at least." We laughed.

"Man," I said, "that old girl got me here from Chicago, and I'll drive her till the wheels fall off."

Sharp pulled up in a new black Mercedes.

"Wow, was that your hunk of junk?" he yelled as he got out of the car. He tossed his keys at the attendant, then handed him a five-dollar bill. "You gots to represent *Hype* better than that, my brother."

"You know, Sharp," I said, "I'll put my new business up against your new car any time. Your car's losing value every minute. It just went down by $500 since you drove up here."

"Could be, could be," he said, "but I bet it gets me a thousand dollars worth of pussy this weekend."

The three of us walked into the restaurant, and saw dozens of people were already partying inside. Tim stepped into a nearby banquet room to speak to the caterer; Sharp and I ordered from the bar.

"It's been a good five years," he said, "thanks to me—and you helped a little, maybe."

"Some of the best writing and editing in the business—clearly thanks to me," I said.

"So what's this new business you been hinting about for weeks?" he asked. The bartender brought him a beer, and soda for me.

"Let's just say things are about to get shaken up."

"Boy," Sharp said with a smirk, "you ain't starting no business or shaking up a damn thing. Quit fronting."

He was goading me, I guessed, in the way a boy needles his brother to throw a rock at a window or jump off a cliff. But I was an only child, unversed in sibling manipulation.

"All right, prick, I'll tell you. Some friends and I started a record company. They'll be here tonight. We're doing some old school type R&B, trying to bring back the soul. I think people are ready to hear *real* music again. I'm betting on it. Big. Twenty thousand."

"Man, you jiving," Sharp said. "Don't you know it's over, son? Nobody wants to hear that 'Baby, I love you' stuff no more. Don't you know it's all about the beat? Haven't you learned nothing in the last five years?" He took a drink. "I hope that was twenty thousand dollars you could afford to lose."

It was my life savings, but I didn't tell him that, and I felt like I had told him too much already. My contract, the thing that kept me wedded to *Hype* all these years, had a vague clause against conflicts-of-interest, which probably included owning a record company. My contract was nearly up, but I could still be fired if someone pressed the issue.

The DJ was ending "Can't Touch This" and beginning "Me, Myself and I" when Tim joined us at the bar.

"Everything's rolling smooth now," Tim said. "We have ourselves a party." He ordered a Jack and water.

Sharp got a twinkle in his eye.

"Hey, Tim," he said, looking right at me, "have you heard about Anthony's new venture?" He smiled a crooked smile.

Was this clown about to jeopardize my job and tell our boss I had a record company? In the time it took Tim to swig his drink, I wondered if Sharp could be that lowdown. He had already done things—and said things—in the past year to make me dislike him, the perpetual playground loudmouth. But he knew rap music like no one else at the magazine, which must have been the only reason they kept him around. I respected him for that, until now.

"No," Tim said after a generous belch, "tell me about your venture, Anthony."

"It's nothing really. I'm just getting back into my music, doing some sessions on the side. Hey, I'm a songwriter first, remember?"

"Yeah. I do remember something about that." Blank look on his face.

He was satisfied with my oblique response. I looked past him, and shot a glare toward Sharp, who nodded his head twice and smiled a crooked smile before looking away.

The three of us finished our drinks, and drifted off in opposite directions. Tim went to talk to some men in suits; Sharp bee-lined his way toward two tight-dressed women across the room. The crowd had doubled in size.

"Anthony," someone called out. It was Cedric, followed by his sister and brother-in-law. "What you doing standing at the bar alone? We in Hollywood, baby, it's a party."

"We're just getting set up," I said. "I'm sort of like a host tonight, being a boss and all. What are you guys drinking?"

"Three Buds," Cedric said to the bartender. "We need to sit down and talk if you got a minute."

I led them to a nearby booth.

"Two things," Cedric said. "First - I don't want you to worry, but we need to get a record out soon, to get some cash flow. I found an act that is ready to blow up the scene big time, and he's got the perfect song."

"The perfect song," I said. "I'm all ears."

"You know how this crack epidemic is tearing apart the black community right now? Drive-by shootings, families being destroyed? You can't drive past a street corner in the hood without seeing crackheads standing there, looking like zombies, searching for the next fix, ready to do anything—*anything*—to get a crack high."

His brother-in-law spoke up. "The song is called 'You Look Dead To Me,' and it's an anti-crack song, an anthem, you might say."

"Nick Valentino is the singer," Cedric said. "I've known him in the business for a few years, and he came up with the concept."

The barmaid brought their beers, as the brother-in-law spoke again.

"We'll have all kinds of tie-ins for promotion. Schools, public service announcements, churches, they'll all eat it up. The song'll play everywhere."

"You Look Dead To Me," I said. The title sounded harsh, but the concept was original, and I wanted to give it some thought.

"Get me a tape, I'll check it out. I want to meet this Valentino guy. Now, you said there were two things to talk about."

The three of them looked at each other, as if wondering who should broach the next topic. The sister remained ever silent, while Cedric took a breath and spoke.

"It's about money," he said, looking into his beer. "Your twenty, plus our forty, together gave us a good start for the office, the studio, pictures and all. But we may come up a little short by next month. And we don't even have our first record out yet. We need to get something out on the streets soon, like I said."

"Are you saying the money's all dried up already?" I asked.

"Not dried up," Cedric said. "We're just trying to keep the stream flowing. Between our other family businesses, I can move money around until we put this new record out. I'm just giving you a heads up about everything. You know, keeping it real."

He tilted his head, and put out his right hand for me to slap, which was an odd gesture after telling me our company was having money trouble. I slapped his hand just so he'd get it out of my face.

True Blue Records was in trouble. Months ago, Cedric had guaranteed that he, and his people, were experienced with running companies. They owned three successful laundromats in Los Angeles, and Cedric had connections and knowledge about the local music scene. I had chosen to start off as a silent partner, to stem the likelihood of a conflict-of-interest, with the goal of being more active after I could leave Hype Magazine. Soon.

But now, I could only hope that the record company would *last* that long, that Cedric knew what he was doing, that my money hadn't flown out the door the way Cedric and his people were leaving the restaurant now.

I looked around for Jason, but didn't see him. *He* was the one who finally convinced me to invest in a record company, and I wanted to pick his brains—literally.

Eight o'clock, and the front area of the restaurant was almost packed. I got up and walked into the banquet room, and filled a small plate with shrimp, crackers and cheese.

As I walked toward the door, I saw a woman, who was as tall as me, entering the room. Her high, angular hat added seven inches to her towering stature. She was with a bespectacled brown-skinned man who looked like a dwarf next to her.

I recognized the woman. It was singer Phyllis Hyman, whom I had interviewed once for my old television show. We had gone to dinner on the night of the interview.

I watched the two of them for a few moments while I hurriedly ate, then I dumped most of the food in a trashcan and stepped toward the mismatched duo.

"Miss Hyman," I said. "Welcome to our party. You probably don't remember me. I'm Anthony Adams of *Hype Magazine*. Thank you for coming."

She smiled and put out her hand, which I shook lightly.

"Of course I remember you," she said, "I did your TV show in Hollywood, a while back."

"Wow, that was six, seven years ago. I'm flattered you remember."

"I never forget a—well, you know the saying."

Her small friend seemed annoyed; he looked at me over his round glasses, then he scrambled away, out of the banquet room. He looked like Rumplestiltskin scuttling away into the forest.

"Come to think of it," I said, "I gave you my number after we had dinner. You never called. I thought we made a connection that night."

"We did. I was going through some rough times. But I liked you—such a trusting face."

"You're a New Yorker. What brings you to L.A.?"

"I'm in a new movie, and I'm doing some recording for a new album—hopefully. Things are good." She paused and looked down. Her mood became dark, like a thundercloud was gathering over her head. "Things are *not* good."

Now I remembered our interview from years ago. It went well, but she was emotional and unpredictable during the three hours we spent taping her segment. Happy one minute, then sullen and sad. She ran the camera crew ragged. At the time, I wrote it off as nerves or artistic temperament.

Now, she was genuinely troubled. I stepped closer to her.

"It's getting really noisy in here," I said, "let's go find somewhere we can talk."

She kept her head down, barely able to walk as I led her upstairs. I took her hand as we went up to the empty balcony area. We stood and looked over the partiers.

I waited for her to talk first.

Ricky Sharp was in a far corner, huddled with two tall men. They gave him a small white envelope, and Sharp slid some money to them across a table. I looked over at Tim, who was standing off with a group of men who looked like him and were dressed like him. In fact, I noticed the whites were on one side of the club and the blacks were on the other. Like high school all over again.

I turned and faced Phyllis.

I thought about our dinner way back, and how we made a striking couple, like king and queen. I wanted her to like me at the time, but there was a lot going on in her head. I knew she wouldn't call me. It was strange now standing next to her, up high, surveying the crowd.

"Things are not good," Phyllis finally repeated as she lifted her chin like Evita, and looked at the scene below. "You can be in a room full of happy people, and feel like the only living person in the world. Do you know what I mean?"

"Uhhh, I've felt that way before, I'm sure. Tell me what's happening with your career."

"It's a struggle," she said. "Everyday—*fighting* with my management, *fighting* to get good songs, trying to get heard on the radio. And here's the new thing: black radio and this rapping business. They won't play a pop song unless it's got a rap break in the middle, ever since Chaka did 'I Feel For You.' It's a nightmare."

"You always seemed so happy when I saw you performing. I've seen you twice."

"Don't believe the hype," she said. "I cry myself to sleep at night. Things are never what they seem. Everyone you see down there at your party? They're pretending right now, and most of them are sad."

She stood up straight and got a tissue from her jeweled purse. She dabbed her eyes. She looked at me.

"The years have been good to you, I see. Running a magazine, still looking good. Your party is a success. I'd better get back down to it, Anthony."

"Are you going to be all right?" I followed her slowly toward the stairs.

"Oh, I'll be just fine. I just had a diva moment. You'd have to be a girl to understand. This business is turning against us. Miki, Regina, Melba, me—we can't compete against hot pants and implants. When all the young female singers start acting like prostitutes, there's no turning back. So, us grown women find other things to do, like Broadway and movies." She put her hand to my ear. "Just between me and you," she whispered, "I don't have a record contract now."

We reached the bottom of the stairs, and heads turned as people saw us together.

"I wonder," she said, putting her hand on my shoulder, "what would have happened if I *had* called you back."

"Where are you staying?" I asked, as we took the final step down. "Maybe we can have lunch."

She just smiled, and disappeared into the crowd, her giant hat looking like a sailboat, lost at sea.

Chapter Thirty-Three

City of Cocaine

TWO YEARS LATER, AUGUST 1990

My boss was high on cocaine. More precisely, he was big on the idea of doing a cover story on cocaine, and how it was on everyone's lips in show business.

I remembered the first time someone offered me coke. I was interviewing a famous singer in his living room back when I worked at the TV station. The interview was over, and the crew was out in the truck packing up. This singer took a vial out of his shirt pocket and began pouring and spreading and dicing and clicking away at the stuff he had put on his glass table.

When I was eight years old my parents had similar rituals with alcohol. Pouring, shaking, mixing, squeezing, stirring, then sipping or gulping, maybe fighting, then sleeping. A handful of times I had to make my own dinner and put myself to bed. It was during one of those nights I decided to never drink or take drugs like the stuff that was shooting up this clown's nose.

Now, it's 1990, and you can't talk about the music business, Hollywood, or the '80s and '90s without talking about cocaine. Every show business player in town was either using coke, selling it, or knew someone who did.

Two kinds of coke were flowing across the L.A. basin: pure, white powder in the hills and the studios, cheap, jagged rocks in the city streets, where crack heads and drive-bys were becoming common. It was too large an issue for *Hype* to ignore.

Cocaine was the topic of an executive meeting one summer morning between me, Sharp and Tim Wilson.

"This coke thing is getting bigger every day," Tim said. "My idea is for us to take a look at the connection between the drug trade and the music business, focusing on rap, of course. This looks like a major piece—weeks of research and interviews. Any volunteers?"

I was intrigued with the thought of doing some serious journalism, but I had other plans. My contract was expired, yet I needed to stay at *Hype*. True Blue Records was sucking my finances dry, and I needed the job just to stay afloat. I wanted to devote every spare minute to my struggling record company. I had no interest or motivation for doing a big article on something I knew nothing about.

Sharp was slouched in his seat, fiddling with a yellow pencil, quiet. Tim began rocking in his chair, letting us sit for a minute, until I spoke up.

"I'd like to do it—get out in the field again - but my plate is full."

"I think it's a bad idea," Sharp said. "Kids don't want to read about the drug trade. They want to know what their favorite stars are up to, see pictures of 'em. What, are we turning into the *New York Times* all of a sudden, Tim?"

"Actually, I *do* want to move in the direction of harder pieces, more reporting. We've been around long enough, we can afford to do some real journalism once in a while."

"Well," Sharp said, "what does Freeman think about all this?"

Tim stopped rocking, and looked at Sharp. Freeman's name rarely came up. For Sharp to mention it now might have meant he was comfortable enough to go over Tim's head to kill a story.

"Like I've said in the past, Freeman's got his own fish to fry in New York. I'm your publisher here, and your boss. Is that clear?"

"Crystal," Sharp said, still focused on the yellow of his pencil.

"Anthony, I want you to do this story. You can bring the right attitude to it. Some thoughts off the top of my head: L.A. streets are a battleground; gangs are making parts of the city unsafe for normal people; is there a connection between rap music and the culture of violence in the streets. Hell, there's even a rumor that the federal government is funneling crack into California, the CIA or somebody, I heard. There you are. Bam. Two thousand words, and you're done."

As I thought about it, it might be good getting into the streets to do some reporting—to take a break from the office and the editing chores, which would now all fall to Sharp. *Yes.*

Maybe I'll make it a major, high profile piece, something worthy of a Pulitzer Prize, stir up controversy. With luck, my record company would start making money, and the article would hit the newsstands in time for my last week at *Hype*, my swan song, my goodbye to the strange world of rap music and all who inhabited it. I wrapped my mind around cocaine and got to work.

I made calls in the afternoon, and set up interviews with a record company executive, a school principal, a police lieutenant, and a few rappers.

I was headed for the elevator to make my first interview at five o'clock, when Sharp stepped into my office. He walked to a chair and sat down.

"What's this all about, anyway," he said.

"What do you mean?"

"This 'you got the right attitude' bit between you and Tim? Don't think I don't realize y'all trying to sabotage me." He was jack hammering his knee up and down as he sat, and his eyes were weird.

"Sharp, I don't know what you're talking about, and I got an interview to do right now..."

"I could have done that assignment—twice as good as you, and with better sources. I just didn't want to. But go ahead and do your little interview. Just don't step on the wrong toes. I'm warning you."

"Sharp, I hope you can handle things on your own around here for a while. And it may not be a good idea to get high on the job, man. You look a mess. Just try not to break anything or start trouble with these folks when I'm not around. I won't be here to cover for your sorry ass."

"Hey, I don't start trouble, but I know how to finish it, if you know what I'm saying."

He got up and walked to the door, looking both ways twice before stepping into the hallway.

I drove to Compton to meet MC Easy. He had been featured in *Hype* once before. On the phone he had agreed to talk about the problems of crack cocaine in his neighborhood.

I had the directions he had given me to a public park near his home: "I don't want no reporters knowing where my crib is," he had said. A street intersection and a description of his car was all I had to go by.

And what a car it was. I saw it gleaming in the sun as I pulled up at Central and Rosecrans. A green and gold Mercedes was parked on the opposite side of the street. I parked, and walked over. The driver's side window came halfway down, and a cloud of marijuana smoke rushed out into the hot summer air.

"Why you writing about drugs, anyway?"

MC Easy was behind the wheel. I could see the shadow of someone else in the passenger seat.

"We're trying to see what the drug trade is doing to our community—the people, the kids, the music."

"White man always trying to make black folks look bad," he said.

"I'm not white, my brother," I said. "Look, why don't we take a walk? I just have a few questions for you."

"We can talk here. This cool."

I was about to ask him my first question, when a bone-thin man walked by and asked me for a cigarette. I thought of the song, "You Look Dead To Me." The song my record company tried to put out a year ago. We were this close to releasing it, but the singer disappeared before signing all the contracts. Haven't heard from him since. L.A. people had a way of vanishing without a word.

This crack head looked dead, to me. I told him I didn't smoke, then he asked me for a dollar, which I gave him just to move him along.

I stood next to MC Easy's two-toned pimp car for twenty minutes while he told me, off the record, stories about L.A.'s gangs, and how drugs were the fuel driving most of the turf violence that was happening. He said Compton was a central distribution spot for southern California, to the point where the little town was commonly know as the "City of Cocaine."

When I was about to leave, he stepped out of the car. A younger man got out of the passenger side.

"This my cousin, Lil' Homicide."

The boy looked about twelve years old, maybe younger; he was wearing dark shades, black jeans and jacket, with a white t-shirt.

"What's up, Lil' Homicide," I said. "What do you want to be when you grow up?"

"I'm already grown, nigga, what you talking 'bout, fool? Hell, I'm a motherfucking rapper. My album be out in little while. Check this shit out." He handed me a cassette tape, which I slid into my pocket. I know my mouth must have been hanging open in amazement at hearing this language from a kid who should have been riding a skateboard or shooting hoops instead of pretending to be a gangster, a future ex-convict. It was getting dark. I wanted to get back to my turf in Hollywood. I said goodbye to the two of them, and got into my car.

As I drove, I thought of the kids I'd seen years ago at Dana's school—how wild and aggressive they were compared to when I was twelve. Now Lil' Homicide, even younger, was showing that same attitude and behavior, in an extreme way. Dana's students: how many are selling crack right now, smoking it, or in prison because of it?

The next morning, I met with Sal Wasserman, president of the nation's biggest record company. He had been reluctant when I spoke to him on the phone, but I was able to convince him to give me fifteen minutes. I brought my small cassette recorder to tape the interview.

His offices were in the heart of Hollywood. I arrived, and his secretary sat me in a large conference room, where I waited. Minutes later, Wasserman entered and sat one seat away from me.

"*Hype Magazine*, huh? You guys have been through some changes."

"Yes, sir. With more changes to come. I'm doing a piece on drugs, and I wanted to get your take on things in general." I turned on the tape recorder and put it on the empty chair that separated us.

"Drugs have always been with us, and they always will be. End of interview." He paused. "Just kidding."

"Do you see cocaine being used, like currency, to get deals made and pay favors in the business?"

I didn't expect him to answer honestly. He didn't get to the top by falling for a J-school trap from a nosy reporter. But he had to say *some*thing. And from what I already suspected, cocaine was practically running through the building's pipes and served in the company cafeteria.

"In any business today, 1990," he said, "you will find problems, whether it's drugs, racism, or any number of issues. The music business is no better or worse than what's happening in the baseball world or on Wall Street."

Full of deflection, each word carefully chosen to avoid the question. A perfect political sound bite for television. The guy was good.

"Let's focus on rap music," I said. "Do you see a connection between the crack cocaine problem, and rap music that glorifies violence, street hustling, the criminal lifestyle, prison culture, gangs..."

"Look," he said, "we don't have any rap acts on our labels here yet. That may be about to change - in fact I have a big meeting in a few minutes to decide if we start a rap music division. But right now, I don't feel culpable for the things you're describing, if that's what you're driving at."

Wasserman was a dead end, but he said I was free to talk to any of his A&R people—men who worked directly with talent and had a better grasp of what was happening on the streets.

Our interview ended when three tanned and suited executive-types entered, laughing at an unheard punch line, my cue to say goodbye and leave.

The next morning, getting ready for work, I realized I had left my tape recorder in Wasserman's conference room. I needed to run by my office anyway. I stopped to pick it up on the way to Santa Monica. Wasserman's secretary led me to my machine. It was right on the pushed-in chair where I left it.

When I got to *Hype*, I tried to sneak into my office before anyone saw me.

I almost made it. "Anthony!" someone called.

Sandy, a staff writer, needed me to approve a feature she had written.

"Rick Sharp is covering everything for a while, you know."

"I know, I know," she said. "But he's really hard to catch, even when he *is* here. Tim is practically doing everything now."

She pointed toward the pit, where four people were standing around Wilson, like elves trying to get Santa's approval. I took Sandy's article and darted into my office. She left smiling.

I closed my door and rewound the tape so I could transcribe the Wasserman interview. Listening to him, I realized his answers were even more evasive than I'd remembered, but at least I had quotes from a big record company president. His responses made him seem defensive and a little clueless; they weren't going to make him look good in print.

The interview ended, and I heard the laughing vice presidents enter. I started to turn off the machine, ready to head for my interview with LAPD, when I realized it must have kept rolling after I left. My eyes got wide.

"Get a grip, you guys. We have to listen to some demos, then we have choices to make, and not much time."

It was Wasserman's voice.

"There's three or four indies out there making a ton of money in rap music, or hip hop, as they call it. We've talked about this before. But the time is right, I think, to make a major move in that direction. A rap music department."

I heard a chorus of agreement from the other men.

"Good. We're on the same page. The big question is, do we step in lightly with the Fresh Prince/M.C. Hammer kid stuff, or more toward the hard edge, gangster sound that seems to be taking over?"

I heard a new voice. "Hal, you gotta love the cars, guns and women thing that's out there. Edgy."

A different voice spoke up.

"Boss, I've been talking to three unsigned acts that are ready to break through. I'll play the tapes for you. They're straight from the streets, poor and angry. Kids will eat it up. And we can sign them cheap."

A third voice spoke.

"I agree. Our black music division is dead. A hip hop label gives us access to a whole new market—black kids who identify with these guys, and white kids who think it's cool and just want to piss off their parents, their ex-hippie parents."

There was a pause on the tape. Then Wasserman's voice.

"I've seen the videos of the popular rappers. And there's a certain minstrel quality to it all that bothers me. The jumping up and down, boasting about nothing, holding their penises. I mean, you have to wonder how far it all will go."

"In a few years," said one of the men, "they'll be covered in gold jewelry, gold teeth and covered in tattoos. There's already a guy with a giant clock around his neck. Kids will go insane over the outrageousness."

Where did I hear this all before? Was it part of a plan?

"Yeah, really," Wasserman said. "And the young ladies, gyrating their asses and basically acting like dogs in heat—I mean, how do black women allow their men to do this stuff? Don't these guys have mothers, sisters?"

He sighed, and sounded ambivalent about the choice he was about to make. "But hey, it's the next big thing. And we're here to make money, not social work. If they want to make it, we'll sell it. If we're all in agreement, then it's done. We're in the rap business now. Cory, I want you to help me find a black guy to head the division. Get somebody who knows what's happening in south central, places like Watts and the City of Cocaine. Now let's hear those demos."

Silence. I could picture the three men nodding their sycophantic heads.

After a few seconds, I heard a familiar drum machine sound, followed by a looping sampled part from a James Brown record. Then came the voice of a rapper. He could have been that kid I saw in the Brill Building back in New York, or MC Easy or Black Ice. It didn't matter.

Shake your butt, girl, shake your booty
I bet it taste like tooty fruity
I got more rhymes than Howdy Doody
Now get over here and shake dat ass

My tape machine made a squealing sound, as if in pain, and then it clicked off.

Chapter Thirty-Four

One Angry Voice

1990

I was angry. Knocking on my best friend's damn door. It took three different series of hits before he answered. Each knock louder than the last.

"Jason, what the hell have you gotten me into?" I looked at his bleary face. "And why the hell are you sleeping at 7 P.M.?"

"I nodded off watching TV. Why are you banging on my door, freak? I am not having a nice day. Come on in."

"I can't stay. I'm meeting with Cedric and his *clan* about this record company. You need to ride with me. This is all your fault, man."

"Give me a break, Anthony. Please." He took a loud breath and let it out. "I'll be ready in a minute."

I hadn't seen him in months. He looked tired - probably worn out from some job that was running him into the ground.

In minutes, we were driving down La Brea Avenue for the meeting in one of Cedric's family laundromats.

"I don't know why I'm so tired lately," Jason said, letting the seat back, "I can't get enough sleep."

"I'm not sleeping too well myself," I said, "between all this crazy drug world research I'm doing, and this record company. How much do you know about what's happening with True Blue Records?"

"Uhhhh, not a whole lot. I hooked you up with Cedric, end of story. I didn't have money to put in it. I'm on the sidelines. But if you sank your money in it, I would think you'd keep a better eye on what they're doing."

I tried to think of a way to refute his comment, but his eyes were closed when I looked over at him. He was correct anyway.

Jason was asleep when we arrived at the Squeaky Clean Launderette. I woke him up, and we walked inside. A small office in the back was where we found Cedric, his brother, and sister, seated around an old gray metal desk. The sister was watching a small black and white TV.

"Anthony, my brother," Cedric said. "And what's up with you, Jason?"

"When you hear '*my brother*," Jason said, "look out." The two of them laughed. Jason sat in a corner chair. I remained standing.

"Tell me the company's doing well," I said, "and that you haven't lost all of my money."

"Unfortunately," Cedric said, "I can't tell you that. We tried to make it work, but none of our acts caught on."

"Music is changed," the other brother said. "We tried to go one way, with soul music, but we just couldn't get distribution. All they're signing is no-singing girls and mean-mugging rappers. Fake gangsters. It's a bad time to have talent."

"The bottom line, Anthony," Cedric said, "is we need to shut down and take a loss on True Blue Records. The funds are gone, and we need to realize we were barking up the wrong tree —unless you want to sign rappers and go into the hip hop business, and I know none of us wants that."

I had been expecting bad news, but I was still shocked to hear what he said. I looked around the room, figuring out how I should respond. I wondered if I could bust these people in their heads and make a clean getaway.

"You mean to tell me you burned through sixty thousand dollars, in a few months time, without making money on a single record?"

"We were under-funded," Cedric said. "We *could* get a bank loan, but do you want to go into further debt behind this? I don't think so. We chose the right company, at the wrong time. True Blue might have worked ten years ago, or ten years from now when this rap thing blows over. I've been beating my head against a wall, but at some point you just have to walk away."

His brother was looking down at some papers on the desk; the sister was watching an MC Hammer video on the tiny TV, rocking to the beat.

"I'm sorry we lost your money, Anthony. These papers are for you. You can still get a pretty good tax write off for the loss."

"You know," I closed my eyes, "I never should have put a single dime into this. What the hell was I thinking? Somehow you people can make money with these damn laundromats, but when somebody else's money is involved, suddenly it's a problem. I don't like this, Cedric, not one bit." I opened my eyes and took a step toward him, not sure what I was about to do. *This creep just cost me a fortune!* I saw his brother sit up and tense his body.

"I don't know what else to tell you, Anthony. It's all in the financial statements right there. Have someone else go over them if you don't trust me."

"But if that's the problem," said his much-bigger brother, "it's probably not a good idea to go into business with somebody you don't trust in the first place."

I felt outnumbered—my one angry voice was falling on deaf ears against the three of them. Why were they taking this loss so lightly? Why weren't they as upset as me? My money was gone, and there was nothing I could do except wake up Jason and leave.

The boy could sleep through a hurricane.

"I should have known something like this would happen," I told Jason. We had gone directly to Queen Bea's, a soul food restaurant on La Brea. We sat in a booth near the jukebox in the front.

"Always keep your money in the bank. That's what Mama says."

"Jason, you're pissing me off. It was *you* who got me into this dumb scheme."

"Let me buy you dinner. You're kind of right; I did bring you all together."

He tried to catch the eye of the only waitress in the place, who was slowly moving from table to table to the kitchen.

"Jason, I just lost twenty thousand dollars. I must be insane. There must seriously be something wrong with me."

"Don't beat yourself up too bad, Ant. The thing about money is, you can always make more."

"Beat *myself* up? I should beat *you* up. I should..."

The dawdling waitress stepped to our table and interrupted me.

"I'm Doreen, what can I get you?"

Jason and I ordered our food, then I started attacking him again. He apparently knew I was letting off steam, and I got in a few choice phrases, until I called him "stupid." His eyes got Joan Crawford, and I knew I had gone too far.

"Now, wait a minute. I'm not going to be called too many more names tonight. It was *you* who took every penny you had and invested with some strangers. And it was *you* who decided to be a silent partner and not even keep an eye on them. If I recall, all I told you to do was make a good choice."

"Don't loud-talk me, man. Keep it down, Jason."

"No, *you* keep it down. The worst part is, you people put money into music that nobody wants to sign, nobody wants to hear, or buy. *Now* who's stupid?"

The nearby jukebox started clicking and whirring. Someone played "The Humpty Dance" while we sat quietly, until the waitress brought our food. Doreen plopped the plates hard on the table, then left without a word.

"I have an idea," I said, "maybe I'll find a white rapper with some street credibility. Call him 'Al Bino' or something."

The two of us laughed at the idea.

"Yeah," Jason said, "a guy with a criminal record, broken family, bad attitude. White kids would eat it up."

"But only if he gets some kind of black seal of approval first. So far, the Beastie Boys are the only huge white act, and they're more of a comedy group if anything. Let's find a white guy—call him milk, or vanilla-something, a food name. What a joke. How's your food?"

He was busy lacquering salt, pepper, and hot sauce over every inch of his dinner. He took a bite of chicken, and nodded his head with approval.

"I know you were joking," he said, "but the white rapper thing could actually work."

When he said the word "work," I suddenly realized I would have to continue working at my job, even longer than I expected. My money was gone, and the record company was out of business.

I reflected on my years in California. I was tired of losing. My band, my girl, a record company, and my money—up in smoke. For a second, I thought about starting another band, but that would be a waste of time unless we did hip hop. Hearing "The Humpty Dance" made me angry: guys were making millions of dollars by talking nonsense and sampling other peoples' material. *There must be something I can do or write or say. Some way to vent this anger.*

All I could do for now, I thought, if I wanted to pay my bills, was to stay at *Hype Magazine*—at least until I found something else.

I dropped by the office the next morning for an editorial meeting. The cocaine article had kept me in the streets for most of the week, and I needed to check my messages and mail. I also wanted to see if the magazine was falling apart without me, knowing Sharp was a lazy buffoon.

Wilson, Sharp, Phoebe, and several writers were sitting down when I walked into the room.

"Hey, look who's making an entrance," Sharp said. "Back from your vacation?"

"You should be a comedy writer," I said as I sat down. "I hear Eddie Murphy's looking for joke writers, and you're a drag queen at night, aren't you? I hear he…"

"We have a small problem," Wilson said, ignoring the banter between me and Sharp. "Andre, you want to tell everyone what happened?"

Andre was a young writer and critic who Sharp hired several months earlier.

"I'm out, y'all. Today is my last day here. Remember the review I wrote about Cypress Mob's new joint? Yo, I got jacked. They said the review made them look soft or something. And—get this—it was a good review!"

"What happened, Andre?" I asked. "You're talking crazy."

"Check it. Yesterday, outside my crib, two thugs jumped me and said they didn't appreciate the things I said in the review. Said I didn't make them look hard enough. I'm not trying to lose my life writing for y'all. I gotta let this go."

"What, they roughed you up?" I asked. "Did you call the cops?"

"I ain't a snitch, man. But I'm not stupid. No more of this for me."

"That's that," Wilson said. "But it creates another problem. Andre was working on the cover piece for the next issue, and we're caught with nothing big for that edition. We need something quick."

Wilson cut his eyes toward me and stared, tapping a pencil against his right temple. It dawned on me: he wanted me to have my cocaine article ready in a few days.

Andre stood up and said goodbye; he walked around to shake hands, and he gave a hug to Sharp.

"Thanks for the break, yo," Andre said.

"Watch yourself out there, son," Sharp said as the young man left the room. "Go back on the porch if you can't run with the big dogs." He let out a sinister laugh.

"Ever the sentimentalist," Phoebe said.

"What do you think, Anthony," Wilson finally said. "Can we get your big piece sooner? 'The Rap on Drugs,' or whatever you're calling it, by next Thursday?"

"Not a bad title," I said. "Not bad at all. Problem is, I have twelve interviews to transcribe, four more to do, and that's even before I start writing. You gave a piece to somebody who knows nothing about the subject. Which is not always a bad thing, it just takes time. "

"I told y'all I could have aced that piece," Sharp said.

"All the help you need is in this room," Wilson said. "Keith and Sierra can help with the transcriptions, and Sharp can probably do at least one interview for you. You guys could even do some co-writing, if you don't kill each other."

"Give me a few hours to figure this out," I said. "I'm talking to a gang task force cop at eleven, and I can be back here after lunch."

The staff meeting went on, but I left early to find the police station in East Los Angeles for my next interview.

While I was driving, I tried to picture Sharp and me, collaborating on an article. Then the picture in my mind dissolved to the scene of Andre being threatened because of a review he wrote. *I remember that review of Cypress Mob. It* was *a positive review!*

I had heard of a similar incident in New York, where a writer was either beaten or threatened (there were conflicting reports) for writing something a rapper didn't like.

Was I putting my neck on the line for this rap and drugs article? I wanted controversy, but I wasn't ready to die for a stupid magazine.

I had collected dozens of stories over the past week painting a grim picture: there was, in fact, a direct connection between the rap world, and gangs, crime, prostitution and cocaine distribution.

And now Tim wants me to rush the article through.

I drove past a huge boarded-up Ford factory. Lots of graffiti-covered liquor stores and nail salons were along the way as I looked for the police station. I saw the words "no snitches," barely legible on the side of the Lucky Star Party Store. Three black men were in front—apparently jobless since it was a workday morning—probably selling crack.

I found the police station and parked across from it, ten minutes early. I finally had time to think.

Let's see. Rappers are threatening writers. Music company execs are secretly comparing rap to minstrel. Reporting a crime is considered snitching. Gang members are building reputations on shooting people and going to prison. And I'm about to write a major article on drugs in the rap business, with a little help from the police.

It seemed like the world was turning upside down, like the bizarro world of Superman comics, where the rules of logic and physics don't apply. Wonder Woman flies an invisible jet. Wolverine had 18-inch retractable claws, yet he can still move his wrists.

A police car pulled up in front of the station. Cops got out, and removed a young man with cornrows and sagging pants he could barely keep from falling. The kid was in handcuffs, yet he was smiling.

I was angry again, but this time, instead of anger at losing all my money, I was angry at a system that glorified violence, prison and ignorance. At a music business that fed kids a steady diet of ass-shaking nonsense. Execs who considered rappers to be minstrels, and rappers too happy to play the part. A business where talents like Phyllis Hyman are pushed aside to make way for sex kittens with paper-thin voices. Most of all, I was angry that rap music seemed to be taking over the world with no resistance—no one to ask questions while it rolled over the soul of music, destroying everything else in sight.

But I had a voice—at *Hype*. I didn't know for how much longer, but I wanted my one angry voice to speak up about what I saw happening to music.

As I got out of the car, still another young black man was pulled from the back of a police car, no doubt with hip hop beats still in his head.

It might be a dangerous thing to do, but I had a voice, and I was going to say something.

Chapter Thirty-Five

The Article

The Rap On Drugs

By Anthony Adams

D-Murder sold half a million records last year. But he'll tell you he made more money selling crack cocaine the year before than he did from royalties. It's no secret: he boasts about his criminal past in interviews and on records. And his drug-dealing past gives him street credibility.

He's not unique. Hundreds of young black men easily float between the worlds of rap, prison and drugs. Some do it proudly.

"Ain't no jobs out here, what else can we do?" MC Easy said while parked near a popular drug-buying spot in Compton. "For most brothers, it's either rap, sling dope, or die. How else we going to feed ourselves? If I ain't rapping or selling dope, I'm robbing your house."

Captain Keith Archer of the LAPD disagrees. "We live in a culture that glorifies violence and renegades—from Jesse James to Scarface. When you put rap, crack and gangs in the mix, you're looking at a formula for destruction of a whole generation of black youth. A lost generation."Archer heads the gang task force in LA's roughest, poorest area.

"Crack and crime are the fuel for this angry, misogynistic so-called music," according to Principal Barbara Miller of Sojourner High School. She's seen thousands of students in her 25 years in teaching.

"If these men had been focused on school, they wouldn't need to be selling dope or calling women hoes and bitches on records and videos. Without the crack explosion," she went on, "you wouldn't have the rap explosion."

"Wow," Renee said as she looked up from the magazine. "This…is intense."

We were in a convenience store three blocks from the Warner Building. Renee worked in the company's accounting department on the third floor, and we had taken a short walk after eating lunch together. I liked her pretty eyes and brown skin, and she liked me. She was girlfriend material.

"I put a lot of thought into writing it, believe me. It's time somebody spoke up about what's happening to music. I decided to be the one."

"And you decided it was a good idea to put your real name on top of an article criticizing drug dealers and criminals?"

"I think I know what I'm doing," I said. "Black music is on a one-way trip down the toilet, girl. The sad part is, I don't even think we've seen the worst of it." I paid for the magazine and two sodas. "By the way, thanks for joining me. Sometimes I like to buy a copy from the news stand the first day it hits the street, to feel what the readers feel when they buy one."

"Now, Anthony, seriously," Renee said as we left the store and stepped into sunlight. "My cousin is dating a guy who sells cocaine. The guy and his drug-slinging partners don't like the light shining on them, and that's what this article is doing."

"Read the rest of the article, will you just?"

"Anyway, I have to get back to work. I'm not a big executive, like some people." She bumped my shoulder playfully as we walked.

"I'm glad I wrote it. It feels *so* good to finally publish something meaningful after doing fluff all these years. It'll be interesting to see the response. But I'll be okay. I'm betting that drug dealers don't read a lot of magazines anyway."

We headed down Ocean Park Avenue, past the office workers at lunch, past streams of Mexican nannies pushing blonde-haired babies in strollers. The sun was bright, and the smell of the sea was in the air. *This* was what it felt like when I first started at *Hype* thirteen years ago.

In minutes, we reached the Warner Building and rode an elevator to the third floor.

"Thanks for lunch," she said.

"I'll call you tonight. If you don't hear from me, just check the morning obituaries. I'm a marked man."

"Not funny," I heard her say as the elevator doors closed.

I was surprised at how concerned Renee was about my safety. Today had been our third lunch date, and I was planning to ask her to dinner soon. I could tell she liked me, which made her worries even more troubling. Had I gone too far in the article?

I got off on the seventh floor, walked down the hall and past the big Hype sign, heading toward the pit. I immediately sensed that something was different.

It was the sound.

Phones were ringing everywhere. Whatever staff that wasn't out to lunch stood beside desks, answering the bleating phones. I even noticed Tim Wilson, who rarely visited the pit, on the phone, standing at a writer's desk. He looked up and noticed me.

"Dive in," he said, and waved me toward him.

I reached for a phone and thought, the magazine just hit the newsstands and mailboxes this morning, like it does every other Tuesday before ten. This is the first time phones have lit up like this. It can't be a good thing. Can it?

"I just got your magazine," the caller said, "and I think y'all are all wrong making hip hop seem like it's to blame for all this mess. You know what I'm saying? Rap just reflects what's happening in the streets."

"Yo," the next caller said, "I'm reading your magazine, and this Anthony Adams is a straight up clown. Why white people always got to tear down black folks and they accomplishments? If he want to talk smack about hip hop, he better get his facts straight, or watch out."

I saw Wilson take a final call, then he headed for his office. I listened for a few more minutes to the guy who called me a clown, then I followed Wilson and sat across from his desk.

"You wanted us to make an impact. I did it with a bang."

"Yeah, we kicked up a lot of dirt with this one. I think it's fascinating. How many more articles could we do on frigging Kris Kross or LL Cool J?"

Sharp entered the room.

"Door was open," he said, "thought I'd join you."

"Good," Wilson said. "I think we can expect a lot of response from the drugs article—some bad and some good. Like I said before, I want us to move toward more news and less fluff."

"And like *I* mentioned before," Sharp said, "I think it's crazy to alienate the very people we're covering: the hip-hop crowd. And I already told you, Adams, some people won't look kindly to seeing their name in the papers linked with coke."

"Since we're all doing 'like I said befores,' I didn't want to write this article to begin with. But after talking to people, the picture was clear. Face it, guys, this is the start of the nineties, and some strange things are taking hold in music. I just pointed them out. I interviewed a damn twelve-year old named Lil' Homicide who dropped out of school to be a rapper. We're glamorizing the most destructive element in our community, and kids are sucking it up. You're right, Sharp, it *is* crazy out there. But maybe *you* should have written this damn thing."

"Everybody just calm down," Wilson said. "Let's take it slow editorially, and only do a heavy piece every few months or so. This next issue we can get back to Vanilla Ice or something."

He was interrupted by a ringing phone, which he answered on a speaker.

"Tim, this is David Freeman in New York."

"Mr. Freeman, how are you. I'm sitting here with your two ace editors, Anthony Adams and Richard Sharp."

"Good. That'll make this simple. I just got your *Hype Magazine* with the whole drugs and rap thing. Tim, we've got problems."

"Really, sir," Wilson said, looking surprised, "what kind of problems?"

"First off, you know *Hype* is designed to be a lightweight music magazine for young people, not *Newsweek* or *Time*. You're opening a whole can of worms by connecting music people to drug dealers. Record companies are our biggest advertisers, and we don't want to alienate them."

Sharp kicked my foot and smirked when Freeman said 'alienate.' Wilson's face looked like the principal was chewing him out. And me? I felt the rug being pulled from under my feet.

"Mr. Freeman, it's me, Adams. Maybe it'll work in our favor. Any publicity is good publicity, I've heard. Won't it help sales?"

Wilson cut me off and leaned toward the phone, "David, I sent you a memo weeks ago detailing my plan to move in the direction of news—slowly, over the next year."

"Now, come on, Timothy, I'm swamped out here. If it ain't broke—you know. Don't put yourself in the position where I have to approve your content every issue. Just stick with the kid stuff for the MTV crowd, and we'll be fine. By the way, nice writing, Adams, but stick to managing for a while. Take care, fellows."

Sharp stood up, holding his stupid chin high.

"I'll be getting back to work, yo."

I didn't know who felt worse at the moment, me or Wilson. He lowered his head, and shuffled papers on his desk, until one caught his attention and he started scribbling on it.

I got up and headed for my office.

Sharp was behind his desk as I passed. He was on the phone, and when he saw me, he waved me in. He put the caller on speaker.

"...don't know who this little punk Adams is who wrote this, but me and my boys on the way down there. I got something I want to talk to his bitch-ass about."

The caller hung up.

"I told you," Sharp said, "I told you a hundred times y'all are messing with some crazy people you shouldn't be messing with. Now what you gonna do, smart guy?"

"Don't be a total jerk, Sharp. He's not the first crank call and he won't be the last. If you're expecting me to run for the hills, think again. Hell, a writer should be willing to stand up for what he puts down. Otherwise, I'd do something safe like run a flower shop and wear a dress. The guy is a crackpot."

Wilson appeared in the doorway, with a whiter-than-usual face. He stepped in the office and closed the door.

"Okay," he said, "I read the article several times, and I knew it was different for us, but I had no idea."

"What happened now?" I asked him.

"Someone in the pit took a call. Guy said he was a westsider or something, some kind of gang stuff, and…let's just say he made some threatening remarks. Anthony, I think you should work from home for a couple days until this article thing cools down. In a few days, it'll be old news. It looks like we shook the rafters of some bad people this time."

"You all just don't listen," Sharp said.

"I can work from home, no problem," I said. "By the way, before I leave, Tim, I wanted to talk to you about my future here. Sharp and I signed contracts at the same time, and they expired a while ago. Shouldn't I be negotiating or something?"

"Don't worry about that," Wilson said. "New York doesn't do contracts anymore. I was going to meet with you guys about it at some point. Basically it all comes down to: we're all day-to-day. Freeman can fire us at a moment's notice. Just go tell my secretary you'll be home the rest of the week, and she'll get stuff to you."

He left. Sharp leaned back and put his feet on his desk.

"You know what this all means, right?" he asked.

"What *what* means? I think it's cool to have some excitement around this joint. You're on your own around here for a while once again. Can you handle it?"

"It means you pissed off the wrong people. Not just the rappers and dope dealers, but the big boss sitting back in New York. Did you *hear* him? He was not happy. 'Work from home for a few days?' No contract? Figure it out, yellow man. Let me know if you need a reference for a new job."

"I'll clue you in on a secret, genius. You know all the articles that come to you for editing? Wilson has *me* go over them again because of the mistakes you miss. You're not a good writer, and you're a piss poor editor. I don't even know why they hired you, other than Freeman's grand scheme to change the magazine. If today is my last day, just know that you're considered a joke around here."

Sharp quieted down, like bullies do when confronted. I wanted to pop the smirk off his face.

I left his office, and checked in with Wilson's secretary; she said she'd have a messenger come by my apartment twice a day to drop off and pick up copy.

I grabbed a few copies of the latest edition from the mailroom on my way out. I got into the elevator, and opened to the article, proudly running my finger across the words:

By Anthony Adams.

Writers never get tired of seeing their bylines or credits. I was happy with what I had written, said what I wanted to say. In spite of the threats, and even if I lost my job over it, the article was on the streets, with a life of its own.

No one could silence what the article had to say. If a two-bit thug wanted to make a name for himself by gunning me down, there was nothing I could do about it. Innocent people were being gunned down every day in LA's crack wars, rap disputes and gang turf battles. The senseless violence was a way of life.

I ran some errands and went grocery shopping. It was after six when I pulled up to the palm trees in front of the El Dorado. I relaxed for an hour. Then I called Renee, ignoring the five messages blinking on my answering machine.

"What's happening, girl?"

"I read the rest of your article. I have to say, you nailed it."

"Really? You think so?"

"I showed it to some of the other sisters in the office, and they were like, right on. It's a shame what's going on."

"That's good to hear. Finally some positive feedback. They want me to work from home for a few days because of a few threats. Who knew my writing could turn the world upside down?"

"There are a lot of knuckleheads out there, but I don't think they're into reading much. It'll blow over in a few days. You just have to watch your back for a little while."

"Wow, you sure know how to calm a brother down. What are you doing tonight? Let me take you to dinner, if you're not busy."

"No, mister, you're staying home. I've already cooked, and I can bring it over." She waited a few seconds. "The only thing I'm doing tonight," she said, "is you."

And she did me well.

The threats at work came and went quickly. But they taught me the written word can be just as powerful as television, in spite of what my old boss told me back in TV. I had made a name for myself in the rap world, and not in a good way. I kept a low profile over the next year, until my conflict with Sharp exploded.

Chapter Thirty-Six

The Dark Side

ONE YEAR LATER

Crackheads were everywhere. It was the summer of '91, and Los Angeles was producing as many crack addicts as it was bad movies. They wandered the streets day and night, willing to do anything to earn five dollars for another five minute hit. It was the worst thing that could have happened to poor black people.

Well, along with open gang warfare, economic recession, and the unemployment and homelessness that Ronald Reagan left behind. He was in Japan giving a speech for three million dollars, while I was stepping over homeless crackheads near the beach in Venice.

I was walking with Renee. She was my only joy these days, stuck as I was in a miserable job, living paycheck to paycheck, watching city life crumble around me, with folks waiting for prosperity to "trickle down."

I was determined not to make the same mistakes with her as I did with Dana and other chicks. As a 35-year old man, it was time to get serious with someone, so I tried to do more of the things she liked.

Such as shopping. On this Saturday morning we were on the waterfront, entering a record store near the boardwalk.

"When I was in college," I told her as we walked down the aisle, "I would buy seven or eight albums a week. Now, I'm lucky if I find one good album to buy in a month. I mean, we get free stuff at the magazine, but most of it's unlistenable."

"You sound like my dad," she said with a laugh, "talking about the way things used to be. 'This ain't music - it's just noise.' Listen to yourself, Anthony, don't be such a fuddy-duddy."

"I'm sorry, but it's true. Respect your elders, girl. People who grew up listening to real music are having a hard time adjusting to this new stuff. Your dad is right."

We wandered down to the dark end of the aisle, then turned back toward the front of the store. "You know," she said, "I'm seeing more and more of these new compact discs around. What do you think of them?"

I picked up a nearby CD. It was by Whitney Houston, who was the singer Jason and I submitted songs for the previous year. They had rejected our songs, but I checked the back of the CD to make sure they didn't steal our material.

"What do *I* think of compact discs? They're tiny, they cost fifteen dollars a pop - I don't know. Everybody's got a turntable and hundreds of vinyl albums at home already. I think we're looking at the Betamax of the nineties. They're going to flop."

We left the dim record store without buying anything, and stepped into the noon sunlight, heading to the beachfront. Aimless in that way new lovers inhaled their happiness.

"I forgot how nice it is out down here," I said. "The water is beautiful." She grabbed my arm as we strolled down the wide lane. Sea birds were circling over our heads, dancing to the sound of the ocean.

When I looked away from the water, I noticed even more homeless people dotting the street. Some had shopping carts, but most either sat or stood in front of stores, begging for money, or quietly holding out a hand.

"The dark side of 'morning in America," I said.

"What?"

"Oh, nothing."

We walked to my car, hugged together the whole way, and headed to Renee's place. But this neighborhood triggered thoughts of Sam Stone and my old band, so I decided to drive past his nearby house.

Sam's garage door was closed, if in fact he still lived there. I thought about La Wanda, Don, and the gang, and wondered what I could have done differently to keep the group together. I told Renee about the old band, and my old dream of being a rock musician.

"Whatever happened to this Sam guy?"

"Last I heard, he was divorced, working at the post office, and smoking crack."

I drove on.

The tony townhouses of Venice Boulevard morphed into the simple bungalows of south central L.A., as I got closer to Renee's neighborhood. She lived with her mom and dad, even though she was twenty-five years old. There was a lot of that in California; back east, they put you out after you finish school.

"See you tonight?" I asked.

"Be over around seven," she said, walking to my side of the car. "My mom'll have me running around all afternoon with chores. So be good till then." She kissed me through the open window. Then she said "Fuddy-duddy," with a giggle, and quickly went up her parent's path.

I was sitting in my office Monday morning, thinking about the great weekend, and the good times with my girl. I tried to motivate myself for another week in a job I needed but didn't want. Kenny, who was now a supervisor in the Office Services department, knocked and came in.

"Yo, yo, boss Adams," he said.

"Hey, Kenny. Been a while." He handed me a collection of mail. "You don't do rounds anymore. What brings you up this way?"

"Check it, man. Your boy Sharp is tripping. What's up with him?"

"What do you mean, Kenny?"

He stepped into my office, and closed the door.

"He just acting strange lately. It's cool that he's down with hip hop and all, but I gotta keep it real about homeboy. I catch him talking to himself and repeating things. Is *paranoid* the word?"

"Yeah, it means you think people are out to get you."

"That's it! That's how he be acting. I don't gossip, but once I caught him on the phone, saying so-and-so wasn't a *real* black man, calling somebody a yellow punk. Man, I hope he wasn't talking about you. That would be so whack."

"Yeah, that *is* whack. Thanks for the heads up, Kenny." He opened the door, looking both ways before rolling down the hall.

I knew Sharp was talking about me, if what Kenny overheard was right. I had known lots of black people in my life that had a problem with my skin color, but I hadn't been called "yellow" since high school. That damn Sharp always seemed to be functioning on a ninth-grade level.

I left my office and headed toward the pit to talk to Phoebe. I saw Sharp was there, talking to a small group of contributing editors—a fancy name for staff writers.

First I saw Sandy Geller, a protégé of Wilson. She was Jewish, but she loved hip hop and had a black boyfriend. Next to her was Ray Simmons: he liked to be called Razor. He had long dreadlocks that all the women in the office loved - so much so that it made me consider growing dreads.

Sharp was holding court, sitting in Phoebe's chair while she stood at her nearby drafting board. "I'm calling it 'The Soul of Hip Hop," he said.

I stood behind him, next to Phoebe, who was working on the cover for the long-form article Sharp was developing.

"The cops," he went on, "beat the hell out of a black man in the streets of L.A. That means every last one of us is under attack. Hip hop is under attack, too. You got fools up in Congress talking about legislation against our music. So somebody needs to speak up. That's what my article will do—fend off the critics and haters. Even the haters who work around here, in high places."

Sandy and Ray looked at me; Phoebe looked at Sharp, as if disbelieving what she had just heard. Sharp, whose back was to me, swiveled his chair around and realized I was standing there.

I fixed my mouth into a fake grin, then there were seconds of awkward silence until Sandy spoke.

"It makes sense that if we're the so-called 'Rap Magazine of Record,' we'd defend against people like Tipper Gore and her kind. I mean, she's got the *president's* ear."

"Yo, yo," Ray said, "Can't nothing hold us down. I'll be hip hop 'till the day I die, you know what I'm saying? You know how that go. Keeping it real. Word."

Sandy spoke again, then Ray, but it didn't matter. I had just caught Sharp talking about me, and I was deciding if I should say something to him in front of the staff. Or I could talk to him in private. Or let it go, like a punk.

There were still a few people who considered my article— "The Rap on Drugs" from a year ago—an attack on hip hop music. The words *hater, sellout* and *Uncle Tom* came my way, in letters and phone calls. But now I was hearing it from a coworker, in front of people I managed.

Sandy and Ray, maybe sensing the uneasiness, melted away toward their desks against a far wall. Phoebe buried her head again into her graphics work.

"Sharp," I said, "is there something you want to say to me?

He mimicked me in a nasal voice. "Is there something you want to say to me. We can talk." In tandem, we headed toward the conference room.

I've tried to tolerate this guy for seven long years now. Since the day we met, he's given me nothing but attitude and bad vibes. I know—everybody doesn't have to be your friend, but I won't have him disrespecting me in front of people I supervise and work with.

We took positions, standing on opposite sides of the table.

"What's on your mind," he asked, "what's up?"

"You seem to have a problem with me. I don't know what it is, and I gave up trying to figure out why. But you *can't* be talking about me to the people I work with. That just won't *do*, man."

"What are you trippin' about? Who said I was talking about *you*? There's a lot of people around here that don't got no love for hip hop. And what, are you threatening me or something?"

"I'm saying if you have a problem with what I write, or my philosophy, you need to come talk to me, not spread gossip like a school girl."

"School girl, huh?" He walked around the table, standing inches from my face.

"Nigga, don't front with no weak shit about 'come talk to me first.' I don't owe you no explanation about a damn thing. I run this shit around here. They just keep you around to protect the white man's interest. Believe that."

"You must be out of your mind, boy," I said. "You don't own this place. Freeman—and Wilson, too—just keep us around here to help deliver black kids to their advertisers. You should hear the way record companies talk about rap. I heard it with my own ears."

"What the hell are you talking about?" He took two steps back.

"When I was doing my big article last year, I left a tape running by accident at a big record company conference room. I taped the head of the freaking company calling rappers "minstrels and clowns." That's what they think of rap, and that's probably what they think of the people who buy it."

Sharp backed farther away, and leaned against the wall.

I folded my arms. "Hard to believe, huh, that corporate America would exploit black people. That they'd take our music and use it against us by sinking millions into the sickest possible images. Didn't hip hop used to be about more than just gangsters, big butt women and shiny cars? You gotta know these pimp-and-whore images are doing damage to us as a people, especially kids."

"I don't know what you talking about. That's just the way it is out on the streets, and all hip hop does is tell the truth - our stories. We ain't all grow up in a nice midwestern house with a mommy and daddy like you."

"This ain't about me, Sharp. It's about what we can do at this magazine if we work together."

I was getting nowhere with him, so I tried to lighten the mood; maybe he could relate to a movie analogy.

"Remember what Darth Vader said to Luke at the end of 'Empire Strikes Back?' How they could join forces and overthrow the evil emperor? Sharp, think about what's happening to the music, to hip hop. We can work together to overthrow the evil corporate empire that's turning music into a joke. From the inside, with our voices at this magazine."

He looked at me with a puzzled expression, stood up straight, and headed to the door.

"Like I said, son, I don't know what the hell you talking about. I'm writing *my* big article on hip hop, and maybe it'll teach you a thing or two, even if you *do* know everything. I'm just telling you—don't be fronting me around my people up in here. Don't get yourself fucked up."

I opened my mouth to speak, but he left the room quickly, leaving me standing alone.

I reflected on the seven years we had worked together, and how we could have made a difference. We had a chance to make *Hype* something special, other than a shill for record companies. As enemies—threatening each other—there was no hope of changing things. In fact, one of us would have to go.

Chapter Thirty-Seven

Get Along

APRIL 1992

I was on fire. So was *Hype*. So was Los Angeles.

I was burning with joy from seeing Renee everyday - and most nights. She was easy to talk to, and the sex was great, but even better, she could cook like crazy. She had learned from her aunt, who owned a restaurant. Fried chicken, fried catfish, pancakes—if you could fry it, she could tear it up in the kitchen. Then in the bedroom. It was Renee who made me forget about music, just like my father warned me.

1992 was *Hype Magazine's* best year to date. Rap music was showing staying power, and Warner was behind us in every way, with budget, marketing and personnel support. Every two weeks we were fat with glossy ads. As circulation went up, David Freeman started making regular quarterly visits to our office.

He happened to be in town on the day of the Rodney King verdict, when the city burst into flames over the acquittal of four cops who beat King.

Freeman and Sharp were sitting on one side of the table in Wilson's office, while I sat with Wilson on the other side.

"They're going to burn down this God damn city," Freeman said. We were watching live coverage on Wilson's TV.

"That's what happens," I said, "when people get fed up."

"I think it's a damn shame, Mr. Freeman," Sharp said.

Wilson got up to turn off the TV, but Freeman said, "Leave it on, leave it on. I want to see if I'll be able to leave town shortly. They might burn down the airport."

Wilson turned down the sound. "Who can concentrate with this on?"

"I didn't get where I am, boys," he said, "without being able to do two things at once." He pulled out copies of a one-page memo, and handed a sheet to the three of us. It was titled, "The Hype Music Awards."

"And I sure didn't get here without having a clear view of the field ahead. This paper outlines our next big thing. Take a minute and read it."

The Hype Music Awards

What: an awards show, in the vein of the Grammys and American Music Awards

Who: produced by the editors of Hype Magazine and an independent producer

When: after Labor Day weekend, to take advantage of seasonal new record releases and artists in need of publicity

Why: to raise *Hype Magazine*'s profile and improve sales; to build relationships with rap artists and record companies

Where: ABC network - Hollywood, California

I read the memo, and said to myself, this was inevitable. Rap music is mainstream now. And like any other performers, they'll love nothing more than congratulating themselves with fake awards and honors. Show business people, after a lifetime of rejection and neuroses, will flock to anything with the word "awards." And for some reason, people at home like to watch them.

"This is dope," Sharp said, nodding his head and smiling. "Aw, man, why didn't I think of this. 'The Hype Awards.' I'm just the man to produce it, too, with my TV background."

"Interesting idea," I said. "Take a lot of work to get it flying, but we can do it. Sure, why not."

The three of us looked at Wilson, but he was still staring at the memo. After a few seconds, he spoke up.

"I'm sorry, my head is killing me. Hype Awards, yeah, solid idea, the kids will love it."

Freeman's eyes darkened, showing he was unhappy with his publisher's sarcastic tone.

"Maybe you need to take some time off, Timothy," he said. "This is a major move at helping turn the name 'Hype' into a brand. We need to make this happen for the fall season. ABC is highly interested, and I've got an outside TV man lined up to co-produce. You guys work out the rest on this end, let me know what you need. Any questions?"

My only question was, how did these two men work together and get along for all these years, with their opposite personalities?

I shook my head "no questions," Wilson was rubbing his temples, and Sharp still had a happy little grin on his face.

"One other thing," Freeman said. " Ditch the big editorial pieces. I thought we talked about this last year. Sharp, I liked your 'Soul of Hip Hop' article, and your 'Rap on Drugs,' Anthony. But face it, kids don't care about that heavy stuff. We need to focus on two things: the personalities, and the music.

Our goal is simple. Leave out all the preaching. I don't want to say it again. We're not the *New York Times*."

Freeman swiveled his chair to look directly at the television screen. "Now, how much longer is this riot thing going to go on? Enough is enough; we get the message. I mean, jeez, they're burning down their own neighborhoods."

"No way to tell," I said, looking at the silent screen. "People are angry. It'll take some time before things get normal, if they ever do. You can't pummel a man like that with no justice and expect black people to just take it. That King video hit a nerve."

"Yeah, those cops hit more than a nerve, but I think it'll be fine," Sharp said. He looked at Freeman. "I do want you to consider letting me produce the awards show."

"Young man," Freeman stood up and looked at Sharp, "call my car around so I can head to the airport and get out of this fucking madhouse."

When I got back to my office, I had an urgent message from Renee. I called her.

"They got us, Anthony. Mom said she was in the kitchen and she heard glass break. Then she said smoke was everywhere. She had to run from the flames."

"Are they okay?"

"They're safe, for now. They jumped in the car and drove to my auntie's house."

"My God, I can't imagine what you must be going through. We need to go see what's happening out there. Can you get away from work? I'm swamped here, but I can take you to your aunt's house."

"I'll talk to my supervisor. You'd think they would give you the day off if your damn house gets burned down." She started crying.

I've never heard Renee cry before. Well, except for the 'Color Purple' movie and other films and plays.

I hung up and left my office, running to the stairwell. From the seventh floor to the third, all I could imagine was neighborhoods in flames, homes of hardworking people, up in smoke, and my girlfriend among them.

She was in Charles Roth's office. He was head of the accounting department. I went to Renee and wrapped my arms around her. Her face was still wet from tears. Roth just nodded and motioned his head toward the door. Renee got her purse, and the two of us went down to my car in the garage.

I drove us to her aunt's house, near Normandie and Pico. The closer we got, the darker the air became, as smoke mixed with the usual toxic L.A. haze.

Aunt Fran was peering out a front window when we pulled up; she opened the front door and waved for us to hurry in.

Renee's parents were sitting in the living room, watching the TV news. Everyone hugged, then I sat next to Renee on the long sofa.

"If you need to stay with me, or need *anything*, you let me know, okay?"

She nodded. We watched the screen images of flames and smoke.

Renee wanted to stay the night with her parents and aunt, so I left when it seemed the neighborhood was calm.

The city of L.A. shut down, with the exception of newspapers and T.V. news - they were orgasmic in their breathless coverage of the violence - and Hype. I avoided Hollywood, and drove back down to the safe and quiet streets of Santa Monica. I worked for a few hours, then laid on the sofa in my office, and went to sleep.

The next morning, with flames still in my head, Sharp and I were sitting in the conference room, waiting to meet the outside producer who would be working on the awards show. We were both going over copy; I was editing a profile of a female rapper; he was editing Ray's profile on an upcoming star, Tupac. The quiet was broken when Wilson walked in. He was followed by someone who looked like a bulky version of Michael Jordan. His name was Jay Rivers.

"What's happening, fellas," he said before Wilson could introduce him. "I'm Jay. I'll be working with you on the Hype Awards." He reached out to shake hands. "This rioting is crazy. You all are wildin' out here."

"Jay just got in from New York this morning," Wilson said. "He's produced a lot of live comedy shows for HBO, and plenty of other production work. He's Freeman's man."

Jay winked his eye at us, as if to say, "I'm Freeman's man, and I'll be running the show."

Wilson left the room.

"Have a seat, Jay," I said. "Sharp and I agreed that I'll be writing the show, and he'll co-produce with you."

"Sounds good, Big Time," he said. He snatched the back of a chair and sat down; he rubbed his shiny bald head, and put his briefcase on the table. "Here's what I need to know: what—if anything—have you all lined up for the show so far, in terms of venue, acts, personnel?"

"Not much," Sharp said. "We just found out about it yesterday, homie."

"Cool, cool," Jay said. "You from back east, blood?"

"Nah, bro," Sharp told him. "West side 'till I die." Sharp flashed a "w" with fingers the fingers of his left hand, and Jay nodded his head with approval.

"Well," I said, "I'm from the Midwest, so we got the whole geography thing covered. Why don't we talk about this show."

Sharp and Jay sniffed around each other for a while, tossing ideas out and testing each other's knowledge and connections in TV production and hip hop. I sniffed myself for funk, having not taken a shower, but all I could smell was smoke in the shirt I'd slept in. Jay directed a few shots at me, until he realized I wasn't going to compete, or play the alpha-male game. *I don't want to be here. Renee is on my mind. Awards shows are corny and stupid. My manhood is not at stake here.*

He focused on Sharp.

Jay was a few years older than us, and his personality was perfect for being a producer. New York attitude, sharp dresser, willing to step on toes. I was content to simply be the writer, to put cute and clever words into mouths of award presenters, letting these two guys design the concept.

After a short while, Jay began to dominate Sharp. He was a big guy, physically intimidating. During the meeting, he would get up and stand over Sharp from time to time. Funny, watching the power play between them, even though there would soon be no humor among us. Events were about to become as violent as the rioting on the south side of the city.

Los Angeles was under a dusk-to-dawn curfew. Rioting and looting were still happening in the lawless streets. Anger was thick, moving beyond just the outrage over the King verdict; now there were white, Hispanic and Asian people caught up in mass hysteria. Those brave enough to go to work had to rush home to avoid the looming threat of police, or gangs, or other dangers.

I wanted to see Renee, but it was late when I got home. I called her at eight.

"The smell of smoke is getting worse, Anthony," she said. "I can hear fire alarms everywhere. I'm upstairs, and I see flames. It's terrible, absolutely awful."

"Tomorrow is Saturday - maybe things will settle down. Try not to think about it, babe. Play some music or something."

"Play some music? My tapes and records all got burned up. I just hope they don't burn up my aunt's house or her restaurant." Her aunt owned a big soul food restaurant and bar on Crenshaw.

Renee was working herself up, and she started crying again. I didn't know what to say when women cried. After a few seconds, she said, "Tell me what you did at work today."

"Let me think," I said. The day flashed through my mind.

I edited a profile of a female rapper who had a top ten record. She was a lesbian, but everyone in the industry tacitly kept it quiet. Then I made plans for a TV special where we'd give awards to rappers. Words like artist, musician and legacy were being used to describe people who weren't artistic, weren't musicians, and were leaving a legacy that glorified violence. The same kind of violence that was burning now in the streets of L.A.

"Not much, boo," I said. "It was a slow day."

The next day, all the TV stations were still showing Los Angeles, live and in flames. My Saturday morning cartoons were missing. *"The Smurfs" and "Hammertime" are being preempted to bring you this special coverage of 'The Verdict: L.A. Under Siege.'*

I invited Renee and Jason to my apartment for lunch. It was risky, asking them to drive through the madness, but I knew we'd feel better if we were all together. Renee arrived first, and I gave her a big hug and kiss at the door. Jason arrived soon after, with the new boyfriend he wanted me to meet, Demetrius.

I had fixed a good meal—baked fish, rice and salad, and we sat at the dining room table with our plates, the TV playing in the background.

"Anthony, baby, turn that off please," Renee said. "It's nerve-wracking, and enough is enough."

"I hear you," I said, "but don't we need to know exactly what's happening, which neighborhoods are burning? Hell, our lives could be at stake if this gets any more out of control."

"He's right, you know," Demetrius said. A different type brother for Jason, I told myself as he spoke. American and outgoing, he was a teacher and also a musician, he later revealed.

"This must be what it feels like to be at war," Jason said. "Look at that."

He pointed to the screen. Two armored tanks were rolling down La Brea Avenue. Then firemen were being shot at while putting out blazes. The riot was flaring up.

No one was eating; we had all lost our appetites. Renee got up to change the station. She landed on BET, which was showing an old episode of "Good Times." I tried to get us to talk about something else.

"I think I have a job for you, Jason," I said. "My company is producing a rap awards show, and we need to hire a musical director. I told them I had someone in mind."

"Really. Me? What do I know about rap?"

"Most of the music will be prerecorded anyway. They just need a small orchestra to backup one or two R&B acts, and to play music going into commercials. It's good pay for a few weeks work."

"And I play a mean bass," Demetrius said.

"And I can sing," Renee said.

And I can sing. Dana! My old girlfriend who wanted to sing but sounded like a wounded cat? Oh no.

"That's all well and good," Jason said. "I'm just wondering if we're going to have to spend the night here. It's like a civil war out there."

We heard a siren going down nearby Melrose, and everyone's ears turned toward it. No one knew if the violence was spreading, or exactly what was happening. J.J. Evans was wearing a red skintight jumpsuit and a stupid smile on the television. I wanted to turn to the news, but I also wanted my friends and I to relax and enjoy the Saturday—to forget about the raging city.

The four of us mingled around the living room and dining room in nervous silence, until Jason said, "We have to know what's going on."

I had hoped to talk to him about working on the awards show, but that topic lost all meaning now that people were being killed in the streets.

I tuned the set to a news channel, and turned up the sound. We were startled to see Rodney King himself, live before the cameras, tearfully asking people if there were some way we could all just get along.

The same question would soon apply to Jason, Sharp and Jay.

Chapter Thirty-Eight

A Song Can Change Everything

AUGUST 1992

Renee's parents were heartbroken, seeing their house go up in flames. So they moved back to their Texas hometown after the riots.

My girl and I had thought about living together, and talked about it for weeks, before making a decision.

"You're at my place every night anyway," I remember saying.

"But what if it doesn't work? What if we can't get along?" She was more nervous about it than I was. But I was in love. Wow. I don't know when I broke down and admitted it, but I was in love with her. She was stuck in my head, like a song you can't get out of your mind. When we were together, I'd dread the approaching moment when we'd have to part; when we were apart, I worried if she was okay and what she was doing.

"I tell you what," I said, "if we get on each other's nerves after four weeks, you can always move back in with your Aunt Fran. Maybe we'll end up hating each other; maybe we'll be together forever. Let's go for forever."

That last line was from a song I had written ages ago, and I think it closed the deal.

The Hype Awards show was a few weeks away, and things were not working out between Sharp and Jay.

Sharp had come up with a complicated system of selecting winners. It involved readers mailing in a ballot from the magazine, with the votes counting toward each nominees' percentage, along with the choices of him and Jay.

It was a screwy scheme, and there was no time to get the ballots out.

Jay wanted the show to include a special tribute to an R&B pioneer, "the Legacy Award," but Sharp thought old school R&B would dilute the concept of a hip hop awards show. It wasn't a bad idea from Jay, but then again, would hip hop and R& B mix?

They had other disagreements: break dancers or not, a single set or several, a live orchestra or a DJ. *So* many conflicts that Wilson bumped me up to executive producer.

Executive producer.

I was in charge now. I put up a weak protest, but I knew it was the only way to save the show. The three of us were equally experienced producers, but Wilson knew I had the skills—of personality and peacemaker—to make this stinking thing happen under pressure.

With three weeks to go, the three of us arranged to meet downtown at the Dorothy Chandler Pavilion, annual home of the Academy Awards, which we had booked for the show.

(David Freeman had to pull some strings to get the place on short notice.)

I got there first, parked in the main lot, and went through the curving glass and marble front entrance. I walked the length of the fancy red-carpeted lobby. Busts of Louis Armstrong, Barbra Streisand, Frank Sinatra and other Hollywood greats lined the wall. Their eyes followed me as I passed.

Louis Armstrong seemed to say, "Boy, how you gonna fill up this great big hall in just three weeks?" Then a hearty laugh.

Barbra Streisand said, "Anthony, my boy, what *are* you doing?"

Sinatra smirked and shook his head. "You got talent, kiddo. Use it and quit messing around."

Sharp and Jay arrived soon after. They waited while I checked in with the theater manager in the front office, then followed me down the long, sloping aisle of the auditorium. Someone in the control booth turned on the house lights for us, along with a single spotlight on the stage. The three of us climbed the steps on the side of the stage, formed a triangle and started our meeting.

"Before we leave here," I said, "we have a lot of decisions to make. Some things need to be nailed down to avoid a disaster. We go live in 22 days, and my name is all over this show now, so I don't want to screw up."

"Word," Jay said.

I looked at my clipboard. "Let's talk about staffing. Who do you guys have on board so far?"

"I got a full tech crew from HBO," Sharp said. "Cameras, lighting, sound—everything covered. Leon, my crew chief, might be stopping by shortly."

"I'm handling talent," Jay said, "and I got a director lined up. People are geeked up about being on the show. For most cats, this will be their first award. Everybody'll be here. You know what, Big Time? I might have to turn people away."

"That's cool, man," I said. "I'm writing the script, and I also have a music director. He's a good friend of mine—waaaay talented, and he should be here soon for you to meet. So, I've got music and writing, Jay is doing talent, and Sharp is technical."

My juices started flowing. Nothing compared to the pressure of live television, and I was back in it. In a music band, the control is in *your* hands up on the stage. But as a producer, I depended on a hundred people to do their jobs well. *We're under the gun, and I love it.*

I looked down to make some notes. From the corner of my eye, I saw Sharp walk to the front edge of the stage. He was peering out, through the glare of the spotlight, looking at something.

"My man—Leon," he said. Then he squinted his eyes tighter and said, "Wait, that *ain't* Leon."

Jay and I walked to the edge of the stage, and saw someone coming down the aisle toward us.

"Who is that?" Jay asked, peering through the bright white light. "Look like some faggot."

I looked out. I could tell by the walk who it was.

"This is my boy, Jason Brown. You don't need to call him that, Jay." He made his way onto the stage. "I'm hiring him for musical director. Jason, this is Rick Sharp, my coworker from the magazine. And this is Jay Rivers, producer, from New York."

"We're both Jays, huh," Jason said, shaking hands, "that's *one* thing we have in common."

Sharp and Jay exchanged glances.

"Are you up for this gig?" Sharp asked. "Don't bite off more than you can chew."

Jason looked at him, and took a visible breath. "I used to play for the L.A. Conservatory of Music, and I've been M.D. for over a dozen stage productions. Anthony told me you want a twelve-piece orchestra. I already have a contractor lining up the musicians, and I'm just waiting for a rough script so I can start scoring. I need a cue sheet for the show." He walked over to the spotlight where Sharp had been, and looked down. "Nice orchestra pit. I also need a rehearsal schedule as soon as possible. You guys are *really* cutting it close."

"I think *he's* up to it, Sharp," I said. "He could ask *us* the same question. Let's all take a walk around and check the facilities. We should meet back at *Hype* around one and come up with a final production schedule."

I was surprised at how easy it was to step in and take over the show. I simply fell back on the tools I learned while producing at KCBS. They boiled down to two things: confidence and execution.

Sharp and Rivers were a bad mix on their own; their high-powered personalities canceled each other out. But our three-way chemistry got things moving, and the show was on track.

Faggot.

Back at the office, I took a short break at my desk after meeting again with the other producers. I closed my door, and reflected on the way Jay Rivers had called Jason a faggot, and whether I had said enough. *Should I confront him about it? What would be the use?* Not a day went by without a remark like that from Sharp or someone else in the rap world. Homophobic, misogynist, anti-Semitic remarks. *BUT NOT ABOUT MY FRIEND*. I decided to check Jay hard if he said it again.

I heard two knocks at my door, and yelled, "Come in."

"Hello, Mr. Adams." Kenny came in the door with a small batch of letters. He liked to personally deliver mail when he wanted to get out of his office—or to gossip. But for the first time, he was dressed in a conservative suit, and a tie that matched his short red hair.

"What's with the suit, Kenny, who died?"

"There's no funeral," he said smiling. "I got another promotion, a new job. I'll be up in the corporate office, working in the legal department. I always wanted to be a lawyer, and it could happen one day. This is my last day here, boss."

I stood up, and walked over to shake his hand.

"That's great news, man. But what happened to all the hip hop dreams?"

"Time to grow up," he said.

"Wow. Well, good luck to you up there, son. Stop by and visit some time."

He dropped a batch of mail on my desk, and I followed him out the door.

I went to the pit to check on the writers, since we still had a magazine to produce.

Ray handed me an article he was working on. I glanced at it, and shoved the papers under my arm.

"Have you heard about Kenny," he asked. I just nodded. "Funny how a white boy can play at hip hop while it's fun, but drop it and put on a suit when it's convenient."

"You got a point," I said.

I looked up and saw Kenny, among the offices circling the pit, saying goodbye to coworkers. He was pursuing his dream, moving on, and I was still at a job I didn't want to do. I felt lazy *and* old. At 37.

Sharp's voice broke my contemplation.

"Anthony," he called in a loud whisper. He was standing in the conference room doorway. "Anthony. Come up here."

We stepped into the room and closed the door. "Look, I just got off the phone with some of my boys in New York. There's all kind of drama going on between the east coast cats and the west coast. I'm hearing there's some serious beefs going on. Shit could all hit the fan at the awards show. *My* damn awards show."

We were still standing behind the closed door in the big room.

"I have a budget for security," I said. "Maybe we need to double it. What about metal detectors? Wow, at a Hollywood awards show. That'll go over big."

"I don't know," Sharp said, "but I'm also hearing things about your boy Jay Rivers. He's tied up with a east coast set that *don't play*. I dropped his name to my boy, and he was like, whoa, dude is connected. Don't cross him, yo. I *knew* there was something about him I didn't like. That's why we didn't get along."

"Where does Freeman find these people?" I said. "First you, now Rivers."

"Man, screw you."

"All we have to do is make it through this freakin' show. A few more weeks, that's all. I'll work on the security thing, you keep your ears open and let me know what's going on with those fools out there."

The entire staff was working overtime to put out the magazine, along with whatever was needed for the awards show. David Freeman's harebrained one-page idea turned our office upside down. But we were going to make the show a reality, even if it killed us.

The next afternoon, I entered the Vine Street Talent Agency. It was time to audition dancers for the show. Talent was Jay's domain, but I felt I should at least check his progress for a few minutes.

I walked up a flight of stairs, turned a corner, and saw a long line of young women sitting in chairs, waiting for what they thought was their big chance—to dance on the first annual Hype Music Awards Show. The hallway was packed with pretty girls.

Inside room 201, Jay and the choreographer he'd hired were seated together at a long table that was pushed against a wall. A girl assistant was sitting at a smaller table near the door.

"You must be Anthony Adams," the choreographer said. She stood up and came around the table to shake hands. "I've heard so much about you. I'm Pasha. I'm very happy to be working on your show."

"Good to meet you, Pasha. I've seen your work before. You've been all over the TV."

"I've been around the block a few times, if that's what you're saying. And *I* must say it's wonderful having two brothers in charge of a big magazine like *Hype*. And *now* an awards show—a feather to add to your cap."

"It pays the bills. I've been around that same block a few times myself, and it's killing my back, I gotta say. Tell me, what are we doing for the first dance number?"

Pasha winked at me and sat down. I sat next to her, with Jay on the other end.

Jay spoke up. "She worked out a bomb-ass opening number, a hip hop routine to a medley from 'The Chronic'. And we better start looking at these chicks now."

Jay gave a thumbs-up to the assistant at the small table; the young lady stood up and peeked her head out the door, beckoning the first dancer into the room. The dancer nervously walked to an 'X' taped on the floor. She was gripping a cassette tape and a big headshot.

"Tell us a little about yourself, baby girl," Jay said.

"Me? My name is Lyniece, I live in Inglewood, I'm a dancer and a singer, and I want to be a star one day."

"That's beautiful, sugar. Give your tape to the girl, and let me see what you got."

The dancer handed over her tape and picture. The assistant fumbled with the picture, the tape, and the cassette machine, while Lyniece untied the long white shirt she was wearing around her waist.

I saw the shock on Jay and Pasha's faces, and my mouth dropped open, too. The dancer was wearing the tightest red hot pants and had the biggest behind I had ever seen. She wasn't fat; in fact, she had a slim waist, which only accentuated the size of her behind. *What an ass!*

Music began.

"I like big butts and I cannot lie..."

She did a sexy freestyle dance: arms flailing, knees going up and down, neck swiveling from side to side. But her butt was clearly the centerpiece of it all. I couldn't take my eyes from her, glancing only for a second to see Jay and Pasha, who showed equal amazement.

The song ended, with beads of sweat on the girl's forehead and a few on mine. My partners and I were quiet for a few seconds while Lyniece found her way back to the black 'X' and stood there.

What in the hell! What kind of dance is Pasha planning to produce? This girl is hot, but her movements were frenetic, tacky and showed no signs of technique.

"Damn!" Jay finally said. "Baby, that was on the one. We can definitely do something with you. Pasha, what you think? Cause if you don't want her, I definitely do."

"I like the way you move," Pasha said. She was matter-of-fact and strictly business. "I'm just not sure if you can learn combinations and take direction. Callbacks are tomorrow, and you might hear from us. Thank you, dear."

"I *might* hear from you? You don't like the way I dance or something?"

"Okay, honey," Pasha narrowed her eyes and leaned in, "you dance likyour pants are on fire, and that's not what I'm looking for. That will be all."

The girl snorted and turned her back. And stormed out.

That's when I knew Pasha could get the job done.

I had another appointment to make, but I also wanted to see more dancers, maybe even a catfight, so I sat through two other auditions.

"I like big butts and I cannot lie..."

"I like big butts and I cannot lie..."

Each of the next two dancers brought the same song; each one wore extremely tight pants.

Before leaving, I whispered to Pasha, "Is this the new style or something? I mean, I appreciate a big butt like the next guy, but what's up with the tight pants?"

"I have no idea, sweetie. These kids are in their own strange world."

I waved goodbye to her and Jay, as another dancer entered the room while I left. In the hall, I looked down the row of young women anxiously waiting, and saw they all had on equally tight jeans or hot pants.

I stepped out of the building, onto Vine Street, and walked to Sunset, where my car was parked. I stopped at a pay phone to call Jason about tonight's music rehearsal for the show.

We were talking, when suddenly *"I like big butts and I cannot lie"* popped into my head, and the song started looping in my mind, stuck. The words forced me to take special notice of the way women on the street were dressed as they walked by. The street was crowded with tourists, and most of the women were wearing super-tight pants. Some of them were sexy; most of them were not.

"Jason, man, you have to explain this new fashion thing to me."

I told him what I had noticed at the auditions and on the street.

"It's that song," he said. "It's empowerment. I've seen some huge, huge ass women in pants they knew they shouldn't be wearing."

"It's not just me tripping? Sisters weren't dressing like this a few weeks ago. Damn, a song can change everything. For me, it was "What's Going On." Now, I guess it's "Baby Got Back." Got women thinking obesity is hot. I wish they'd make a song about voting or the homeless or something."

I finished my business with Jason. As I walked away from the phone booth, I passed by a heavyset woman—again, in ultra tight pants. I looked back, and saw her turn sideways and slowly, carefully squeeze her way into the phone booth. She barely made it.

One song—was it true? Did that silly record, and its cartoonish video, teach women that guys were crazy about giant butts in tight pants—that no butt was too big, and no pants too tight? Renee had a nice sized behind - I decided to ask her.

I like big butts and I cannot lie...

Wait a minute: the guy who did that song is up for a Hype Music Award. After all this, I might be honoring him with an award.

All right, Frank Sinatra, I'm ready to take your advice.

Chapter Thirty-Nine

My Girl Can Sing

LABOR DAY 1992

I remember when I first saw her. I was with Jason in Hollywood that night. She was brown, beautiful and curvy. Long sexy neck. She was hanging up on a wall. I got her down and played her; she had quick action, and when I played her, I knew I had to have her.

I was still in bed, at home, on a lazy holiday morning, when I realized I hadn't picked up my guitar in years—didn't even know where it was - but I knew I was still in love with music. I thought about all the other times, when I'd be in bed in the early morning, a song would flow through my semi-sleep head.

Aretha singing "Wholly Holy."

The piano part at the end of "Layla."

Any guitar solo from Jimi Hendrix, Steely Dan, or Prince.

On this morning, in that hazy real/dream place, I was hearing Joni Mitchell paint a picture with "Song for Sharon," singing about romance and art, when the voice morphed into something else—something deeper, blacker and more soulful. I pulled myself into the waking world, and I realized it was Renee.

I don't recall ever hearing her sing before, and if she had, never like this.

She was in the adjoining bathroom, singing an Anita Baker song—amazingly, better than the original. I sat up in the bed and turned my ears to hear better. Her voice was a rich alto; she was singing on key, and she made beautiful vocal runs at just the right parts of the song.

The water stopped, and all was silent.

Then I heard her step out of the shower and walk toward the bedroom. I plunked my head back down onto the pillow, and pretended to be asleep.

With one eye, I peeked and saw her drop the towel. She started putting lotion all over her still-wet body, deliberately rubbing the cream-colored cocoa butter into her smooth brown skin. I felt myself getting excited.

My girl can sing.

A busy day was ahead. In spite of the fact it was Labor Day, we had a final dress rehearsal scheduled for the evening. All the Hype Awards pieces were set to fall into place at six o'clock: twelve musicians, thirty nominees, ten presenters, and eight dancers. And several beefs between famous rappers.

On top of that, some of my neighbors on the first floor were having a barbecue at three o'clock.

The day rolled on. Renee and I were on our way down to the party when the phone rang, with yet another awards show problem. One of our nominees had been arrested at the airport, with a loaded gun in his bag.

"This shit is wild," Sharp said on the phone. It was hard to hear him: music was loud in the background. "The big man's lawyer back east is trying to get him out, but they don't know if it'll happen by tonight."

I opened the closet door, looking up and down for my guitar, and said, "I thought this thing couldn't get any crazier, man. He's worth a million dollars, and he's carrying a gun."

"I don't know if this joint is going to come together, son. I ain't never tried to do a show with so many out-of-control people before. And that fool Jay is just, well, a damn fool. I heard he took one of the dancers to his hotel room last night—a seventeen year-old."

"We go live in 36 hours, then this will all be a memory, man. A producer can only do so much—you know that, Sharp."

"Yeah, but live TV, nationwide. Stakes is high, brother. Stakes is high."

I calmed him down as much as I could. I had never seen Sharp so nervous as this show was making him. His bark, as I had always suspected, was louder than his nerve.

Dark smoke from dead meat was in the air. Renee and I arrived at three-thirty, stepping into the hot sun of the courtyard, holding hands. Ten to 12 people from the building were already there, and I could tell the alcohol was in full flow.

"Thanks for inviting us," I told my downstairs neighbor, Teresa. "I want you to meet my girlfriend, Renee."

Teresa cocked her head to one side. "Hi, Renee. You are so pretty. Wow. We always thought you were gay, Anthony. What a relief."

I bugged my eyes at what she said.

"Teresa, I'm the furthest thing from being gay. Not that I have a problem with it. I mean, what is it with people? Someone at work just called my best friend a faggot." Renee squeezed my hand. I heard the place grow quiet and felt eyes on me. "We can only stay for a short while. I have to work tonight."

I got sodas, and followed Renee to a bench where we retreated under the shade of a magnolia tree.

"Does it bother you that much? I mean, what's the big deal?" Renee asked.

"I don't know. It must be the pressure of getting this show done. Plus there's all this dumb conflict with Jay, Sharp and Jason. All the rappers want to kill each other. My back is going out on me. Now all this gay stuff. I'm trying to not let it get to me."

Then she said something that was supposed to make me feel better, but didn't.

"Baby, I know you're not gay. And that's all that should matter."

Twenty minutes later, we were all seated around a banquet table, eating and talking, when the conversation turned to music. Zachary, the professional pianist, was talking.

"I did some sessions on a David Sanborn record. Folks, let me tell you, that cat can play. Best time I ever had in the studio."

"Mmmmm," Teresa said. She kept eating, and there was a lull.

"It's too quiet," I said, restless and bored. "That must mean the food is good." A few giggles and grunts of agreement.

We finished eating, then Helen said, "Let's play a game. Finish this sentence: my biggest regret in life is—who wants to go first?"

Mario spoke up, and talked about his divorce. Then Helen talked about her distant relationship with her children.

I thought about the topic, until I found something to say.

"Funny you should bring this up. I was just thinking about it this morning. My biggest regret in life is not giving my music career a better chance. Sometimes you wonder what would have happened 'if only.' If only you could have stuck it out longer, or if a break would have gone your way." I felt Renee put her hand on my back, and rub lightly. "I got more, but I'll shut the hell up."

"No, Anthony," Helen said, "Go on. I want to hear more."

"Please. Talk," Teresa said. "Let us get to know you better."

"Fine. I regret sinking money into a bad business deal with a bunch of shady characters who just wanted a tax write-off. I regret not playing my guitar more often, or calling my folks enough."

I was full of the nervous confidence I always got before a show. In fact, I felt like I was back on stage.

"I also regret what's happening to pop music these days. There was a time when a good song almost seemed to bring the country together. Everybody everywhere knew 'Bridge Over Troubled Waters.' You might not have anything in common with a redneck in Tennessee, but you knew he'd heard 'My Girl' or 'Let it Be.' Now the whole industry is fractured. Singers who can't sing and artists who can't play a fucking note."

I stopped. Helen said "Wow," then all I heard was the sizzling of a lone burger on the dying grill fire. After a minute, people spoke up again. I listened to each one speak about failures and missed opportunities. Most of them had already *had* show business careers in the past, but I learned that everyone regretted something they wanted to do in life. Wasted youth, bad choices.

Renee spoke last. She wisely changed the somber mood of the party.

"I regret not becoming a stripper. I always fantasized about dancing for money for horny guys. My friend made a ton of money in college stripping. But 'good little Renee Love' couldn't bring herself to do it."

"It's not too late, honey," Zachary said.

"I got a pocket full of tens if you want," Mario joked, and everyone laughed.

The discussion made me wonder if age 37 was too old to focus on another career; I knew it was time to end my days at *Hype*.

After the barbecue, I drove alone to the theater for dress rehearsal. Sharp, Jay and I had spent the past three weeks doing our best to bring the show together, but there were still a handful of unresolved issues. The biggest question was: would violence break out between feuding rappers, and could we keep a lid on it for just a few more hours?

I turned on the car radio. The rap music station was playing "Cop Killer." I listened for a few seconds, then turned to the classical station.

The drive downtown gave me a chance to think about other things. The morning music in my head; voicing my regrets to the neighbors; the fear in Sharp's voice on the phone...

Did he call me brother? Did I hear that right? Sharp never called me brother before.

The thoughts didn't help me relax - they just fed my anxiety.

Traffic was holiday-light. I parked in the theater's underground garage.

I took the stairs up to the stage entrance, and heard the taped music of the opening number as I got closer.

Pasha and her dancers were front and center, running through their first piece. When she saw me come from backstage, she stopped the run-through and walked quickly toward me.

"Anthony! Baby!" She gave me a welcoming hug.

"What's going on, Pasha. Is everything all right?"

"Yes, it's just a pleasure to see you. We need your calming presence around here. People are a little bit tense."

We walked, arm in arm, to the front center of the stage, where she had been giving direction.

"It'll be just fine, baby doll," I told her. "I'm just looking forward to my first live show in years." I spoke loud so the dancers could hear. "And we're going to have fun, right?" The eight of them said 'yes' or nodded their heads with the cat-like nonchalance dancers have. They were dressed in their outfits: sagging jeans, bandanas, t-shirts, hot pants and sunglasses. *Not exactly an M-G-M production*.

Talent and crew started arriving. Jason came with several musicians. I hugged him, and they went directly to the orchestra pit and huddled over the piano, with Jason in charge.

The show director, Lionel Pierce, came with a half-his-age wife. His white hair and skin were stark next to her dark complexion. We had been working closely with Lionel over the past weeks. He was an old pro at live television, and he had a way of instilling confidence in his crews. Lionel liked to be called "captain." He and his wife headed up to the control room.

Soon everyone was present, and the huge auditorium was buzzing, until stage manager Abby called for quiet. Lionel spoke over the p.a. system.

"If everyone is ready, we'll take it from the top, people. Places in five."

"Wait a minute, wait a minute," I said.

Everyone froze.

I stepped out to the edge of the stage. "We can say more than that, Lionel. Tomorrow night we make history. The first major awards show for hip hop on national television. All of us have worked our asses off to put this show together in less than four weeks."

I looked over at Sharp, standing in the wings to my left, and Jay, standing on the right. Both of them crossed their arms.

I saw the plainclothes security men I had hired, standing at the back of the theater, black silhouettes against the lighted wall.

"I want to thank all tonight's presenters, dancers and musicians, technicians and crew. You guys have done a tremendous job on short notice. And we're ready. Have fun, and I know tomorrow night will be a great show."

Applause rang through the hall, startling me.

People resumed their scrambling. Abby walked onto the stage and screamed "Places!" at the top of her voice, jolting my ears.

I realized I hadn't yet seen our Legacy Award recipient. I walked toward Jay, who was talking to a presenter on the side of the stage. Before I reached him, he bent down to pick up his bag, and I clearly saw a black gun, tucked tight under his belt. Light hit its metal trigger as his jacket draped clear. The sight of the gun stunned me for a second, but I composed myself enough to ask my question, and he responded.

"She just got here. I put her in dressing room A. I *got* this, Big Time."

"Looks like that's not all you *got*. You brought a gun to rehearsal? What the hell's going on, Jay?"

"Aw, man. I forgot to drop it in my glove compartment. Where I'm from, it's second nature, being strapped. Don't sweat it, son."

I headed for the elevator and rode up to the control room. Sharp was already there at work, whispering something into Lionel's ear. He looked up at me, and we sat next to each other, between Lionel's wife and a guy from ABC.

"Jay's staying backstage, right, handling the peeps?" Sharp asked me.

"Just like we planned, working the talent. Everything's ready to roll." I leaned in and spoke quietly. "On the phone did you call me 'brother?"

"Watch the monitors, fool."

Lionel spoke into his headset and asked Abby if everyone was ready. Then he said, "Music, hit the lights, cue dancers," and our final rehearsal was underway.

I got home just before midnight. Renee was in bed, watching "The Arsenio Hall Show."

"How did it go?" she asked, sitting up against the headboard.

"Oh, it was fine—a few kinks to iron out, but we made it through. This Jay-person was carrying a gun." I went to brush my teeth.

"A gun? Wait a minute, come back here. Who's carrying a gun at a rehearsal?"

I returned to the room, and gave her a kiss before climbing into bed.

"This New York cat who's co-producing the show had a gun tucked on his waist. I saw it myself. I was going to tell Rick Sharp, but he's already a wreck. I *have* to get out of this racket."

Snoop Doggy Dog was performing on the screen, rapping about gin and juice. The audience made barking sounds in approval.

"What have you gotten yourself into?" she asked, slumping back into the covers.

"I don't know, but were you serious about the stripper thing?"

"Be real, baby, I could never strip. It was just a crazy fantasy. Like you wanting to be a rock star."

She might as well have stuck a knife in my stomach.

I sat for a while, reflecting on the day, and thinking about what she had just said.

"I was *supposed* to be a musician, you know. Somewhere along the way, I got sidetracked. Maybe it's not too late, maybe it is."

"I support you, baby," her muffled voice said.

"As far as this hip hop thing is concerned, I don't know how much I can take any more. I feel like a fake, a total fraud, promoting something I hate and don't believe in. I'm up on that stage tonight being a cheerleader, and half the people there are probably carrying guns. The producer had a gun! I just have to put my smiley face on for one more day. I want to get through this show."

She didn't respond, but the Arsenio audience started barking their approval.

Why isn't it me and my old band, Modern Man, on TV right now? Instead of these…these minstrel music comedians? I thought about the first song I wrote when I got to California, "I'm On My Way." I never finished that song, and now I wondered if I were on my way down another path. Through the years, the jobs and the women, I had lost the cohesion I used to have with my music.

My woman, the woman I loved, fell asleep while I was pouring my heart out. But it would be another woman—a great artist—who would help me straighten my way.

Chapter Forty

Alone In A Red Dress

David Freeman's memo was clear and direct: rap music was changing, and *Hype Magazine* needed to change with it.

I was standing in my office Wednesday morning on the day of the show, reading what Freeman had sent from New York:

The music is harder and edgier, and to stay relevant, we have to reflect what's happening in the streets.

The Rodney King verdict, Reaganomics, the riots, gangs and crack - these elements have moved music into the realm of the gangster, or should I say, 'gangsta.' Even MC Hammer has changed into a thug. Our coverage needs to move in that direction, too.

His words were the last straw for me. Freeman—a white, millionaire executive—was helping push black music in a negative direction for strictly commercial reasons. Finally I knew. It was time to turn in my resignation.

The decision sat in my mind, sure and unflinching. *Thirty-seven.*

I walked out of the office, and went to take a look at what was happening in the pit.

Sandy was working on a piece about a feud between rap music's two biggest stars. East coast against west coast. Both were coming to tonight's show.

Ray was making calls for a story about the word "nigga," and how rappers were using it freely and trying to change its context.

Sharp was going over some photographs with Phoebe. He was laughing about something, one of the few times I remembered seeing him laugh. Again I wondered what Sharp and I could have done at the magazine if we had worked together, instead of being adversaries all these years.

I walked back to my office, reminiscing about Wendy Robinson, the woman who started this whole thing and gave me my first big break. Back then, she envisioned a small, informal magazine covering rock and entertainment, barely acknowledging black music. What would she think—to see this big, glossy, corporate magazine we had become, full of pictures of snarling black men and stripper-like women. I could just see Wendy now, living in Maui or Spain or somewhere, very rich—and still very weird.

I sat at my desk, and turned on my typewriter just as Sharp came in.

"Maybe we should have done the metal detectors for tonight. 'Cause some of these beefs are gettin' wild. Hey, I just saw you, floating over the pit, looking around. What's up with you?"

"This is it, man. I've had enough. It's time for me to do something else. I'm typing up my resignation."

"Wow, dude, no joke." He sat down, and I moved the typewriter closer.

"My girl said some things last night, got me thinking. I don't know, man. I'm ready to grow up, but I don't think hip hop is. I been waiting, but it's just getting worse."

"Yeah, I'm making a change, too. I'm in a drug program. I'm kicking this problem I got. Don't *tell* nobody what I'm telling you, though."

"Sharp, I don't think it's a big secret around here that you've been using. But, good luck to you, man. We got a big night ahead, and I need to type this letter before I change my mind."

Sharp left, and I hammered out a one-paragraph letter to Tim Wilson.

I took it to his office, where he was standing, looking out his window.

He read it.

"I don't suppose there's much I can do to convince you to stay. You haven't been happy here in a long time. I have to say, your timing sucks—resigning right before the show. What are you going to do with yourself without all *this*?" He spread his arms wide.

"I got a few pennies saved up, and my girlfriend is paying half the rent, so I have a minute to figure out some things."

"You're still young," he said. "Me, I'm stuck with a mortgage and a kid in college. Stuck like a pig in shit. Whatever you do in your life, Anthony, don't get trapped. It's the worst feeling in the world."

He walked from behind his desk to shake my hand, then he said "Aww, heck," and gave me a hug. "You'll be fine. Maybe you can come back next year and do the awards show again."

I smiled, and headed for the door. "Just let me get through tonight. Stakes are high."

Twenty minutes before six, twenty minutes before showtime. Everything was falling into place at the auditorium.

I wanted to take a quick walk through the audience, the way Don Stone and I used to do before our band performed. But there was no time, so I just peeked through the curtain from the side of the stage. I could see most of the people I invited.

Renee and her aunt were in the third row, talking and laughing. Aunt Fran was like an older version of Renee—dark, beautiful and regal. Tim Wilson and his wife were a few seats away. She was quietly reading the program, and he stared ahead blankly, silent.

A few rows back was Dana, my old girlfriend, sitting with what must have been her husband, who looked like a preacher or a schoolteacher. They seemed happy together, with the same controlled energy, same peaceful containment.

I scanned the huge crowd until the house lights dimmed, and I hurried upstairs.

I walked into the control room just as the curtain opened. The stage lights came up, and the music started. We were on the air.

The show was in Lionel's hands now. Our "captain" was either sailing the Mayflower, or the Titanic.

ABC's man was seated next to me. He was on the phone and chewing on a pen. I had met the guy once, back when I was at KCBS. I remembered he got his job because his father was a network executive. He was here to "protect ABC's interests," which meant telling Lionel to hit the delay if anyone said a curse word or violated the network's puritan standards.

Sharp came in, and sat on my other side—out of breath from running up the stairs. He had just handled a last-minute technical problem down on the stage.

Pasha's dancers were getting the show off to a good start: a combination of break dancing and modern dance moves that was energizing the crowd.

"You sure you want to pull the plug on your career, smart guy?" Sharp said in a quiet voice.

"Yeah, there's other careers to be had. I'm still young enough to bounce somewhere else."

"Shhhhhh!" Lionel said. "Ready camera two, take two."

The dancers finished their three minutes, and our comedian host, who went by the name Aladdin, stood at the podium to read from my script on the prompter. It was hard to tell he was reading - his delivery was smooth and natural.

"The Hype Awards," he said, "are here to recognize excellence in the world of hip hop music. But enough talk. Are you people ready to pump it up?" Half the audience said "Yeah," with a sprinkling of whoops and barking sounds. "Put your hands together for Melanie Felony and the South Side Ganksters."

Sharp motioned for me to lean toward him.

"Just so you know," he said, "this chick Melanie got a beef with MC Sheba. We need to keep them apart if they show up at the afterparty, most def."

"Two women? Beefing? What the hell."

"Shhhhhh," Lionel said again. He shot a quick look over his shoulder at us. *We* had hired *him,* yet he was in charge here, like a traffic cop stopping the president's motorcade. I put a finger to my lips, hoping Sharp would be quiet so I could follow the show.

After a commercial break, the host introduced the Donner Party, a group of five men who took turns rapping on their nominated song, "Criminal Behavior."

Then the first award was given out, to Mike Machete, for best new artist, beating out the "Baby Got Back" guy.

"I wanna thank Jesus Christ," he said at the podium, flanked by six other men. His speech went on, but I was thinking of the new direction my life was about to take.

A direction away from songs like "Leave 'Em Wanting More," Machete's hit song where he says

"Not too much time do I spend with my bitches,
I cum then I go, leave 'em laying in stitches."
Yes, it was time for me to go.

Carina, a 19-year-old singer, took the stage to lip-synch her hit song, "Do Me Again," based on a sample of Steely Dan's first hit. *"Come back, Jack, do me again…"* She was surrounded by ten of her own dancers, three rappers, fog from a machine, and flashing lights. One of the rappers had a live Rottweiller on a leash, and stood frozen midstage with his arms folded.

It was a dazzling, garish production—a spectacle—thanks to Jay and the girl's manager. The crowd went for it. I just had to wonder: *does anyone else notice how her paper-thin voice barely breaks through the sound mix?* She was the center of the production, yet she was the least dynamic element on the stage. She was cooing and kept saying "oh-baby;" she was fake as a ten-dollar hooker.

Her song was top five in the country.

"Don't get trapped," Wilson had said. I looked over at the red exit sign above the door.

More commercials were running. Ads for McDonald's, Nike, Chevrolet, Cheetos, the new "Malcolm X" movie and Mountain Dew. Some of them had rap music or a rap theme.

Corporate America's full weight was behind this music. I bet myself that none of those companies had a black person on their boards, yet they were backing rap music. *They're using hip hop to get into the pockets of young kids.* The rappers were like black Africans delivering their brothers and sisters to slave ships docked on the coast of Sierra Leone. Only this time, the performers were the ships. Minstrels, as I overheard a music exec say once. Minstrels dancing outside the tent, luring kids into a youth of cool consumerist servitude.

The Hype Awards were humming along toward the final few segments, and I was resisting the urge to bolt out of the door, to go stand in the hallway, or jump in my car and drive to Venice Beach.

Then I heard her voice.

"Hhhhhmmmmmm."

Like warm water about to boil, it was the unmistakable voice of Gladys Knight, who was there to receive the Legacy Award. Her humming alone was enough to grab my interest. The voice was chocolate-rich, and without a word, she had said more than any of the youngsters who preceded her on the show.

I remembered what she had done during rehearsal, so I leaned over and spoke to Sharp.

"You got this under control, man. I'm going down to the wings to check her out."

I ran down the stairs, and emerged into a wide hallway where rappers and young singers were congratulating themselves and making plans for the night.

Approaching the stage, I had to push past people who were listening to the show. They were standing - transfixed by Gladys's performance. She was singing a medley of seven songs from her long career—alone in a red dress on the stage. She had obviously held back during rehearsal; right now she was on fire.

I walked closer, and I saw Jason conducting the orchestra, looking back and forth between Gladys and his musicians. Of course, *she* was conducting *him*, as great singers do.

The audience was on its feet, honoring her talent and long career. She was like the sun: singular and powerful. *Finally I'm proud of this show.* I felt goose bumps when she reached her high notes. She was enjoying the moment as much as we were; love was looping back and forth, between artist and audience. *What a joy it must be to be in her shoes.*

She finished, bringing the loudest applause of the night from the three thousand people in the audience, and she did it without dancers, background singers or animals jumping through hoops.

Gladys received her award, to a standing O, and gave a short, gracious speech, talking about her musical journey, and the strength it took for her to make it this far.

After a few more commercials, the comedian made his final jokes, said goodnight, and the show ended. My time with *Hype*—coming to a close.

The curtain was down, and the stage lights dimmed, but energy started to swell backstage. Most spectators headed out, but dozens of people flooded from the audience, up the side steps, into the stage and dressing room areas.

I saw Jason on the far side of the stage, and squeezed toward him, between the hugs and the handshaking people. I finally reached him.

"We did it," I said, and we hugged.

"You did it, boy. This is all you."

"You know what? You're right." We laughed. "I have to find Renee, then we need to get this after-party started before everybody runs off. Don't forget, look for the 'Louis Armstrong Room' upstairs."

I walked toward the steps of the stage to find Renee.

She and her aunt were still in their seats when I finally made it to their row. They stood up when they saw me, and we made a big group hug.

"You did it, baby," Renee said. "All that worrying for nothing."

Yes, we did it, I said to myself. We put together a live music award show in less than a month, and got through it without a fight breaking out or gunshots.

Then I remembered Jay Rivers and his gun.

Chapter Forty-One

Last Words

Twenty people—maybe twenty-five—were in the after-party banquet room. I was standing with Jason, his friend Demetrius, Renee, and her Aunt Fran.

"I have an announcement to make," I said. I was still charged up from the show, which had just ended minutes ago, and I wanted to indulge in the moment. "This is perfect, surrounded by my favorite folks in the world, after a great show in front of all those people."

"I thought the show was over." Jason said. "Skip the dramatics. What's the news?"

"I put in my resignation from *Hype* today. Two weeks, and I'm out. A free man."

"Finally," Jason said, "after all these years of complaining. Well, it's about time."

"Wow, baby, what are you going to do?" Renee asked.

"I have no idea." I thought for a second. "And it's a good feeling."

Behind me, I heard a loud group of people coming through the open doors of the banquet room. I looked over and saw three men. Jay Rivers was at the center of the group; they were laughing and moving through the small crowd, toward the food table.

"Anyway," I continued, "that's my big news."

"Takes a lot of courage," Aunt Fran said, "jumping out there without a job." She stroked her hair once and said, "You're only young once, Anthony. Let me tell *you*." She took a gulp from the glass of red wine she was holding.

"*This* is the party?" Jay yelled from across the room. "No bartender, no VIP section? You Cali niggas got no style."

"Excuse me," I said quietly to my group, then I walked toward the food table where Jay was standing.

I held out my hand to Jay as I walked. "Congratulations on a great show. We got through it, man."

He glanced at me, shook hands, then he looked over my shoulder at my friends.

"Just another paycheck."

He went back to talking and laughing with his group, so I returned to my friends.

"Aunt Fran," I told them, "everyone, help yourselves to some food. It's not much, but it's free."

"What was that all about?" Jason asked.

"The man has some serious issues," I said in a low voice.

Jason looked over at him, and I saw Jay look directly at us, just as my friend said, "He's actually kind of cute."

"Don't do that, Jason," I said. "Be careful. We're dealing with a different kind of people here."

"What? All I said was he's cute. What's the big deal?"

"Lord," Aunt Fran said, "he trying to get us kilt in here."

"Everybody just be cool," Demetrius said. "Anthony, you ever think about doing that music thing again? 'Cause you know I play a mean funky bass."

"Do I think about it? I wake up every morning with songs in my head. All I ever wanted to do was play music for people. I just never figured out a way to make it happen. Wrong time and place, I guess."

After a few minutes, the crowd started to thin out, and it was clear the party would never get off the ground.

"Tomorrow's a work day," Renee said, as four more people left the room. "And it *is* getting late. It's been a long day."

"Fine," I said. "Let's call it a night."

I kissed Renee, then she left to drop off her aunt.

Jason, Demetrius and I talked about the show for several minutes, then the three of us walked to the door.

We went down the hallway and turned a corner, heading for the stairs down to the garage, when I noticed Jay and his group had followed us.

"Yo."

We stopped and turned around. The only sound in the wide hall was the squeaking from their shoes as they walked toward us.

"Hold up," Jay said. He was centered in front of his two friends. "Yo, I don't like the way your *boy* here be looking at me. I ain't no motherfucking punk, and I don't play that shit."

"Jay," I said, stepping closer, "nobody's looking at you, nobody's got a problem. We're just going home."

"Going home to fuck," one of the men said. They snickered.

"Get out the way, Big Time" Jay said to me, "I need to deal with your little friend."

My mind raced.

Good thing the women are gone.

This is like a schoolyard fight, and I've never even been in a fight.

Three of them, and three of us.

They're built like defensive ends; we look like their lawyers.

These guys are drunk. Or high.

Demetrius looks like he can handle himself. Not so sure about Jason.

I probably have one more shot at reasoning with these clowns.

"Man, here we are, worried about rappers getting into beefs, and it's the producers fighting. My boy got no problem with you, Jay. All right?"

"Well, he about to have a problem."

One of the big men points at Jason; he whispers in Jay's ear. Then he lunges forward, and hits Jason hard in his left temple. Jason falls to the floor, his head making a cracking sound on the stone cold tile.

Next comes the melee. The men pounce on Demetrius and me, but we fight back. Something tells me to aim for stomachs and private parts. Demetrius lifts one of the guys and throws him against the wall, dazing him. The other two guys target me, and one of them is Jay. He swings wildly at me, but he's drunk, slow and stupid—I can easily dodge his punches. I'm worrying about Jason - who's knocked out - and hoping no one falls on him.

I sidestep a punch, but my right foot comes down on something slippery and wet. Jason's blood. I lose my balance and fall backwards to the floor. Jay plops right on top of me, collapsing the air out of my lungs. I work my arms under his midsection, and push him up an inch off my body so I can catch a few shallow breathes. But I'm getting weak holding up his weight, trying to keep him from pinning me down again. I hear a faint sound from Jason; maybe a death knell, and I know I'm his only hope for survival.

Jay slowly pulls his left arm up along the floor, and grips my neck with a sweaty, cold hand. Sausage fingers come together until there's no space between them, and no air. He's blocking my air, my throat is explosive. I'm getting lightheaded.

I see pictures, scenes of my life in my head.

I'm playing guitar. *Anthony, play your guitar.* My fingers are strumming, but the guitar is cold hard steel.

It's Jay's gun. I remember his gun.

I pull myself out of the haze, and reach in to pull the gun from his torso. At the same time, to distract him, I smash my left knee up into his groin. He lightens up and recoils, letting me tumble away until I reach a wall. I use the wall to pull myself up, coughing, steadying myself, then I point the gun at Jay.

I see bullets in the chamber, and I aim down at Jay's nose. The human sounds fall silent as everyone notices me. *I'm standing here pointing a loaded gun.* The blended bodies separate, and Demetrius pulls himself away from them, coming to stand by me, allied with the power of the gun.

Now we're all on our feet, facing off.

"Three against two, motherfucker." Jay's eyes are blood red. "You better get ready to use that, and don't miss."

Can I shoot this man, these men? My father once took me out to shoot a rifle, a lifetime ago. The thing recoiled and sent me back on my ass.

Demetrius is a good fighter. If this were the end, I wished I could thank him for hanging in there.

There are footsteps coming around the corner. I hesitate to look away—the five of us, two against three, are locked in each other's eyes, waiting for the next move.

"What the fuck are you niggas doing?"

It's Sharp.

He looks down at Jay on the floor. He looks back and forth between the two groups. Then he walks and stands beside me, tensing his body to fight.

The next move is up to me. Now I'm full of the adrenaline rush you get when standing on stage. But the rush ends when I see blood gushing from Jason's forehead.

Jay's men now have defeat in their faces. Wordless and wounded, they fish for wallets and gold chains spread around the floor. I keep the gun pointed at Jay, and step back as they walk past us and hurry out the stairwell door, with Jay leading the way.

Three days later, on Saturday afternoon, I picked Jason up from the hospital. He had a concussion, but his vomiting and dizziness had stopped, so the doctor said he could come home.

He sat quietly in the passenger's seat while we drove down Fairfax Avenue toward my apartment.

"How are you feeling, man?"

He didn't respond, keeping his face turned toward his window.

"The doctor said the stitches probably won't leave a scar. Aunt Fran said to keep cocoa butter on it."

"Where's Demetrius?"

"Uhhhhh," I had to think quickly, "He said an emergency came up. The doctor also said somebody should keep an eye on you for a few days. You should stay with us, at least through the weekend."

"Hmmm." He lightly touched the bandage on his head.

We arrived at the El Dorado, and I parked on the street. I got out quickly and ran over to help Jason out of the car. He steadied himself after just a few steps, and we rode the elevator up to my floor. I put the key in my door.

"Surprise." Renee and Demetrius said it softly, as not to give him a heart attack, I guess.

Red balloons and a red cake were on the dining room table. On the cake was written "Get Well Bloody Soon."

Jason smiled. "This is awful," he said with a laugh.

"It wasn't my idea," I said with a shoulder shrug. "I don't even like red."

"Blame me," Demetrius said. "I *knew* it would make you laugh."

Renee went to turn on some music, choosing among the compact discs to play on my new CD player. Then we ate cake, and sat in the living room talking.

"I still have the gun," I said out of nowhere to Jason. Then I kept eating. They each stopped and looked at me for a second. Apparently they had forgotten about it. "Any ideas on what to do with it?"

"Keep it," Demetrius said. "No police, no problem."

"I could sell it at a pawn shop. Might be needing money, unemployed and all."

"Anthony," Renee said, "that thing might have been used in a crime. Like I told you before. If they trace the serial number to you, you could be in trouble. We're going to Santa Monica tonight to drop that thing in the ocean."

Hours later the four of us were standing on the pier, watching the sun as it finally dropped below the horizon. We were leaning on the railing, watching the water and the orange sky. The gun was now tucked into *my* waist, under my Dodgers jersey, wrapped in a white plastic bag. I pulled it out.

"Any last words?" Demetrius said.

"Last words? Let me think. This gun represents my final chapter in hip hop, and the beginning of a new career. I'm pulling the *trigger* on my days at *Hype Magazine*. I was quite a *pistol* there, but now, I *aim* to move on."

"Sorry I asked," Demetrius said.

I coiled back my arm, and threw the bag into the water as far as I could. We stood for a minute, as the white bag sank into the blackness, then we walked back toward the parking lot, got in my car and drove away.

"Where do we want to eat?" I asked.

"Let's try my aunt's restaurant," Renee said. "You all should like it, good stick-to-your-ribs soul food."

We headed east. I saw the Warner Building on the right, peeking its corporate head over some nearby trees.

Fifteen minutes later, we were standing in Fran's Place, near the front door, on a crowded Saturday night. Renee spoke a few words to the cashier, and minutes later Fran came out and led us to a booth in the middle of the restaurant.

"Nice place," Jason said after we sat down.

"This one's on me, folks," Demetrius said. "To celebrate the new fighting team—Demetrius and Anthony. I mean, we kicked some *ass* Wednesday night, bro." He put out his right hand, and I slapped it vigorously.

"New team, D?" I said. "All this togetherness reminds me of being in a band."

"What would you have done if your boy hadn't shown up? Were you going to blast old dude?" I looked at D and thought about it.

"I guess I'll never know, man."

"It looks great in here," Renee said. "They gave out loans after the riot, and my aunt used one to expand the place. You should have seen it before. The kitchen is all new, and she broke out a wall and put that stage in."

I hadn't noticed the darkened stage. I wanted a closer look, so I slid out of the booth and walked across the floor to the performance area. A new piano, sound system and lights. *Not bad.*

I walked up the two steps and looked back at everyone.

"Demetrius, I guess we'll never know."

What I *did* know was a feeling, like home, on the stage.

I thought about Gladys Knight's words, about music and the journey. How she said the love of the music was often the only thing to carry her through. I thought about that vision I had three days ago - me playing guitar when Jay was choking me—that saved us all.

The stage was dark. No one noticed me except Renee, Jason and Demetrius, who were looking at me with smiling bemusement.

Wait a minute. Renee's voice—singing in the shower. Jason's world class piano-playing. Demetrius plays bass.

I'm free from *Hype*, and I have a chance to make music again.

Music saved my life.